Salvage

Salvage

CURT CRAIGHEAD

RESOURCE *Publications* · Eugene, Oregon

SALVAGE

Resource Publications
An Imprint of Wipf and Stock Publishers
199 W. 8th Ave., Suite 3
Eugene, OR 97401

www.wipfandstock.com

PAPERBACK ISBN: 978-1-7252-6304-8
HARDCOVER ISBN: 978-1-7252-6305-5
EBOOK ISBN: 978-1-7252-6306-2

Manufactured in the U.S.A.   03/13/20

To Teresa,
without whom this book
would be forever on my desktop.

Chapter 1

I'm turnt, turnt 'round,
And I can't find my road back home.
Lord, I'm turnt, turnt 'round,
And I can't find my road back home.

—MEMPHIS JOE McRAY

DAWN BREATHES LIFE INTO the day. A restorative puff filling the lungs of that diurnal course, that daily resuscitation, once again opening the locked eyes of the world's quiet, daily death. For Tom, the notion of the day beginning in darkness never made sense, and while his clock and the world both told him midnight was the hallmark of the new day, the feeling of wrongness in that could never be overcome. Every morning he felt the world must be surprised by the gasp of renewed life, as one struck by lightning or pulled lifeless from a river is surprised to find they live again, determined to make this portion matter. This day would matter, he knew, as the first time on the road in a very long time.

And that road, that glistening black stretch-and-bend, stretch-and-bend, stretch-and-bend—undulating and cool, like the warped 78 records he listened to in his youth, the needle rising and falling in an endless left-hand sweep, writhing almost, as did the shimmering black rat snakes in the hay barns and canebrakes of his boyhood. On pebbled asphalt, the surface almost imperceptibly bowed and endless, he made out the first mile before it twisted north, lost behind the damp loblolly pine, bald cypress, redbud, white oak, and magnolia. The dank earth steamed to give the forest back to the sky, releasing the sweet aroma of pine needles,

1

pungent undergrowth, and turning leaves. The soaked bark and fallen needles deadened the sound of the old motorcycle, hushing the staccato rumble like an embrace. He thought of it that way—an embrace—one he'd given or gotten with intent as he hurtled through the magic of the east Texas Big Thicket on the edge of the Davy Crockett National Forest.

Easing into the throttle he took advantage of the light and the straight away, the pipes humming an aubade while he hoped his afterlife held this for him. At seventy-seven and one-half, most people would have thought Tom had figured it out. Still, he didn't know whether he had no business whatsoever on a motorcycle, or if that was his only business. It had always been this way for him—all or nothing—and while he often considered what he had given up and what he had gained, he liked to believe he had given more than he'd taken.

While the balance was in his moral favor, giving up this motorcycle, in his mind, should not yet be penance. At his age, he made few apologies and even fewer excuses, but not because he was too proud or set in his ways. He had just gotten very good at resisting anything needing apology. This too had always been the way for him: be a good man, a better man, do the right thing. Indeed, do the right thing.

Blobs of fresh orange sunshine squeezed between east Texas pine trunks, the sun's crescent silhouette stretching to clear the horizon. Sun up but unseen as it rose behind the trees; orange, amber, gold, silver, and white shafts slicing through first the ground cover, then the vines, then the forest proper to dapple Tom as he rolled on. That glowing orb, welcomed by the good of heart, cursed by the philistine, took away all hiding, took away all fear, took away all unknown in the brindled early morning light of east Texas. The northbound tarmac wouldn't feel the sun directly for another two hours when it would rise above the treetops, but Tom had felt it even in the dark. Tom had felt the coming sunlight always, in fact, even while he slept and for seventy-seven and one-half years.

Overhead the morning shone blue; a cloudless, powdered azure specked with cowbirds, grackle, coots, and cormorants, phoebes and flickers, and far more sparrows than the rest. None of which reap, none of which sow, none of which store for the winter. This was his path, his duct, his endless channel cut from the trees and covered in tired asphalt. This road was built for him, he thought, as was the morning, as was the hour, as was the sun.

He'd spent so many years—seventy-seven and one-half it felt—swimming upstream that days like this were rare and glorious. In the groove, so to speak, Tom reveled in the sound, the vibration, the movement. Silenced were the hecklers of his psyche, those faraway voices shouting doubt from the caverns in his mind. Absent were their echoes, bouncing between memories of a lifetime as reminders of what had been, could have been, would have been, and how little there was left.

He'd ridden motorcycles more than sixty-five years, on and off, and had owned more than four dozen all told. While he had three in his garage that very day, his ride of choice was clear: a 1969 Triumph Bonneville he'd modified as a younger man. It was a custom-built machine meant to gain speed very quickly, handling the power nimbly and assuredly. He came to build the bike in the summer of 1971, with his then twelve-year-old son, Jonathan, a smart and curious boy grown into a smart and curious man.

This machine was an exotic beast in its time, a holdover by a British company who'd never seen Japan coming. While Harley Davidson, Triumph, BSA, and Norton had been competing with one another, Japan snuck in and took them by surprise, effectively ending all talk about which western manufacturer would dominate. The answer was none of them. Japan won, would win, still wins.

His machine, Tom's machine, his time machine, was all his. Created from the factory as a multi-purpose commuter in England, he'd disassembled and recreated it as an individual, stripped-to-essentials, personal rolling cannonball. Tom, enamored with the innovation and the very notion of creating something whereby the sum was greater than the total of its parts, had begun piecing the motorcycle together almost fifty years earlier, rode it until he couldn't, and parked it just three years before this day. Now, with time on his hands and Roseanne gone, he set about disassembling the motorcycle bolt by bolt and restoring it to its former glory, finishing just days before this morning ride. Some fifty years later, it was an old exotic beast, out of its time, out of its element, and far away from home, much like Tom himself.

Even when he'd finished it the first time, the motorcycle was out of place in Houston's oil heyday, when pickup trucks and station wagons gave way to Mercedes Benz and Cadillac. Even then and always still, Tom had no interest in fitting in. It wasn't that he made an effort to be a dissenter, he was just different. Just was, pure and simple. Part of being different meant interest in everything from science to medicine to art to history to animals to machines. But mostly machines. And part of being different compelled in him a deep and abiding love of blues music, Cajun food, old people, firearms, philosophy, theology, literature, engineering, architecture, humanity, and motorcycles.

When he brought his first motorcycle home in 1944—a 1939 Whizz-er motor mounted on a 1940 Schwinn Superior bicycle—the matriarch of the Sunday school class had chastised his mother for allowing it.

"Tom goes his own way," was what his mother had said. And indeed, she was right. Until he had met Roseanne, his mother was the only one to know what that meant, and since Roseanne's passing, there was no one. This motorcycle, this Triumph, was strange and strong and precise and authentic. It was stout and powerful and nimble and honest. The bike was odd and built to perform. The same could be said of Tom.

He hadn't ridden any motorcycle in three years; eighteen months to hold the hand of his withering bride and eighteen more to restore the Triumph. For the first time in three years, Tom felt Tom-ish, again in his groove, in the world but not of it. Whole and alone, not lonely but solo. The black-and-white diamond-quilted seat was right, the pegs were right, the soft white Biltwell grip rolling under his hand and wrist was right.

His jacket, worn white leather with a black Triumph breast and back patch, was chaffed at the cuffs and waist after years of wind, dirt, and rain. The collar was tinged ecru from the sun and sweat, and the red satin lining was beginning to separate at the seams. The zippers, heavy brass Talon brand, were solid still, even better than new, tinged and worn with the joy of going on and coming off, while the rest of the jacket held every mile, but couldn't keep them a secret. His helmet came new with the bike, and even after replacing the lining and padding many times he knew it was long past its life but couldn't bear to separate the three. And with him being part of the ensemble, he couldn't separate the four.

That morning he would have said he was as giddy as a schoolgirl had there been anyone to listen. Anxious and excited, he put the jacket on and looked in the mirror. It first shocked him, then made him laugh. Nearly hairless, and thinking his face looked like a bearded catcher's mitt, Tom couldn't rectify his mind's self-image against the old man staring back at him. When had that happened? Why hadn't he noticed? When had his beard gone from distinguished salt and pepper to white? Do his children think of him this way, or the way they'd known him in their youth? No matter, as he was simply grateful to throw his bony leg over the bike and ride it, when a lot of men his age couldn't check their own mail. Some-how, he knew the little things become the big things.

Tom had had seventy-seven and one-half years filled with introspection, curiosity, and enlightenment with this one exception: he'd spent the last eighteen months restoring this instrument, not because he needed the bike, but because he'd needed the distraction. After forty-five years of marriage and eighteen months of handholding, Tom put a wrench where her hand had been, somehow hoping to retrain the shape, as though his empty hand was far worse than anything he might put in it.

Forced to trade warm and familiar with cold and familiar, he was somehow hoping late nights and weekend swap meets would occupy him. Somehow hoping that being busy would make him miss her less. "Time heals," he would say to himself; the same mantra he'd recited countless times to his own patients or his patients' loved ones. And every day he felt less like a liar.

"It is getting better," he thought as he rolled on. Tom was alone in the world. No one left to take care of; no one to take care of him.

The straightaway was an invitation; an invitation he accepted by ducking, tucking in, and holding on. The heat blowing off the motor felt good on his early spring legs, drying the damp and warming his shins and knees. He'd given up wanton recklessness after college and had given up subdued recklessness—for the most part—after his first child was born. By the time his third baby entered the picture, he had conformed to relative safety and responsibility, and while peppered with the occasional high-speed straightaway, he'd distilled his riding to nothing less than and nothing more than the sheer joy of separating space with his body and bike. Nothing more and nothing less than bridging the lacuna between what was behind him and what was before him. Upright, alone, clear-headed. Besides, his reflexes and eyesight weren't what they once were, so his interpretation of rowdy was reduced to simply being crazy enough to ride the thing. At seventy-seven and one-half years, sixty miles an hour felt like flying, and for the first time in many months Tom found himself grinning, because flying does that.

Strapped to the back of the seat Tom carried a Thermos of coffee, a Pride Pistolero cigar, a box of strike-anywhere matches, ibuprofen in a plastic film canister, two oranges, a Case pocketknife, and a thick leather-bound notebook, all neatly packaged in an old Pentax camera box held down with twine. As was his tradition, he'd ride out to some undetermined or predetermined destination, eat something, drink coffee, smoke a cigar, and spend some time alone with his thoughts. If he had a good one, he'd write it down. He had missed this more than he realized, and on this day—his first day back to Tomness—his heart was light and anxious.

In logging country, somewhere between Crockett and Woodville and south of Perdition, Texas, the roads were well-maintained but lonely. Perfect for slow drives in the country, logging trucks, and motorcycles. Pocked with small towns, most folks in a hurry couldn't bear the pace, so the roads were left to locals and to people whose intent was to be gone, not to get there. Tom belonged here now, in "the betweens": between dawn and dusk, between east and west, between wilderness and waste, between coming and going. This road was built for him, after all, as was the morning, as was the hour, as was the sun.

Clearing the last rise before the curve, Tom was tickled when his stomach rose and fell, then he began to lean left on a long westbound sweep. The tarmac rose again with the curve but was gentle and predictable; it was a road he'd covered dozens of times before at even higher speeds. Higher speeds on a well-worn 1969 Triumph, in bygone years on bygone days. At no time before, however, had it been just past dawn on wet asphalt, riding with tires that had become glazed and hardened after sitting up for three years. At no time before, however, had he been seventy-seven and one-half years old; a little slower, a little weaker. So, at the apex of the curve, first his back then his front tire turned loose the road.

It was just a slide at first, beginning with simply gliding through the lane with the bike upright at the same angle. Not realizing he'd lost traction, Tom leaned further to make the curve, causing the bike to slip out from under him entirely. In that instant, that slow-motion instant, Tom's first thought was the bike and how much damage the drop and scrape would do to the paint and chrome and mechanical bits. In that slow-motion instant he worried whether the bike would even be repairable. He saw Jonathan, twelve years old, wearing the white jacket and pretending to ride it. All of those hours, all of that effort, all of it falling away.

As he hit the ground, he heard the mirror and clutch lever snap as did his wrist, the left side of his helmet slapping the pavement, the sky and road a muddled blur of black and of blue, as both man and machine slid from the pavement and separated. They then cleared the shoulder of the road and breached the tree line—spinning horizontally at sixty miles an hour.

PART II

Troubled, troubled, troubled, I can't get satisfied,
Screamin' and cryin', reckon I'll dust my broom.

—*SWEETWATER JEFFERSON*

"Johnny, have you heard from Dad?" Hannah asked when he answered the phone.

John was taken aback by the alarm in his sister's voice. "No," he answered, "Am I supposed to have?"

Hannah was calmed, as always, by her older brother's demeanor. Three years her senior, she'd begun taking his lead early on. At two, she followed him like a duckling, now at forty-eight, he was still her first call when the world wasn't right. All through school he was the popular older brother, admired by kids and teachers alike, an honor only deepened by the notion he had never, not once, done anything to tinge her adulation. While their mother was sick, John had been the organizer of help, the information conduit, and the unshakable generational pillar she and her younger sister, Grace, had needed, even more than her father, as he was going through his own mourning. Now in his early fifties, John seemed, to her, the heir to the throne. What throne she didn't know, but he bore the mantle of royalty.

"I've been calling him since yesterday and he doesn't pick up," she said.

John was her hero. Both brother and friend, but a pillar surely, she was confident in his intellect and moral example. He had composure not because he had to have composure, but because he struggled to have it, and by virtue of his father's example, had never betrayed himself. He was strong, upright, and humble. He was interesting and adventurous. He was the high school star athlete and scholarship winner. As a doctor he had saved countless lives, winning award after award after award as a leader in the medical community. His kids were happy and well-adjusted. He cooked and played guitar and was always laughing. He was that leader; trustworthy and smart and articulate and grand, certain to bear the coat of arms she and her sister had turned over to him in deed if not in word. Her big brother in every sense, he had earned it.

He, on the other hand, had grown weary of these and other expectations, electing to move to Galveston where he taught biology to pre-med freshman at Texas A&M. While he couldn't articulate it, he'd grown uneasy wearing the crown and mantle, prompting him to start his life again on the beach. He could articulate, however, that he'd found Houston to be overbearing, with the added complexities of family management and maintaining his reputation as avid golfer, exotic car owner, and surgeon.

In Galveston, he spent his days teaching, fishing anonymously at the pier, walking the sea wall with his second wife Dianne, or working in the yard with her. Balding and with a paunch, he looked nothing like royalty. John grilled a lot of meat, made berry wine, read incessantly, dabbled in writing music, and missed his grown children and grandchildren, whom he'd call several times each week just to say he loved them.

Still, and as adulthood often masks, John would naturally fall into a role when his sisters called on him. That is to say, when he got the call from Hannah, he found himself as he always did: twenty years old, dean's list, Eagle Scout, golden gloves, a semester painting harp seals for Greenpeace and the planet. Standing beneath his patio cover in cargo shorts and gardening gloves, his nearly hairless white legs in contrast to the dark mud on his bare feet, he pushed the newly dug wet earth over top an earthworm.

"You know Dad, Han', he's probably in the garage, or went somewhere and didn't take his phone."

When she didn't say anything, he continued. "He was gone two weeks in January, and we didn't even know it till he came back. And he was out of the country!"

Never rattled but ever aware, John's mind began to scour the possibilities. If Tom was home, he definitely would have called back. If he was doing something that would make them worry—a very distinct possibility—he would call after he had finished to bear the post-event, what-could-have-happened conversation.

Their father was very much like that, as John's grandmother had known; as Roseanne had known. Tom went his own way.

"But he usually calls back," Hannah answered and was right.

John replied confidently, "I wouldn't worry about it, Han. He's just starting to enjoy himself again, so let him." But inside he was alarmed as well. Then, asking about their youngest sister, "Have you talked to Grace?"

Grace, three years Hannah's junior and six years younger than John, lived in Fredericksburg, Texas running a bed & breakfast with her grown son Tom and her second husband Eric. The family called Tom "Tommy" or "Tommy-Boy" or "Tom-Tom" as a way of discerning between the boy and his grandfather, embracing him as the family mascot, the family concern, the family's soft spot. Grace's first husband, Todd, had become mostly legend in the eighteen years since his death, having been diagnosed with testicular cancer just weeks after Tommy was born. He'd been a strong, strapping med-school student, full of promise and hope and the realization of Grace's schoolgirl fantasies. Then, without the family ever getting to know him very well, Todd passed on ten times as many years ago as they had known him.

For four years thereafter, Grace had lived with her father and mother, Tom and Roseanne, until she met and married Eric. Eric was a sweet man she'd met at church, fifteen years older than Grace, and he held for her the notion that they would be okay. She loved him for that, and for his kindness and love for her son, carrying for him a tenderness and gratefulness she would never be able to express. Still, it was never mentioned, and Eric would never know, but she sometimes wept when thinking of what might have been. She loved Eric, but might catch a glimpse of Todd in Tommy, or stumble across a misplaced picture, then lie awake that night to linger and to weep. She would cry for Todd, cry for Tommy, cry for herself and everything they'd missed together. These are the secrets we keep.

"No, not yet," Hannah answered, "Do you want me to?"

John thought for a second and said, "Not yet. Let's give him some time before we panic."

After hanging up, John called his father, somehow having to verify Hannah's lack of answer with his own. The siblings had never had the nerve to ask their father to change his answering machine recording, making John ever-startled when the ghost of his mother answered. "You've reached the Welton's," she would say with past generations' well-mannered south Texas Spanish charm. "We're sorry to have missed you. Please leave your name and telephone number, and we'll return your call directly."

John hung up without leaving a message.

PART III

I'm okay now, ya'll knows I'm okay.
Sun on my face in the mornin', moon on my face at night,
Wet when it's rainin' and dry when the sun is bright,
I'm okay now, ya'll knows I'm okay.

—*JOHNNY FLATT*

Tom, heart and mind racing with adrenaline, sat upright in a mad rush to escape the wreckage. Not that he would have identified his motive, only that the abrupt cacophony, the sparks and scraping, the ten-foot drop between the road and the forest, winging thirty feet deep into the trees, the impact and bounce all came together instantaneously, causing Tom's fight-or-flight instincts to ignite. It was just a glint on the face of Tom's watch; that immeasurable rest between clicks of a second hand. "An instant," as they say, to define some length indefinable. An event measuring the least in time but the most in consequence, as those instants often do.

On the fringe of shock, before the dirt had settled and with shook leaves still showering from the trees, Tom put hands to damp earth, then pressed to bring his body and legs under him.

In that fleeting second, that gap between motivation and movement, that instant, Tom felt his regret and embarrassment. He felt the dread of calling a wrecker and of telling his children. He felt the self-loathing over losing control of this machine, and of having the reason be his fault or worse, a result of his age and reflexes. But, also in that fleeting second, with hands to damp earth, pressing to bring his body and legs under him, he felt something worse. Far more terrible than the sacrifice of his pride, Tom felt the sacrifice of his body. As he pressed to push himself up, flush with panic and adrenaline, Tom felt a burning flash in his wrist and forearm, his left radius shattered just above his watch where it had collapsed under the weight of the fall.

Worse, far worse, a jolt of pain fingering from his hip to all points beyond. Intense, searing pain like an arrow's bolt piercing and emanating from the top of his right leg, but reverberating through the soles of his feet, tips of his fingers, tops of his ears. The pain was such that he blacked out just long enough to collapse, and as he came to rest there in the east Texas Big Thicket, behind the loblolly pines and under a great umbrella magnolia, Tom knew what he had done.

Spinning vertically off the road, man and machine had both launched into the air, the momentum taking them from tarmac to tree line in a blink. The ten-foot drop began without event, even as luck and providence allowed them to easily hurdle the barbed wire fence, past the first few trees, striking only smaller limbs and whisper-thin, outstretched saplings. Four feet from the ground, however, as he came in to land, the rear wheel of the Triumph hit an eighteen-inch, unassuming burr oak, causing the machine to spin violently in mid-air, with the seat and rear fender striking Tom at hip and mid-torso. The impact not only fractured his pelvis in dozens of web-like cracks but broke the ball of his femur from the socket.

"Oh God! Oh God! Oh God!" he cried out, not an expletive but an entreaty, settling back into the soft earth as the pain moved through his furthermost extremities, escaping through his teeth and hair and eyelashes.

As the pain washed over him and away, the wake slapping the shore of his consciousness, Tom felt his shoulders and back relax, and it actually felt good to have the wave pass. As light won out over darkness, and breathing deeply to clear his mind, he fumbled for the strap on his helmet, loosed the d-ring and pushed it up and off his head. The impact of the road on the helmet had exposed the interior hard padding beneath the worn lining, which abraded a clean bloody line an inch over Tom's brow from temple to temple. The compost beneath him accepted his head like a cradle, cooling his pulsing pate, reassuring his racing mind.

"Think Tom," he said aloud, somehow invigorated by his predicament. "Just relax," he told himself as he inhaled deeply, then exhaled through his nostrils.

He knew he wouldn't have much time before the flush of adrenaline left him, so he took a massive bite of the moist air and sat upright on his left hip. The left side of the motorcycle had landed on his right foot and shin, his leg winding up under the rear of the engine cradle, and the chain with the weight of the swingarm pivot cutting off the circulation to the bottom half of his lower leg, still a safe distance from the hot motor and oil. He was amazed to find almost no pain from his lower leg, as the ground had accommodated the weight by simply pressing his calf and heel into the dirt and leaves without breaking anything else. He moved his toes to know he still could and flexed his lower leg as well. Holding that same bite of air, Tom leaned forward to lift the back of the motorcycle with his right arm, hoping to drag his disassembled femur from the wreckage.

With a heave, he used what little leverage he had to attempt lifting the bike, which weighed 475 lb. in total. The backend, he knew, couldn't be more than a quarter of that, but at seventy-seven and one-half years, broken femur, one arm and no help from his legs, Tom simply couldn't budge it. Convinced the left foot peg and handlebar had been embedded in the earth making lifting the bike impossible, he scanned the ground around him for a limb or a branch. He had no way of knowing, and would never know, that the peg had broken off, now a roadside bibelot resting on the shoulder of the road where the bike had gone down.

Truly, he had no way to admit he was seventy-seven, and simply didn't have the strength. The bike may as well have been set in concrete or attached to a cable through the planet and tied off in a knot above the earth's surface in Qamdo, Tibet, where the antipodes map said it would emerge.

Beside him lay a branch from the magnolia above him, crossed over a stout limb from a pine that had washed down the embankment during a storm. Grabbing first the magnolia, he grasped it in his armpit and stripped it of leaves and twigs, wedging the end in the ground beneath the rear tire. Easing into the lift, Tom was nowhere near the fullness of his might—only a fraction of the whilom might he once had—when the branch snapped hopelessly in the middle. Unpanicked, Tom raised the pine limb from the ground. From the top it had appeared stout and capable, but from the underside, however, it was brittle, weak, and ineffectual. So weak, in fact, Tom broke it with his hand.

Taking the two magnolia halves, he again wedged one end under the wheel of the motorcycle, taking the other half and crossing it beneath at the base. Using the cross as a lever, Tom leaned over the top of the branch, which now wouldn't budge. With all of his weight upon it and all of his strength behind it, the motorcycle was unwilling to get up and off of him.

An old joke came to mind, a joke made of graduates of his alma mater. In the joke, both engines had quit in an airplane carrying one of his alum. The punch line was, "Oh well, I guess we're stuck here." Lying back down into the ground Tom considered that joke and considered himself stuck there.

Chapter 2

PART I

My woman like my Mama,
Take a switch to hide if'n I wasn't home before dark,
Sweet Moses, the sun is goin' down and I'm still miles to go.

—SLEEPY BILL OWENS

JOHN WASN'T QUICK TO worry, having seen enough and experienced enough to know better. But with a geriatric father, particularly a geriatric father who wouldn't acknowledge his age and refused to stop riding those damned motorcycles, John knew better than to let it be. He found himself on the side of the house, hurriedly washing his feet with the garden hose amidst his border collie's wagging and panting, doing his best to simply do what he does—take action. His father's house was three hours away; forty-five minutes further than where John had lived in Houston. John had tormented himself with this when considering the move but chose his sanity over the self-imposed sanctity of family obligations.

No one had ever asked John to be the pillar. He had just one day noticed himself holding the roof up, so to speak, and once there, found it near impossible to move for fear it would cave in. In his late forties he spent a lot of time thinking about this, knowing he had to be some-where, and had to be someone. He'd just decided he didn't have to be in Houston, and didn't have to be a surgeon, and more importantly, he didn't have to hold up the roof. It struck him early one morning while sitting in traffic. How could he be sitting in an insulated Audi listening to Voodoo Child without feeling ridiculous? Would he give up the Audi, or give up the Hendrix?

His preemptive consideration over what-if gave way to his need for peace, so he had moved to the beach with a woman he loved, and a refusal to be anything more than who he was. He expected this rebellion to be an alarm to his parents and siblings. In throwing off the mantle, he expected their worlds to fall apart. Instead, and to his surprise, they saw his newfound freedom not as an affront to their vision of him but rather as something the heir would do, and they didn't question it. As it turned out, John went his own way as well.

Tom's house was located near Trinity, about twenty-five miles south of Crockett, on the western edge of the Davy Crockett National Forest. Nine-hundred square feet on seventy-three acres, Tom bought the place in 1978 and moved there with Roseanne when they'd retired at fifty-five. They lived there well over twenty years, but John still thought of it as a weekend place and was always sort of surprised to see things there that indicated occupancy like gardens and garage projects and leftovers in the fridge. Twenty-some years later, John was just coming to understand this would be the last place his parents lived, and in a real way, the only place they'd ever lived.

Toward the end of his mother's illness, she stayed in a hospital in south Houston and Tom stayed with John. His father would drive to the hospital every morning and return every evening, when he would sit on the deck with John and Dianne to eat dinner and to worry.

With furrowed brow and experiential clairvoyance, he would say to them, "She won't be long now, I'm afraid. She won't be long now."

John knew enough not to placate his father with anything less than truth, so he would sit in the quiet holy gap left by Tom's predictions, while Dianne would reach out to pat the old man's speckled hands. After Tom went to bed, John would call or email his sisters, give them the day's status, and make his best effort not to be somber.

John knew some of his father's friends up there, as few as they were. He'd spoken with the county sheriff's office, the nursing home too, and local EMS providers, and had felt good about being able to call and have them check on his father should the need arise. His father was getting old after all, and the ever-vigilant first born had to consider these things. Just months earlier when taking his own granddaughter, Courtney, to visit his father, John had tried to hire a housekeeper and a local kid to mow the lawn. His father wouldn't hear of it.

"The day I can't cut my own grass or dust my own furniture is the day I'm done," Tom said. Then with a smile he said to Courtney, "I'll give up my feather duster when they pry my cold dead fingers off the handle." And that was that.

Now with clean feet, John entered his own house where Dianne was reading, and said only, "Dad's not answering the phone."

Dianne was a good woman; a woman who knew her husband and adored him the way he adored her. There wasn't a nuance she didn't respect or forgive in him, was attentive without being subservient, and cherished him in ways steeped in trust and admiration. She knew him as a flawed man, loving him for the flaws, knowing above all he had honor. The honor, the kindness, his ultimate motives; these things he'd learned from his father.

These were the things she'd seen, and despite her best efforts—despite her countless self-reprimands and her moral retributions—everything in history's past, she felt, pushed her toward him, and everything in time's future pulled them there. She simply couldn't resist him, and while there had been no tawdriness or compulsive sexual temerity, the chemistry, the universe, and seemingly all of God's angels gave them no choice but to rest within one another. And they did.

Five years his junior, Dianne had unwittingly fallen in love with John when he was chief of surgery at St. Mary's Hospital eight years before. She was a surgical nurse, and while their story sounded typical, even predictable, it wasn't. It had started with coffee and ended with John filing for divorce and moving to Galveston with her. She wasn't a home-wrecker, wasn't a husband stealer, wasn't a harlot or seductress. She was a good woman who would have loved him with or without the money, with or without the prestige, with or without his divorce, even with or without him. Oddly and reassuringly, his parents, siblings, and even his own grown kids came to recognize the fit, and while rough for the few months between filing and final, she slipped into the family as though she'd always been there. With two faraway kids of her own, she was now exclusively John's.

Slight but not frail, with thick premature silver hair and a small white scar above her left eyebrow, she could curl up to read in a chair and occupy almost no space at all. She was certainly a better fit than his first wife; kind where she'd been abrasive, accepting where she'd been judgmental, sweet where she'd been demanding, satisfied with simplicity where she'd been hallmarked by avarice. Dianne accepted him as he was, with no expectation of improvement or alteration. She wanted him to be happy, because that's what love does.

Love does not say, "Change for me, to be more to my liking, and my liking is your sacrifice." Love does not say, "Provide me with my whim, and heed my fickle humor." Love does not say, "Service me, as it is your duty, as I am your spouse." Love does not say, "Bend, but don't break, because in that breaking you can no longer be my provision of all things material, all things emotional, all things psychological." Love does not say, "Bend to my liking, because only in that bending can my ego flourish, and only in that bending can I manipulate. Bend to my liking, but do not break to yours." In fact, love says nothing, but simply is.

So, as it turned out, John's love for Dianne rested not only in what she said and did and in the way she treated him, but also in what she did not say, what she did not do, and the ways in which she did not treat him. Simply, she was who she was, and they fit.

When John walked in, she was doing what he would have expected, curled up and reading *The Atlantic* with their cat on the top of the chair behind her. Upon hearing Tom was missing, and knowing John's intent, she put the magazine down on an end table and said simply, "I'm going with you."

PART II

What evil have I done? What evil have I done?
Lord, I'm askin' what evil have I done?
Now when the moon crawls over them trees out yonder, I'll pack my bag and go.
—*LEONARD KING BEE WASHINGTON*

The pain came in tides now, sending waves up through his abdomen and body with no seeming regularity or reason. It simply came on, almost as a motivator for Tom to move, to fight or flee, to get himself some help. His body compelled him to choose, and while Tom had always been prone to fighting over fleeing, being pinned under the motorcycle allowed neither. The first time the pain rolled over him, Tom tensed his entire body, every muscle straining against the assault, causing him to arch and flail. This only made it worse, grinding bone on bone, marrow on marrow, causing chasms of fracture throughout his hip. He knew too that if he couldn't control himself, he'd bleed to death without ever leaving a drop, pooling instead in his abdomen as it poured from his hip and leg. He'd become a giant bag of blood, filled to bursting by the very machine it enclosed.

Having spent forty years as a geriatric physician, he knew too well what was at stake. Beyond the immediate injury, he'd endure surgery complete with pins or plates, then rehabilitation. Even then he'd have concerns over thrombophlebitis, mental confusion, and pneumonia. And that's if he lived through it at all. He was, after all, seventy-seven and one-half years old, having lived too long to recover quickly, but not long enough to quit. So, the second time the wave came he took a deep breath and held it, blacking out as the pain washed over him, which wasn't nearly a perfect answer either. Thinking about this, he was certain he wanted to avoid the passing out, equally certain he would eventually not reopen his eyes.

Instead, between the swells of anguish, he focused on the pale blue sky above him: a window framed by three limbs of his umbrella magnolia, where they stretched and crossed three limbs of a neighboring live oak. There through the faraway framework of limb and limb, branch and branch, cross and cross, he focused on the cotton clouds, drifting into and out of sight as they moved from one end of his wooden horizon to the other. He followed the hawk or the grackle or the sparrow passing through, making every effort to detach from the problem at hand. He watched a spider, ten feet above him, busying itself with a web stretching from one branch to another, and wondered how a spider managed a web that high and horizontal. A tightrope, he thought, with no penalty for falling.

Waiting for the telltale signs, he drew deeply through his nose, inhaling all the musk and glory of the east Texas pine, held it for a few seconds and exhaled as it came on, drawing again and again until the pain passed. Then when it had, he began moving his three free limbs in a way that resembled prone jumping jacks, fanning his arms from above his head to his waist and his left leg from the end of the motorcycle seat rail in a three-foot arc. In doing this, he discovered the very ends of his limits, somehow working the tension and adrenaline from his body, while also discovering how much he could move without disturbing the broken pelvis.

"Keep moving," he thought, "because moving means living."

"Move or die, Soldier! Move! Move! Move! Move!" Tom, barely eighteen, rose from foxhole to full sprint in seconds, reeling mindlessly toward North Korean tanks at the Battle of Osan. Unafraid with righteous intent, Tom had peeled away from the rest of Task Force Smith, made up of men from the Twenty-First Infantry Regiment of the Twenty-Fourth Infantry Division, and Battery A of the Fifty-Second Artillery Battalion, to take his post behind sandbags and a mounted machine gun. Five hundred and forty men strong, Tom had gone in good spirits, understanding completely that his odds were not good, but knowing he was meant for the job.

Task Force Smith, first firing Howitzers at a range of over a mile, then 75mm rounds at a half mile and finally bazookas at the battle line, found themselves helpless but for courage and training. Overwhelmed by eight heavily armed Soviet-made tanks and 5,000 enemy soldiers, their only hope was to buy time until help arrived. Taking both ordnance and small arms fire from the opposite army, Tom's command was to stall the invasion of the column of tanks and troops, which smacked of Poland just one war before, and the Alamo a hundred years before that. The same idea—to stave off an onslaught long enough for help to arrive—seldom bode well for the soldiers committed to the task. Such was the case for Task Force Smith.

America then, replete with pride and the favor of God over stopping the evil of Germany and Japan, had every expectation that this war, Korea, would be short and uneventful as wars go. Short or not, Tom preferred to live through it, because short or not, dead is dead. Short for one man is eternity for another, and he had too many things yet undone.

At eighteen, he didn't yet know how unusual he was, didn't yet know what valor meant, didn't yet know how reassuring it can be to find out what you're made of. Over coffee and rations that morning, July 5, 1950, his companions had been somber and afraid but brimming with bravado and nervous laughter. Most of the boys had segmented themselves into groups, if not by state than by region, because that's what people do. Southern boys with southern boys, northern with northern, and western with western. Among the groups there was further subdivision: Louisiana and Arkansas and Mississippi boys together, New York and New Jersey and Pennsylvania boys together, New Mexico and Arizona and California boys together. Then there was Texas. Then there was Tom.

While equally adept at fitting in with all of the boys, he felt an alliance to humanity and his own sense of morality more than he would ever feel an alliance to a region or a dialect or a skin color or a religion. Even more than an alliance to his flag or country.

"You ain't gonna eat neither, Welton?" said a voice from behind him. Turning, Tom found the voice belonged to Percy Daniels, a skinny red-haired kid from Florida. His skin, forever white, glowed nearly translucent in flushed nervousness. Tom could see blue veins straining from within his iridescent biceps. His thick orange hair was a close-cropped shaved flattop; a festive carrot-colored lawn belying the tension beneath it.

"I want to be fast in case I have to be, Daniels," Tom answered, spinning on his haunches to face him, "Just coffee and toast for me. You?"

"Hell, I been up half the night in the latrine. Tallahassee two-step, nearly crapped my skivvies," Percy came back. He was smoking unfiltered Lucky Strikes that had come in his C-rations, the pack itself rolled up in his shirt sleeve and resting on his gossamer shoulder.

Percy continued, "Probly that nasty potted meat from yesterday. Potted meat and nerves. I ain't scared, mind you, just sorta nervous is all."

Fear in battle, Tom had decided, was something you either did or didn't have, something you invited or rejected, and seemed to have little to do with faith. After all, there were good Christian boys as afraid as the heathens. Fear could get him killed, however, and while he was of course afraid, he kept it at bay rather than entertain it. Death was a possibility, but in no way reflected whether he was right to be there.

His fear, Tom's fear, was more a fear of what would happen if he wasn't there. A fear for innocent people, defenseless against their aggressors, and certain to suffer and die at the hand of their invaders. For Tom, it was less his willingness to fight for country than it was his willingness to fight for people. Strangers, to be certain, but also his mother and sister, who'd already lost too much to war as it was.

"Ain't you scared, kid?" Daniels asked. Like a lot of young men Tom knew, Daniels referred to everyone as "kid" or "cousin."

Tom looked at him, understanding fully Percy Daniels was looking for a word to hang on; looking for some inspiration and hope. Daniels was looking to him to assure him they were all going home.

"Scared as anybody else," Tom lied. "Don't worry, Daniels, we're better trained than they are."

Then beyond the fear, beyond the faith, beyond the pride and glory, he knew in his short eighteen years everyone picks a side. Some actively, some passively, and that the better parts of courage come in the choosing. He'd already chosen early on, so when the war—the police action—was imminent, Tom signed on.

While the other boys, like Percy, needed the bit of security offered them by friendship, Tom embraced the friendship independent of the choices he had made, independent of his need for protection, independent of side arm and certainty. He wouldn't have called himself fearless, but that is the way it was interpreted. Percy and the other young men saw Tom calmly drinking coffee, offering no nervous chatter, no wish to be anywhere but where he was. This they read as courage while Tom wouldn't have seen it that way. He had no way of knowing he was alone in this, as he was in most things, for at eighteen Tom thought everyone thought as he did.

His comrades had diverted themselves with talk of what they missed about home, from sweethearts and family to Sunday-after-church base-ball and fruit preserves and friends from school. Missed food became a differentiator for these young men; a distraction to argue over terms or pronunciation. Many had never been exposed to crayfish versus craw-fish, you-uns versus y'all, hoagies versus subs, pops versus soda versus the ubiquitous "coke" in the south.

At first blush the "missings" were tangible, people or food or places. But in them Tom could feel a fear of never seeing them, tasting them, or visiting them again as if the last time was truly the last time, and "miss-ing" being regret over not embracing that last taste, that last hug, that last look. And while the lists were as long and as varied as the soldiers, Tom thought of only three things: his family, the 38th parallel, and his BSA motorcycle left under a tarp in his mother's barn.

Focused, intent, and with a hint of vengeance, Tom turned off ev-erything in him except the task at hand, as he had done since he stood in his father's absence. In fact, these three things would occupy most of his thoughts for the following five years. While many of the boys prayed, worshiped, held hands and stood vigil over their own mortality, Tom, with no disdain, saw this as fear not faith; saw this as a lack of focus, as weakness endured as a symptom of self-importance.

Tom had grown up going to church like every good Baptist kid. His mother put his Sunday clothes on his bed Saturday night, washed and pressed, with the expectation Tom would have his shoes polished and hair combed in time to leave early enough for Sunday school. After his father passed, he would walk the mile to the church with his sister, Ruby, and after Sunday school meet his mother for the "big" service. She, flanked by her two children, would sing harmony from the congregation while Tom marveled at her voice. He would close his eyes and listen, oc-casionally crying over the sheer, wild beauty of it.

"Amazing Grace," she would sing, "how sweet the sound," and Tom would well up.

When they saw him cry, the adults around him thought he was feeling the Holy Spirit, when truly Tom was feeling the relief in his mother's peace for one hour every week. She was shy, beautiful, and smart. He'd spent the better part of his memory watching women pity her and men steal glimpses of her. He'd watch them bathe her top to bottom in wanting, disregarding him as an appendage or a pet. His status as a decade-old non-entity gave him the unique perspective of a hidden observer, wherein he saw those men for what they were, and vowed he would never be one of them.

"Brother Richard," one would say, shaking another man's hand. And the second man would respond with "Brother Elwood or Brother John or Brother Percy." He'd then see them follow his mother's curves, and while he didn't yet know what that meant, he instinctively knew it was a secret about her that she didn't know, and one that would ruin her if she did. Stunningly beautiful, his mother was too old for the single young men, and too young to be dismissed. When the men were together, he would hear them say the same thing the women said, but it felt different. And that thing was: "what a shame."

Tom modeled himself after and looked up to the handful of men that seemed to genuinely engage his mother, his sister, and himself. These men did not betray their witness, but they also didn't stick with Tom the way the other men did. Though young, he carried the mantle of man of the house, and he was assured enough of the honorable men's intentions that he dismissed them, instead alert and diligent over the less honorable. Protective of his mother and sister in his father's absence, he didn't have the luxury of trust. Tom knew who he could look up to, and who rubbed him the wrong way. He paid little mind to them men he respected, as they weren't a threat. The others, however, had his attention.

In 1944 Corpus Christi, Texas, Tom saw the same people every day. He saw them at church to be sure, unless they were Lutherans or Catholics, but all over town as well. The Lutherans were tolerated, but the Catholics were feared and disparaged by people who were not Tom or Tom's mother or Tom's sister, and a few others. Transubstantiation and images of Christ on a cross were more than the Baptist sensibility could bear, after all, so saying nothing meant condoning that aberration.

This Catholicism was misguided from a good Baptist perspective, but again, 1944 made it easier to dismiss because many Catholics in Texas were Mexican, leading the Baptists to write Catholicism off as a Mexican religion. Tom's mother, Esther Welton, was half-Mexican, his grandfather

having married his own Spanish Rose, so at his house he knew no difference, but every place else he suffered the subterfuge of dichotomy: the
need to dismiss Catholics and Mexicans when they weren't around, but
embrace and love and sincerely respect them when they were.

"I got a mezkin comin' out Friday to help me roof," he might hear, or
"Who helped you roof?" and the answer would be, "A wetback I picked
up over't the dock."

Some may have thought Tom too young to understand this hypocrisy, but in truth, he actively ignored it. He couldn't articulate the confusing
notion that his role models could do one thing and say another, or vice
versa, but he knew what felt right. And what felt right was to treat people
with honor and respect in and out of their presence. How could a man
work side by side on a shrimp boat or dock with a Mexican man, share
their lives with them and seemingly love them, but speak of "crazy Catholic Mes'cans" and "spics" and "wetbacks" when they were alone? Speaking
fluent Spanish himself, Tom heard the same thing among the Mexican
men, referring to their white friends as "bolillo (white bread bun)" and
"crudo" and "gringo" and "white eye" when they weren't around.

He saw that same behavior from many men when it came to his
mother. How could these men betray his mother's trust with the kindness
of personal conversation, but treat her so disparagingly when she wasn't
there to hear? Fly on the wall, he was, but he was a fly who would one day
grow a beard, one day ball a fist, and a fly whose notion of Christian ethic
was shaped by the hypocrisy of what he witnessed.

This idea, the very idea of not betraying who you purport to be—
not bearing false witness—rang a bell in Tom that echoed his entire life,
prompting in him an integrity and grit and earnest compassion that
would be the hallmark of his existence. Tom was a good man, by any
standard. Conversely, the disparity he witnessed in the words and deeds
of the adults of his youth ensured he would dismiss their religious con-
victions as well.

Essentially, the disparity inspired in him the belief to be good
trumped any message he got at church. While there were Christian men
and women in his life who legitimately embraced and practiced the tenets of their conviction, Tom grew to think of them as ancillary. Their
kindness was independent of their Christianity, with Christianity being
the beneficiary of men and women who were good anyway.

"I am the way, the truth, and the life," said Jesus Christ. Tom's sense
of fairness had less than a dozen or so years to reflect on that, and as

such, rejected it. As a child, he knew no better than to trust his own innate sense of fairness, and many good churchless women and men he knew seemed more entitled to heaven than several of the attendees that shared his pew. Of course, his innate self-awareness told him to keep this to himself. He would rather die than break his mother's heart with the news he wasn't buying it.

Mr. Leon Springs, one of Tom's examples of a hypocrite, owned the hardware store down the road from Tom's house. He was a man who rubbed Tom the wrong way. Springs was Baptist as well, so Tom saw him as much as any man in the county, what with church and Tom's mother selling eggs that Tom delivered to Mrs. Springs, Leon's wife. He wasn't a bad man, law abiding and nice enough, but because Tom saw him behave differently amongst different people, he didn't trust him. Mrs. Springs, mostly known as Mrs. Florence, worked in the store as well, baking and selling pastries from a glass case in the window. She was big-hipped, always talking about getting her figure back, kind and loving, hugging Tom with every new delivery of eggs.

Outside of his mother and sister, Ms. Florence was the only person who hugged Tom. She would say, "Tom, would you like a slice of yesterday's pie?" then proceed to cut a slice of the warm, fresh-baked pie for Tom. Many years later it would occur to him she'd said "yesterday's pie" so her husband didn't know she was giving away the good stuff. Between the ages of ten and seventeen, Tom ate hundreds of slices of pie given him by Ms. Florence.

Ms. Florence was scandalous for only one reason, and she clung to it: she listened to American Blues and "the colored's" music. When she was younger, she'd found a 78 record in a train yard while on her way to visit her sister in Beaumont and recognized just one of the songs: *Amazing Grace*. The record's jacket announced "Southern Folk Ballads and Gospel Music Sung by America's Newest Colored Stars!" and featured shining blue-faced and teenaged John Lee Hooker, whom she'd never heard of before. Thinking it was a recording of church music, she put it in her handbag and off it went to her sister's house along with nylons and white wax and lanolin.

Her sister Maybell was in Beaumont for nursing school bound for Houston after, and would never return to Corpus. Ms. Florence, a year older, had never moved away and never would. Their adult relationship consisted of weekly letters, monthly telephone calls, and yearly visits. The church and the town missed Maybell, and every Sunday Florence was asked about her.

"Well, Florence," they would say, "I wanted to ask after Maybell. How she's doin' and such." And every week Florence would report the happenings of her sophisticated sister.

On that day however, the first day of their first visit as independent adults, Maybell and Flo, as she introduced herself all week, would have their lives changed by the blues. When Maybell saw the record she gleefully squealed over their coming sacrilege. Without speaking of it, the picture of the shiny-skinned black boy on the jacket was enough to scream "forbidden," and in their youthful rebellion they put the needle down on church music that was enrapturing if not rapturous.

The next week saw nightly visits to over-the-tracks blues clubs for the two young women, and included their first gin, first cigarettes, and first dance. They were Baptists, after all. On Flo's last night they took the ferry across Lake Pontchartrain to a blues club in Louisiana called simply "Music and Dancing." The first white girls ever to darken the door, Ms. Florence came home from her week away with a dozen blues records and two dozen sins, including:

1. One "damn that colored boy can play a piano" (a sin for the damn and not for the colored).

2. Two packs of cigarettes (she classified this as a sin but wasn't sure of it).

3. Six nights of drinking. Drinking was bad enough, but drunkenness was heinous.

4. Dancing and more dancing—strictly off limits for Baptists.

5. A long French kiss with a handsome young policeman who lived in the apartment next to Maybell.

The kiss happened after midnight, after four gins, after dancing and cursing and after cigarettes. She was in her bare feet and tipsy, holding her shoes in one hand and her bag in the other with salacious lyrics filling her head. The young policeman was coming home from his shift, and Maybell introduced them.

She'd said, "Elmer, this is my sister Flo, and she's never been kissed by a boy! Will you kiss her?"

And just like that they were locking lips next to the fire hose on the second-floor walk-up. At that moment and for many moments after, Florence would have gone inside with the handsome young policeman. Would have bed him. Would have clung to him; had him; held him from that day forward. Would have married him. So lightheaded and taken, she would have vanished behind the mosquito clouds and refineries of southeast Texas, having babies with the handsome young policeman from Beaumont, whose voice was deep and cavernous, whose late-shift whiskers rubbed hard against her soft cheek. She could feel her nostrils twitching as she kissed him. He smelled like sweat and honor and she felt like a flower in a fist.

Maybell had pulled her arm, "C'mon, Dolly," she said, dragging her back into the world.

The next morning brought a headache and a cigarette burn on the sleeve of her favorite blouse, but more than that, the shame of her desire. How ready she had been to abandon all virtue to sleep with this stranger, to drink more gin, to dance, to grow up. More than the guilt of her actions, however, was the guilt of her desire to do it again. The shame of her longing. The guilt of repentance without conviction, of doing the right thing—rather, not doing the wrong thing—simply because she trusted that God knew what was best even if she hated it.

The guilt passed but the music didn't, playing softly in the back room of the store for the rest of Ms. Flo's days. She would hum when Leon was there and sing when he wasn't.

"You like that, Tom?" she would ask, followed by the names of the singer and band members. When she sang, she sounded like Bessie Smith, and on the rare occasion she danced it was like nothing Tom had ever seen. She would grab his hand and twirl in the big room, where dry goods and tools were stored.

"Cigareetes, whusky and wild, wild women!" she would sing while dancing.

On Sundays, when the congregation was singing *The Old Rugged Cross*, Ms. Flo couldn't help but bring her blues roots with her, ending the chorus with "Mmm, hmmm, mmm, Lord, Lord, Lord, sho' 'nuff, sho' 'nuff, Lord."

One morning when Tom arrived at the general store, Leon was out front unloading a truck with two Catholics. "Tom," Springs asked, "how's your momma?"

"She's fine, Mr. Springs," Tom answered as he did every day.

"She shore is," Springs replied, looking at the two men for affirmation. They all laughed as though Tom was furniture. Tom felt a disrespect he didn't like.

Two weeks later, Tom was standing in the foyer after church with his sister. His mother was visiting with several women from her own Sunday school class, laughing and happy and glad to be with people who loved her. Lord, she loved that church! The foyer was crowded with folks talking and planning and shooting the breeze, like any Sunday afternoon of Tom's short life. Working his way toward the door, Leon Springs, in light blue cotton church pants, walked behind Florence as they stopped to talk with everyone they ran into, including Tom's mother. Simply hearing Ms. Florence's voice was reassuring, as she gave her weekly report on Maybell.

And while Mr. Springs seldom talked to his mother, on this day he did, saying simply, "How you doing, Esther?"

Tom knelt to tie his glistening, polished shoes and for reasons he would only know later, suddenly balled a fist. On his knees, he was half as tall as the shortest adult in the foyer, so he had room to gain speed. Now a strong, growing twelve-year-old, he came off the floor with every bit of strength in his legs, swinging his new fist upward into Leon's crotch.

On that day, fresh from revival, Mr. Springs spoke in tongues.

PART III

Look down the valley, I see my burying ground,
Look down the valley, I see my burying ground,
My mother and my father, strong and young to let me down.

—TREE TOP WHITE

Six years later, on July 5, 1950, Tom was ordered to take position on the west side of the encroaching North Korean army. He embedded himself in a stand of pine trees, crouching behind a .30 caliber Browning machine gun, alone but for a West Virginia radioman, Ernie Wilkerson. Ernie had never worn shoes until he joined the army, which was common in those days. Outgunned and outmanned, Tom, Ernie and the whole of Task Force Smith listened as the great rolling tanks, their tracks and gears clamoring up the hillside, approached their position. Ernie, over

and over and over, muttered the changed words to a children's prayer he
had learned in boot camp:

> Now I lay me down to sleep
> I pray The Lord my soul to keep
> If I should die before the morn
> Let it be in courage born
> With gun in hand and in the breach
> Between the wicked and the weak
> In triumph, Lord, if I should perish
> The honor I, forever cherish.

Tom prayed as well, as he had all morning but with no sense of a
listener, desperate to be heard by a God he'd come to believe was somehow there, but disinterested in the minutia of men, even though his hope
remained. Or, if He did have some faint interest, He had better things to
do and greater concerns than to pay attention to the fervent wishes of an
eighteen-year-old soldier on a violent hillside in Korea.

"Why would He listen? Why would He care?" Tom thought.

Certainly, the countless prayers of multi-millennia young men on
battlefields from Britain to Bangladesh had to have grown tiresome; had
to have grown a bore. Tom's remaining hope, however, was grace for the
notion he believed he was doing the right things for the right reasons,
thwarting his own fear for the benefit of others. Surely, he could have
hope in that. This remaining hope that God was not only there but might
have noticed his predicament compelled him to purposefully avoid ending the prayer in some way. It compelled in him the urge not to sign off
with "amen" or crossing himself. If he was to die, he wanted to finish the
conversation in person. He'd prayed not to live, but for courage; not for
life, but for honor. He prayed not as one entitled, but as a grown man
hopes and prays for meaning and to die well.

"Dear Lord," Tom said, staring into the distance for his first look
at the enemy. "Dear Lord," he said again. "Dear Lord, make me brave.
Protect me from my enemies. Give me victory here in this life, and if I
should die here today, Lord," pausing when tanks broke the horizon, "if I
die, please let it be fighting, and take care of mama and Ruby."

When the American Howitzers, then the 70mm rounds had no ef-
fect on the tanks, Tom's heart sank, as did Ernie's, knowing they would
be bare-knuckle fighting in a matter of minutes. His mouth was dry,
and he struggled to swallow. He could smell the exhaust of the engines,
the breeze carrying it in through the trees, the odor telling him the

carburetors' fuel/air mix was too rich for the altitude. For a half-second, he wondered what a tank carburetor might look like. He looked at Ernie, whose elbow rested on his bent knee and whose eyes were locked down the barrel of his raised M1 Garand.

Determination flexed in his jaw and his lower leg shook in fearful, angry anticipation. When he was close enough to see the same determination and fear on the Korean boys' faces, the order came. With only a hundred yards to spare, Ernie got word to fire and without hesitation Tom cut loose. Unable to determine the machine gun's location, the tanks and infantry fired recklessly in all directions with enough firepower to matter until they could find their targets.

Tom drew down on two soldiers crouching behind an advancing tank and killed them both while the swarm of enemy soldiers advanced, closing in on his left flank. With only five seconds of active combat, Tom swung the gun to a third soldier when Ernie was struck in the throat. Standing up and clutching the wound, he was cut down with two rounds to his chest and shoulder, his last vertical word less a word than an exclamation, less an exclamation than a guttural sound, a sound less of panic than of recognition, before dropping dead in the only pair of shoes he'd ever worn. With Ernie crying out behind him, Tom swung the gun around to fire on the wave of attackers when he was himself shot through the jaw.

The pain and the fury made him forget himself, and dropping his rifle, he reared up with both hands in fists. That's when he took a second round, grazing the back of his skull and knocking him to the ground. Blinking and half-conscious, choking on broken teeth, he registered a red-flanked blue-tail swallow frantically racing through the sky above him, and blacking out, could smell the damp earthy smell of early summer and pine needless. Pine, not unlike the loblolly pine of the east Texas Big Thicket.

PART IV

Big-legged woman, throw your big leg over me,
God made me a woman, big-legged honeybee,
The lips 'round her mouth, the sweetest sting I ever known,
Sting me one more time agin, big-legged honeybee.

—MISSISSIPPI ENGOL JEFFER

Dianne said goodbye to the dog, named Hambone Happy Cheese by a grandchild, as he whined at the gate, nearly certain she and John would be back before nightfall. She was wrong, as plans and predictions and intentions often are, but she couldn't have known it at the time. Many hours later she would be calling their neighbors, Angel and Rachel Garza, to ask them to feed and water Hambone, and to open the side garage door so he could sleep inside. At that time, however, she had only her purse, her phone, her knitting and a book—standard for any car ride longer than an hour.

Of course, Hambone only knew they were leaving, having come to understand car keys and shoes and locked doors meant something, and whined and yelped accordingly. She placated the dog with kind words and kissing sounds, certain Hambone was comforted but of course he had no idea what it meant, despite her conviction otherwise. She loved the dog, as did John, going so far as to personify him in word and in deed. Hambone knew words like sit, speak, treat, and shake, and proved it often in exchange of bacon-smelling goo chunks or pieces of Dianne's sandwich. She sensed his coming sadness and fear during their absence, assigning the dog some mystifying psychic intuition that would portend the grief of their leaving.

It is important to love and to be loved, and with the kids grown and gone, she had come to believe she and John were central to Hambone, and that his only desire was to love them and be loved by them. She had assigned this to him, and he, naturally, wallowed in it. She imagined him curled up and depressed after they left, trying to sleep in the shadow of the picnic table, whimpering while all manner of beast and bird did their best to comfort him. So convinced he was suffering, she made promises to him as she would a person, in the hope that the projection into the future—their projected reunion and petting and kind words and treats—would tide Hambone Happy Cheese over until they got back.

"When I get back we'll play ball, Hammy. I love you very mu-uch. Yes I do, Yes I do, be a good boy, ooh-youbeagoodboy," followed by a bacon-flavored chunk of goo.

The dog, on the other hand, had no understanding of "soon." Without a watch and never having studied the Gregorian calendar and without any clear understanding of tides and lunar cycles or etymologic gestation or even the regular comings and goings of mailmen and neighbors, and despite the current conviction of people that dogs are humans without a voice, this dog knew only three things: his name, where his loyalties were, and where his food was. Anything remotely discernible beyond that was gathered by way of sniffing, peeing, and rolling in odors unfamiliar to him.

Likewise, Dianne had no way of knowing Hambone's true behavior, true motivation, or true degree of anxiety. Many times every week they enacted this ritual as the humans went to the grocery store or movie theater or dinner, and each time it was the same. As they drove away, Hambone would bolt to the picnic table, jump on top of it and turn circles as fast as he could. He would run the fence line, joyfully chasing anything he could put his eyes on, from birds to rabbits to neighborhood kids dragging sticks along the pickets. He would leap from the ground in a futile effort to catch the birds and would sometimes knock down the garbage can in the hope of finding something delightful. He did all of this in the span of three or four minutes, followed by sleeping under the picnic table.

When John and Dianne first noticed the scratches on the table, Dianne had said, "Oh poor Hammy! He must stand up here looking for us. I feel so bad about leaving him."

John would always follow with something reasonable like, "He'll be okay. We've had him this long. If he misses us, that's not terrible."

And while it is true John loved Hambone Happy Cheese, he saw the dog as he saw every pet: practice in the way to best treat people. Be kind, be gracious, be generous, be patient and most of all, take them for what they are. His father taught him that. This sensibility—John's realism—kept the dog from wearing sweaters and going to the groomer.

PART V

I'm broke, broke and crumbled like walls at Jericho.
I'm done broke, broke and crumbled like walls at Jericho.
Won't somebody come save me, 'fore I'm kill't and gone for good?

—SONNY-BOY THOMAS

With the latest wave of pain passing, Tom could now consider his wrist. The compression fracture splintered an inch or so of his radius, thrusting it through the skin above his hand. There was little blood, and the pain was more of a creak than a cry. The ulna was somehow intact which allowed Tom to move his fingers but little else. The oncoming swelling seemed to give his throbbing wrist some stability. As the sun streamed through the lower limbs of the trees, Tom checked his watch to find it was still only 8:00 a.m. He was alarmed to find the swelling stacking up against the strap of the watch like a tourniquet, the gold links of his Rolex Oyster straining over his speckled skin. He was only now struck by the age of his skin, and the changes that had snuck up on him while he was busy living: the gray hairs of his arms and hands, the age spots and crepe skin, the translucent hide over his skeletal hand, exaggerating the arthritically swollen knuckles.

With the embarrassment and panic and rush of adrenaline passing, Tom set about considering his options. For a fleeting few seconds he was ashamed; ashamed to be old and ashamed to still envision himself formidable and capable and athletic and strong. Ashamed to have thought there was still something scary about him. Ashamed to have had hubris enough to ride a motorcycle at his age.

"What was I thinking?" he asked aloud.

The shame, as in most things, was over the consequence, not over the call he made to ride. And now, now on the floor of the deep woods in "the betweens," Tom's shame found him. What was he thinking? What was the answer?

The veins of his hand were bulbous and straining, struggling with blood flow as the swelling worsened. The bloated flesh began to roll over top of the watch band. Roseanne had given him the watch on their twenty-fifth anniversary, an extravagance he never would have sanctioned had it not come from her and meant so much for her to give it to him. In Tom's mind, a Rolex could have been more motorcycles, which of course, was no extravagance at all.

"Well you can't leave a motorcycle for the children and grandbabies, but a watch means something." She had said this many times over the years. She finally took it upon herself to give him something to leave. For Tom, a watch was a constant reminder he was dying, a record of loss, a meter showcasing an account without deposits.

Time had become an enemy to Tom in Korea, when five years ticked by with no movement, only static rage and loathing. Where his fellow captives had scratched off the days on cell walls, Tom refused to keep record of what was being stolen from him. It was bad enough he bore witness, so he refused to record the daily withdrawals. He refused to know what day it was, what year it was, what time it was. He refused to watch the days of his life pour out on a concrete floor in a dingy cell, clinging to some meager scratching on the wall. For this reason, he was stunned when he was released to discover it had been five years. Five years stolen from him, and fifty more enraged over it.

Easing the hinge of the strap and slipping the watch off his hand, he flipped it over to read the inscription as he did every time he wore it. "To my love," it simply read, "on our first 25 years."

While the watch had become more bibelot than timepiece, these were scratches on the walls he could live with. These were the debits he eagerly gave. This was the measure that mattered. He gently eased the watch into his inside jacket pocket for safekeeping, just behind the Triumph breast patch, determined to be conscious enough when rescued to tell the EMTs it was there.

Roseanne had given him the watch during a celebration with the kids in a reserved private dining room in Houston's Heidegar Steak House. The restaurant was a regal holdover from a well-mannered, sophisticated era in Houston's early days, complete with mahogany walls and heavy velvet curtains drawn over the private room doors. Built just after the war in 1946, the Heidegar was one Rhodes-scholar-turned-wildcatter's effort to bring some civility to a rowdy, roughneck environment. Making more money selling steak than oil, Raymond "Mr. Ray" Heidegar's dining house became the dinner of legend for anniversaries, birthdays, and any celebration.

Unlike other restaurants and other businesses, Heidegar's had not seen better days, as every day was as grand and special as the day before, weathering every economic downturn and threat because there are always people with something special to celebrate; always people with money. Successfully refusing to change with the times, Heidegar's had somehow managed to maintain insistence on coats and ties and dresses and skirts. Boasting "the most robust collection of scotch and whiskey in the world," and steaks "hand-selected by Texas cattlemen and former USDA inspectors," dinner at Heidegar's was extravagant and occasional at best. To say you'd gone to Heidegar's told your listener how special the evening had been or in some cases, how wealthy you were.

There were no fry batters for there were no deep fryers. There was no kid's menu of corn dogs and nuggets, or starters covered in salt and cheese. There were no dipping sauces or vulgar ketchup bottles. Hors d'oeuvres were choices, not additions, ranging from crab cakes to shrimp in peanut sauce to escargot to pork medallions in wine roux. They only took reservations, even on those evenings the restaurant was not full to occupancy, turning away many hundreds of walk-ins annually.

"It isn't enough," Heidegar would say, "to come here dying of hunger simply because you saw that the lights were on. You must want to be with us badly enough to reserve your own seat."

Sometimes the turn-downs would be outraged, the maître d' having lost count of the number of men and women who'd shout, "Do you know who I am?!"

Still and forever, Heidegar insisted reservation-only meant reservation-only, regardless of social, economic, political, or popular station.

His motto? "All are welcome, if we know they are coming and if they are properly dressed."

Often, however, he would personally wait, free of charge, on the men in the alley, who were down on their luck and hungry. He would set a table complete with linens and china service, seating three or four men who thought themselves unworthy of compassion; unworthy of love. So stricken with gratitude, some of these men would weep as they ate.

The wait staff's average age was forty-five, and the maître d' close to seventy. While elegance was the priority, it was still relaxed and fun.

When bringing the check, the waiter would say with sincerity, "We have an after-dinner saloon in the rear, along with a walk-in humidor. We would love for you to stay and enjoy a cigar or pipe or glass of brandy."

There were no costumes and no gimmicks and no horseplay amongst the busboys at Heidegar's. Everyone was articulate. Everyone was well-read. Many spoke two languages. The bartenders knew Scotch whisky and bourbon whiskey and gin and wine; all were versed in Shakespeare and the Bible and Dante¢ as well as last week's ball game. Between the restaurant and lounge stood a deep, rich vestibule, on the walls of which hung watercolors and mixed media and a few reductionist paintings, but mostly traditional oil on canvas, including a seventeenth century original by Noel Coypel. There were also a handful of framed collectible documents, including a ledger sheet from George Washington's farm and a letter of pardon written by William Barret Travis.

The door at the end of the foyer gave entry to the lounge that the staff called a saloon. If you didn't like cigars you didn't go in, but if you took a chance, you would leave the place liking cigars. The saloon itself was cozy, where people sat in clusters of club chairs or booths upholstered in worn crimson leather. The root beer glass ashtrays were always emptied and clean, with the subtle, painted Heidegar's logo peering through the bottom like a fish through a glass-bottom boat. There was never a rush to seat you, never a rush to have you go.

There were signed photographs on the walls of celebrities and in-fluential, exceptionally smart or exceptionally talented men and women including Bobby Kennedy, Harper Lee, Henry Kissinger, Milton Fried-man, Neil Armstrong, Martina Navratilova, Stevie Ray Vaughn, Walter Cronkite, Muhammed Ali, Isaac Asimov, General Hamilton H. Howze, Lionel Hampton, and many more. Desperate movie stars and singers ached over the desire to be on the wall, some bringing in signed head-shots for the maître d' or having publicists send headshots, but these walls were invitation-only. There were two musicians who'd worked there since 1961, a cellist and a violinist, taking turns in the corner at thirty-minute intervals.

There were no anonymously produced house liquors and no mar-garitas or tequila sunrises; there were no daiquiris or coconut-and-sugar-lemon-candy-soaked cherry and soda pop concoctions. Only top-shelf scotch, bourbon and white liquors; world class red and white wine. Your scotch was neat; your bourbon might have a single ice cube; your gin had a lime; your vodka an olive, and while many a rube asked for a Budweiser, not a single beer was ever served.

"Beer, while not always boorish," Heidegar would say, "and has no place among a gentleman's spirits."

The mature staff represented all ethnicities, because Heidegar cared for caliber over color, but there was clearly some welcomed discrimina-tion. That is, Heidegar's discriminated against the mannerless and the moron, which, after all, was their brand. In fact, the wait staff interviews were more culture quiz than food service and as a result only bright, edu-cated, articulate, engaging people were hired. They were all expected to know everything about every dish, most everything about their liquors, most everything about their wines. They were all expected to have read and remembered the Riverside Shakespeare, the U.S. Constitution, the Bill of Rights, a list of hand-picked novels, a second list of hand-picked biographies and a couple of non-fiction books of philosophy and eco-nomics. Twice every month the staff was given a new book to read and were expected to be abreast of current events, and to have an opinion they could articulate.

There was a man or woman on every shift who knew everything there was to know about cigars and pipe tobacco, and as a group, they traveled with a Heidegar family member annually to Honduras or Ecua-dor or the Dominican Republic to secure the next season's contract. This was an elevated position, one aspired to by the already well-paid waitstaff.

Every Monday Heidegar would tack a handwritten question to the wall in the restaurant's breakroom. While not required, having an answer by the Friday morning staff meeting went a long way with the old man.

The questions might be a simple preference, such as, "Who is your favorite post-war architect?" or creatively challenging such as, "As contemporaries, suppose Cervantes and Shakespeare did in fact eat dinner together. What would they have talked about?"

Heidegar's goal was to have a staff more intellectually prepared for the world than most of the patrons in an effort to elevate the brand, certainly, but more importantly to elevate the role of the waitstaff.

"Only in this elevation," Heidegar would say to his staff, "can we ensure your role as a servant. Only in being smarter, more sharp-witted, more informed is your servitude meaningful. Only in subjugation, humbling yourselves to your customer can you properly treat our guests as honored and loved. And in this, our customers know—without doubt—you could be doing something else but instead choose to make their experience unforgettable."

In all of this scrutiny came many things, not the least of which was a bar set high enough that few people in the industry qualified to work there, but once in, became family. And well-paid family at that. It was well known in Houston and better well known in the circles of elite restaurants that Heidegar not only did not pay his staff, but legendarily, they paid him to work there. The customer checks were so great and the tips so grand, waiters were competing for the chance to pay for their position. The resultant staff looked more like a professorial roster than a list of restaurant employees, and while not all of them were formally educated, all of them were educated, nonetheless.

For this and a hundred reasons more, Heidegar's became the destination for celebrities, political leaders, and the wealthy from around the world. This discrimination extended to the patrons too, disallowing not just the underdressed, but also the loud, the drunk, the rubes, the embarrassing nouveau riche. In fact, the local legend is that Steve McQueen was barred from entering the restaurant in 1968 because he wasn't wearing a tie. He returned the next evening in a tailored navy sharkskin suit and tie, and upon leaving gave the cellist his Rolex Submariner and his waiter a cash tip wrapped in that tie.

To the Welton party's private room their children brought records to be played, all a reflection of their own days growing up in a house full of Muddy Waters and Howlin' Wolf. They'd taken turns praying before dinner, thanking God for their parents, their leadership, and their discipline in raising them. They'd had a round of cocktails before dinner, Tom treating himself to a Beefeater Burrough's Reserve gin and tonic, while Roseanne shared a bottle of red wine with John and the girls. Postwar Tom had never been too enthusiastic about abstinence from alcohol, falling in with a Catholic girl who'd converted to Lutheran. Oddly and happily, his Baptist mother had loosened up over the years and, when visiting, might have a glass herself.

Esther and Roseanne had become very close—in some ways more intimately connected than Tom was to his mother—as early on Roseanne's love for God was evinced in a way that made Esther glad she was Tom's bride. As it was clear Roseanne was much more interested in a relationship with Christ than in a relationship with rules, they'd had a marriage of wine with dinner, beer with burgers, and cocktails when the mood struck, despite Tom's Baptist upbringing. This, as was the case with everything Tom, was a question of moderation and discipline. Self-control was honorable, and there was nothing honorable about drunkenness. In fact, Tom had cocktails maybe once in a week, rarely had more than a single drink, and never more than two. This night, however, this anniversary, was a two-cocktail celebration if there ever was one.

Jerked back into the immediacy of his situation, he could feel the pain in his hip coming on again. He tried to enter his breathing and fanning of arms and leg like a surfer might enter a wave. His desire was to simply go with it as best he could and instead of flail, usher the pain through his body and shoulders and head quickly and with as little fanfare as possible, softly scraping the ground around him of debris as he moved his limbs in semicircles, breathing.

"Treat it respectfully," he said aloud as he moved, "and it will leave you quickly," suddenly shocked to recall that's what he said to himself whenever a guard entered his cell.

"Treat him respectfully and he will leave you quickly." Transfixed in that thought, he—as he had some fifty-five years before—thought of home and of his garden and of his family and friends, of his old BSA and the smell of salt air as he buzzed down dirt roads to the Corpus Christi beach. He could hear that bike, the wide-open "blatblatblat" or the racing engine filling his head as the pain enveloped him. Inhaling through his nose and blowing slowly through his lips it finally passed, while Tom relaxed into his clearing. The clearing formed by the diversion of fanning arms and legs.

The pain passing, fading with the remembered roar of that motorcycle and popping gravel under the tires, he licked his dry lips, his eye
catching his Thermos and fruit and notebooks and cigars, still somehow
strapped to the back of the bike seat. He could stretch to reach the package but had to work on the knot for quite some time because he only
had one hand. When successful, he held the Thermos under his left arm,
unscrewing the cap with his good hand and drinking directly from it.
The Thermos, chipped, scratched, and well-used, he'd gotten when Grace
was a baby, but the coffee was less than an hour old. Had he turned off
the pot? He thought so. Still hot and strong with cream and sugar, Tom
leaned on an elbow and drank. He closed his eyes and focused, slowly
swallowing, savoring one of his longest-held rituals.

Over the years the coffee had stained his teeth but had lightened
his heart. A coffee drinker since he was a boy, it had been a part of every
morning with Roseanne, every morning with the kids, every morning of
his life, barring the five years as a POW. At forty he'd stopped drinking
coffee after dinner and at fifty he'd stopped drinking coffee after noon. At
sixty he'd stopped having more than two cups, and most days now just
one. Still, he savored that cup, the oil from the beans glistening across
the top until it was lost in the cream, like his mind glistened across the
morning until it was lost in the day.

Most days, with no one knowing, Tom would peer into the cup as
he stirred, his long-held fascination with the golden ratio—a mysterious geometric ratio found in abundance in art, architecture, and more
importantly, nature—manifesting itself as he stirred. His stirring, that
thick, reluctant cream yielding to heat and motion, creating the perfect
geometric contrast to the blackness of the coffee.

That swirl, that conical formation wherein the mathematical relationship was exactly that of a tornado, a water spout, a drain hole, a toilet
bowl, a conch shell, wherein the relationship between the center and the
pattern's extremities remained constant, no matter how large the cup or
how quick the stir. He had been studying Johannes Kepler, a sixteenth
century German mathematician, and the Fibonacci sequence as found in
nature for several months before heading off to fight in Korea.

Desperately trying to rationalize his mother's blind faith with the reality of science, Tom was, at eighteen years old, coming down on the side
of Divinity. How, after all, could nature so readily replicate mathematical
formulas all over the world, with such exacting geometry? While evolu-
tionists could make a seemingly reasonable case for natural selection in

animals, and even in plant life for that matter, how could the end result be that of identical geometric formulas? And identical formulas across species, and across the planet? At what point, Tom thought, does coincidence become harder to believe than Divinity? At what point does the obvious outweigh his hubris?

Kepler had written, "For the theater of the world is so ordered that there exist in it suitable signs by which human minds . . . are invited to study the divine works."

This made sense to young Tom and helped him question his atheistic ways. Not surprisingly, Kepler echoed Romans 1:20: "For since the creation of the world God's invisible qualities—his eternal power and divine nature—have been clearly seen, being understood from what has been made, so that men are without excuse."

Clearly, understanding was easier for some people than others, and for Tom, it was necessity. More than adoration for his mother and his sister Ruby, he saw in them and in many people of the community a peace through church and their belief in Jesus Christ that he envied but held in contempt all the while. He wanted their peace, he wanted it, but simply could not come to terms with the exclusionary nature of Christianity, and by osmosis, the belief in an omnipotent, omniscient, all-loving God.

What is loving about exclusion, Tom wondered, and what rationalistic contortions does a "believer" twist into in order to explain away dismissing good, loving people, while Christian assholes get a pass? Tom worked with good and kind men and women in his community every day, delivering eggs and preserves and doing odd jobs, but who also never stepped foot into a church. On Sundays he went to church with men and women too, some of whom couldn't hold a candle to the heathens who bought his eggs, but believed in Christ. This, of course was when he was a child, before he put away childish things.

Funny, articulate, energetic, hard-working, and well-liked by all, Tom was still alone there. Dissecting his existence in a seaside world far removed from Ivy League existential conversation, Tom kept secret his intellect, not with intent, but because he had kept secret his intellect the whole of his life. Corpus Christi in 1940 could accept the fatherless kid who delivered eggs and rode a motorcycle. Corpus Christi could accept the good student and his affection for blues and Mexicans. However, 1940s Corpus Christi could not accept his questions about existence, nor his disbelief in salvation through the son of God.

He read fiction not only as an escape, but because it gave him insight into the human condition, the human psyche, and the human heart in a way only good fiction can. He read philosophy as a way of disassembling motive and to feel as though he had kindred spirits out there somewhere. He read poetry because it was raw and desperate and immediate. He read the Bible looking for reflection and flaws, and while he found none, accepted it as a moral guidebook instead of as God's word. He was validated by Thomas Jefferson, who believed the same thing. He studied geometry because Plato insisted, requiring it before he would even consider instructing a student. He listened to blues because Ms. Flo had introduced him, and because somehow, a few chords and sincere lyrics expressed more about humanity to him than 900 pages of Tolstoy.

Finally, he read *Buzzzzz* magazine and *American Motorcyclist* with more enthusiasm than anything else, because for Tom, a motorcycle represented all of those things.

A motorcycle was the industrial assembly of the human condition, of everything we're born with, complete with promise, ambition, adventure, despair, escape, freedom, secrets, confusion, passion, recklessness, honesty, danger, reward, flux, discipline, rage, and satisfaction. Tom rode that motorcycle, read those books, listened to that music, ate Ms. Flo's pies, and made people feel good about themselves as best he could. He protected his sister from bullies and suitors, helped the poor, translated Spanish when his Mexican friends needed help, and performed countless acts of anonymous kindness because he felt people were good at heart. And in all of it, Tom could not have said whether he was lonely, or knew no loneliness.

While at the age of eighteen, he was unable to congeal all of this, he struggled with it and grew in it, nonetheless. He did it all while delivering eggs and turning wrenches and offloading shrimp and doing odd jobs until he could go off to school in Houston. As he started to shave and put on weight, grow taller and gain depth of voice, he began to have faith in himself, and in that faith, planned to provide for his mother and sister in love and honor. Had his thoughts had time to mature, he would have said faith in God was cowardice manifest as reverence for something that didn't care or help, in an effort to give life meaning in the first place and assuage fear. All part of some grand, millennia-old planning to which the participants have no visibility or insight, and the faithful are simply to trust it's for their own good, or good for the kingdom. We are simply to drop to our knees and pray to the deity that knows what's best for us but keeps us in the dark.

No, sir. Tom was convinced it was all born in fear, and he would not allow fear to make his decisions for him. This mathematical research, however, the hours in the library and books ordered from New York, was his attempt to get to the bottom of the nonsense, whatever the evidence showed. He was willing to give God a chance—not for God but for his mother and sister. He suspected prayers were simply shouts into the abyss, because for most people the alternative was bewilderingly horrific, and that bewildered horror was the very thing that motivated the belief in God in the first place. For Tom, it was all simply self-protective, safety-inspired nonsense with no clear rational save a psychological one.

Still, he wondered, how could something like the Fibonacci series present itself all over the world in pinecones and roses and sunflowers and seashells and dust storms? How could it magically materialize from the minds of designers, long before they actively pursued it, in the Parthenon and Taj Mahal and Volkswagen bugs and in Barcelona chairs and French wine posters?

Da Vinci observed that the displacement of leaves around a stem occurred in patterns defined by the Fibonacci series, as each number in the series is the sum of the two preceding numbers (1, 2, 3, 5, 8, 13, 21...) presented in a spiraled sequence in keeping with the golden ratio. How can this arcanum be the way evolution presented itself all over the world, in the exact same way in the exact same sequence in the exact same ratios? Moreover, how can this pattern be such an indelible part of our collective psyche that it then magically presents itself in art and architecture the world over?

So, while Tom was satisfied not having answers, he was not satisfied with not looking for them. Then came the draft.

Chapter 3

The trail is narrow, my heavy brow,
The woods are deep and we don't know how,
The how's and why's of God's kind hand,
To lead us to that promised land.

—*Maybell "Tupelo" Tucker*

Just thirty minutes out from Tom's place, John called Hannah to let her know he was almost there.

"I'm so glad, Johnny," Hannah said, relieved. "Call me as soon as you know anything?"

John knew exactly when to call. If he had called shortly after leaving, Hannah would have been fretting over John seeing the need to drive three hours. But calling just thirty minutes from her father's house gave her no time to worry because John was on the case. This also kept her from going herself. She lived in Houston with her husband Wayne but was in Brownsville working storm claims for Nationwide Insurance and wouldn't be back for a week. Hannah had earned a degree in Business Administration from Rice University and had worked a few years before staying home with the kids. After twenty-one years raising babies, she went back to work and had been writing insurance claims ever since. She neither loved it nor hated it, but instead simply saw it as the trade she made for spending that time with her children.

"I'm praying as soon as we hang up, Johnny, and you do the same, okay?" John, like his grandmother and mother and father as far as he knew, was a believer.

"I will," he answered, "and I'll call Grace."

While Tom madly loved all three of his children, each was different and held a different place in his mind and heart. They held different dates and days and hours. Different pieces and parts. John, the eldest and life-changer, as are all first babies, had been the leader and protector. First, because he was oldest, and second, because he was the boy.

"Watch your sisters," was a primary directive for John, and an order he never forgot. Desperate to please his parents, John gave all effort to everything he'd ever done, from his kindergarten reader to his surgical tests, and had been at the top of every class he'd ever taken. He'd expected the same degree of focus and drive in his own children by osmosis but had somehow lost sight of them. Working and absent much of their childhood, John hadn't seen it was Tom and Roseanne's involvement with him and support of him that had driven him—not just his intellect or ability.

Support is too often thought to be prodding and pushing, where it is instead interest and allowance. Tom and Roseanne understood that, John did not. For that, John suffered alienation from his kids. Though he spoke with them regularly, he sensed an impasse he couldn't understand. His calls to them were often awkward, rife with small talk about weather and dinner and what the grandkids were doing. He felt the awkwardness from them as well, whereby they struggled with the communication of life, falling instead into conversation about current events or sports. John, while not emotionally articulate enough to bridge the chasm between mundane and meaningful, felt the chasm and mourned the chasm and dreaded the chasm, nonetheless. He had not yet learned the chasm is spanned only by "I love you" but since he considered that a given, it never occurred to him.

Hannah, the studious, no-nonsense pragmatist and grand icon of maternity, sat squarely in the middle, best able to relate to John and to Grace with equal understanding and patience. She held John up as the leader of their small pack, but also knew he was impatient and anxious, and while he was best able to do most anything needing done, she knew the expectation was also his oppression all the while. Too often, however, he got the crown and she got the work. She and Grace both loved and respected him dearly and would ask his advice about everything. Everything, that is, except anything having to do with people.

John's version of morality was much more black-and-white than hers had matured to be, his immovable clarity between right and wrong sometimes appearing as judgment or even disdain, when in fact it was simply pragmatic. Her notion of morality, while centered in the word of God, included an understanding of human frailty and weakness that John could not acknowledge as symptoms of humanity. Advice about stock investments, politics, housing markets, certainly. Human relationship, certainly not.

Hannah was the do-er of the bunch, as a kid keen on chores and keen on people, taking care of anyone needing it. In fact, it was Hannah, who after college, took a job back in Corpus to keep watch over her grandmother. Esther was seventy-five at the time and increasingly frail. Nowadays, Hannah's children all live close by—all four of them—because they love their parents and one another, and because their ambitions were not grand.

It was Hannah who best waited on and fretted over Roseanne while she was sick, to the point of annoyance for Tom (a fact she never knew) but had taken care of everything banal in a way that Tom would have foregone, from funeral arrangements to cleaning Tom's house. Hannah had stepped in and taken charge as was her nature.

Finally, Grace was their artist. Flighty and full of life, she exceled in all liberal arts, hated math, played guitar, and painted. Funny and smart, but unable to sit still, Grace gravitated to adventure and sensuous pleasure, eating chocolate until she was sick at eight, sneaking out at fifteen to see Sonny Terry and Brownie McGhee on a school night, and at seventeen to see Adam Ant. One morning, Roseanne opened the door to get the paper, only to find Grace, at eighteen, passed out drunk on the front porch. Oddly, she reminded Tom so much of Ms. Flo that he couldn't fault her, a fact that drove Roseanne crazy with frustration. When she left for college, she stopped going to church and came home that summer with a tattoo—nearly unheard of in 1984—and told her parents she was dropping out to live life, not study it.

She brought home a backpack full of books and a cigar box guitar she'd waited tables to buy. That summer she was home but absent, buried in books by Pynchon, Voltaire, Shakespeare, Kierkegaard, and Vonnegut. She was aloof and subdued, and Tom, who knew what imprisonment was, saw it in her. He knew what struggle was and saw it in her. He knew what it was to be in the wait; to be aware of the passing, and he was fearful of the reason he saw it in her.

Time waits for no one, but likewise hurries for no one, and while most people dread the passing of time, Tom knew what it was to want nothing more. He saw that anxiousness in his daughter. Not knowing what else to do but love and wait, that's what he did. Roseanne, in all of her loving maternity, could not help but prod, could not help but pry, could not help but make sandwiches and take Grace shopping and try to engage her in every way. Tom did not and left her alone that summer because he knew watching a clock made no difference.

Tom and Roseanne would both die without knowing Grace had been raped over her first spring break, by a drunk junior she'd thought liked her. She didn't know his last name. They'd been drinking and wound up in his tent on the beach at Port Aransas Pass, 1:00 in the morning and throngs of kids in various stages of inebriation shouting and dancing and feeling their youth. On the nylon floor of a zippered, sandy tent on a crowded beach of loud music, drunk people and the numb, muffled gray lucidity of eight wine coolers, "no" did not mean no, and "stop" did not mean stop. She would blame herself for all of it, of course, because she must have led him on, must have sent signals, and must have wanted it like he'd said. What was she thinking? What was she doing there? Why hadn't she gone home?

Between the alcohol and boom boxes and shame, the entire four minutes was a soul-crushing blur scrambling to get out, wrapping a towel around her waist and running back to the rented condo, where she showered and wept repeatedly. She told her friends she was sick, spending the next three days in bed before driving back to Austin. It was a quiet drive, as her friends were sunburned and exhausted and she was on another planet.

After getting dropped off she would never see them again, never talk to them again, never acknowledge them again. She stopped going to work, stopped leaving her dorm, stopped going to church, stopped calling her parents, stopped praying, and largely stopped going to class altogether. She lost weight. She spent hours in bed.

Struggling to focus, Grace somehow managed to finish the semester, but none too soon. She drove a 1976 Pinto Tom bought for her in high school, and after her last exam she walked out to the car and drove away. She left her dorm and everything in it, from hot plates to clothing to Madonna cassettes to photo albums. She left her youth, her naiveté, her innocence, and her wonder. There she left herself.

In her car she carried a three-string cigar box guitar, her schoolbooks and nothing else. She drove to Galveston, taking the ferry across the bay to Bolivar Peninsula. She drove with the window halfway down, a soft drizzle gathering on her windshield and window, blowing over into her back seat. The beach houses, stacked ten deep from the water to the road, stood defiantly on spindly legs, daring the storm and tide that would one day come. And it would come. On the north side, only dunes and grass. It would be two weeks yet before public school was out, so the road was empty, houses were empty, beaches were empty. As the houses thinned out, she came upon an ancient general store and washateria, which she knew was there, having stopped many times while on motorcycle rides with her father.

He would say, "Grace! You wanna go get an ice cream bar?" which meant a day on the beach by way of Triumph or Moto Guzzi or Honda or Norton or Suzuki.

She stopped the car. Called simply Ice House, the white, glittered linoleum was worn through to brown before the counter, the soft buzz of coolers and incandescent lights a barrier to the silence. On the counter-top was glued a silver half dollar, the owner promising any kid ownership if they could get it off with their fingers. When she was ten, she would dream of claiming it for herself, but there it was still and yet and eternally. She would lie awake, convinced if she'd had more time, she could do it, could pry it up; convinced the treasure was there for the taking, if she could just figure out how to take it.

The screen door was propped open with a case of orange soda and windows across the front were open too. The inside smelled no different than the outside, that late spring combination of salt air and salt grass and pollen and heat, sometimes punctuated with diesel fuel from the pumps out front or the clean smell of laundry next door.

Grace didn't smoke, or hadn't, but bought a pack of Benson & Hedges and a book of matches. With no judgment from the clerk, she simply said, "Thank you Hon, mm, hmmm. Come back, okay darlin'?"

The parking lot was paved in oyster shells, and, leaving her car, she walked the pocked road five blocks to the gulf, past jon boats and shuttered windows, rusty screened porches draped with cork buoys, cabins built on tar-covered stilts. A few were lifeless, windows and stairs gone fourteen years to Hurricane Celia. Tattered curtains blowing in the breeze, the doors, oddly ten feet from the ground, still locked; forever locked.

She walked past the last cabin, fresh blue with white trim sporting a 1950s porcelain Coca Cola sign on the wall facing the road. Above the sole parking space was a handmade wooden sign, simply, "Pawpaw and Mimi." She had sand in her shoe. Between the berms and over the hard-packed wet sand, she opened the pack and lit a cigarette. She didn't even know how to smoke, but learned quickly and, after the first was gone lit another. The waves were breaking low and close, not three feet high and fifteen feet out, so she waded out to them. She couldn't feel the cold of the water.

Her hair and shoulders were wet from the drizzle. She continued wading past the breakers, where standing in the moving tide would be easy. But she didn't stop. She dropped her cigarette, matches and pack into the surge, walking until the swells lifted her from the ocean bottom. She began to breaststroke, fifty yards then seventy-five and at one hundred put her head under the swells. The tobacco in her mouth and sinuses was still pungent and strong. Her clothes were heavy. She could feel her right pocket fill with water and empty again as she stroked like it was breathing, that cotton lung rinsing itself of the filth of life, forever diluted in the abyss: one part per million, one part per billion, one part per trillion.

As she swam, she began keeping time, her strokes measured against the only lyrics she could remember from a 78rpm record—shellacs, as her father called them—she'd heard many times: *Walk that path down in the meadow, just wide enough for one; when you come up on the river, your swimmin' has begun.*

Swimming out, as she had many times before, Grace knew there was a sandbar high enough to stand on. The goal every summer had been to swim to the second set of breakers, the sandbar directly before them, the brown Texas ocean rife with Mississippi runoff, brown and thick and dirty if you didn't know better. You couldn't see your hand five inches underwater, and it was that lack of visibility, the fear of the unseen that made it scary, that made it thrilling.

"Keep an eye on your sisters," would be John's directive and off they would go, paddling out on surfboards or inflatable rafts.

As she grew older, she'd go out with church groups and friends, her high school boyfriend, and of course, Hannah. There was always talk of sharks and crabs, jellyfish, and stingrays. Always talk of the scary things they couldn't see coming, but that was part of the draw. And always, they would get close to where they thought the sandbar would be, hold their breath and sink to the bottom. Sometimes the bottom was six feet down, sometimes ten; they would swim further until they could stand.

On this day Grace dropped, hoping the bottom wasn't there at all. Dropped, knees drawn to her chest and in a ball, dropped, blowing air from her lungs to speed the descent. Dropped, weighted in hopelessness and despair.

She was startled by the sandy bottom, finding she was directly over the sandbar in chest deep water. She stood, the breakers there coming in sideways and crashing over her, the offshore storm drizzling where she stood but pushing the ocean from many miles out. The storm was changing the sea, the sea pushing hard against the shore, the shore changing as it always had and would, battered by these unending waves. She'd never intended to swim, in fact, never intended to stop, in fact, never intended to drive to Bolivar, in fact, never intended to drive to Galveston, in fact, had no intent about anything at all. She took a bite of the ocean and gargled it, reminding her of the saltwater her mother gave her when she'd lose a tooth as a girl. The sun was low on the gulf's horizon now. Between the breakers she could see the lights of the offshore rigs.

She whispered, "Jesus."

The first person she'd told was Hannah, followed three years later by her husband Todd, followed one week later by her therapist, followed three days later by her minister. These would be the only four to ever know, because her secret, like a lot of secrets, are only meant for a few. A few, but seldom one, as some crosses are simply too heavy to bear alone.

Hannah had been the reason Grace straightened out, righteously and prayerfully giving her the space she needed but not too much, talking about it but not too much, loving her and coddling her but not too much. Hannah had been given the intuition to know what too much was, to transcend time, and to put Grace on humanity's pedestal of worth.

Grace began keeping a journal, sometimes writing words or sentences over and over until, one, two, ten pages were covered in a single thought. Sometimes she shared these with Hannah; sometimes she did not. Hannah could keep a secret. Hannah could hold a hand. Hannah, like Tom, had a clear understanding of humanity, but unlike Tom, she didn't blame the failures of people on some shortcoming belonging to God. It was obvious and clear to her—and befuddling when it wasn't obvious and clear to others—that free will enables evil as much as it enables righteousness.

On a blistering June Wednesday, Grace opened her window to the backyard, the still, angry heat of the Houston summer rushing in and over her. It waited out there, she thought, the heat, patiently watchful for open windows and open doors. She could almost smell the humidity, the yard laden with the white, feathery seeds of a cottonwood tree that had been there before there was a yard, a house or a neighborhood. Towering above the house, the cottonwood cast a grand shadow, cursing the yard to grassless patches starving for light. Her father, having tried every hybrid seed and every fertilizer, gave up on the grass, instead planting ferns and caladiums and elephant ears to grow in the shade. There was a mature pecan tree against the fence and another in the front of the house, giving the family many pounds of pecans every fall to share with friends and neighbors and patients and church members.

Grace sat staring at a yard she adored, through a window she'd crawled through many times when in high school. At the base of the tree she watched a robin, pounding its beak into the soft dirt of her father's landscaping, searching for earthworms.

In that gaze, that blank gaze someplace between consciousness and daydreaming, she startled herself, saying aloud, "How could God let this happen?" Then repeating her woefully illogical question, "How could God let this happen?" she began to cry, softly, almost as if leaking.

Again, this time in her journal, she wrote, "How could God let this happen?"

Both simple and horrifying, she was at an impasse, but in that impasse tore the page from the journal, folded it in half and slid it under Hannah's bedroom door, the rough edges of the spiral paper catching the carpet in an inelegance that required her stuffing it through the gap with the tips of her fingers. Hannah had been jazzercising to Soft Cell's *Tainted Love* but stopped immediately upon seeing the folded sheet with ragged edges slip between the door and the gray shag. Grace, not surprised and eager for it, knew and heard the music stop and the springs of Hannah's bed creak under her weight. She could hear or envision Hannah opening a notebook and a Bible, other books. She could hear her think. Those sounds and that interruption; the seriousness with which Hannah embraced her sister's desperation felt like love, and it was.

Two hours later Hannah answered, sliding her own sheet of paper under Grace's door. It was in an envelope. "He allows it to happen because it stems from our collective free will," she answered. "That doctrine allows humanity's individual latitude in everything from philosophy to action, from kindness to cruelty, from where to go and what to say to which sandwich you will choose at lunch. That doctrine allows belief in Him, or not; belief in salvation through Christ, or not. That doctrine allows the willingness to help or the desire to hurt, because as free people with free will, evil abides beside the righteous, each action pregnant with consequence."

This was her mother's turn of phrase, "Each action pregnant with consequence," which only held depth of meaning for Hannah after

Grace's rape. Until Grace came home raped, Hannah had always thought it meant doing bad things ensured bad things coming back, a la Galations 6:7, you reap what you sow.

To a younger Hannah, reaping and sowing made perfect sense and this is what she thought her mother meant. A warning of sorts, she thought it was Roseanne's version of Christian Karma. Before Grace's rape, the relationship between reaping and sowing and Roseanne's notion that every decision is pregnant with consequence made little sense, sounded so canned, sounded so ludicrous, like the boogeyman or an old wives' tale. A prohibition to be good "or else." It seemed tantamount to believing that by being honorable and moral and righteous, one could guarantee honor and goodness coming back. A nebulous notion that if one put goodness out into the universe, one will be paid back in kind; a myopic, lifespan-centric interpretation.

That summer, however, Hannah came to see the difference. Reaping and sowing is an eternal planting, not a temporal one. Struggling with understanding how this darkness could descend upon Grace, who invested good in the world, she came to realize the reaping doesn't come to us as we sow, because that is not a reflection of the metaphor. No one plants in the morning and harvests in the afternoon. All of life is the sowing, while the reaping is eternal.

Her mother's insistence, on the other hand, wasn't a warning to be good, no; it was entreaty to consider what can come of any decision, good or bad, from eating too much bacon to taking drugs, there is always a consequence, be it good or bad or neutral. It was an acceptance of risk. It is not necessarily that evil begets evil, pain, pain, kindness, kindness, ignorance, ignorance, love, love, acceptance, acceptance. Instead, it is the idea that terrible things can happen to people of honor and sweetness, and it is not the Karmic fault of the victim. If a lion devours a lamb, it is not the lamb's comeuppance. These are the things Hannah considered that summer, and these are the things she talked about with her sister. These are the things she came to write in notes.

When Grace, her mind changed about returning to school that fall, packed her Pinto in late August and was pulling away from the house, Hannah flagged her down and ran to the window.

"Someday try to forgive," she said, "You'll know when. That's the day you get back what he took."

Grace teared up, not in memory but in love. "I know I'm supposed to, Han. I know God tells me to."

Hannah could feel the epiphany of her own understanding, her own realization as the idea itself formed in her mind. She heard and felt it leave her mouth just as she came to believe it. By the time the notion left her lips, she had never said a truer thing: "Grace, forgiveness isn't a command. Forgiveness is a gift you receive as you give it away."

Now Grace was crying, grateful to be loved by her sister. "How did you get so smart?" she asked.

Hannah smiled, "I learned it from my sister."

While all three kids had their rebellious phases, Grace's lasted the longest and expressed itself more fully, but it ended that summer. Though over time she gained wisdom and peace and grace and honor, her fearless, confident innocence was lost forever. This was the mystery of Grace; a secret Tom could not have known.

Of course, he then thought he knew about everything that mattered. He thought his love as a father would mean they shared their deepest secrets and desires. He thought he would have been asked to help or offer advice for any and all of life's tragedies and opportunities. As doctor and father and honorable man and the turner of wrenches, he could always help fix anything broken, and could always help lead in the right direction. He thought he'd led by example, and as true as that was, wrongly assumed his close relationship with his children meant they would include him in all of their rites of passage, their grand schemes, their hopes and dreams, and fantasies and failures. He'd thought his example would mean they would not make, or even seek out, their own mistakes, and by being the very best father he could be might somehow shelter them from some of life's pain.

It took their teenage years and early twenties to teach him otherwise, and to understand that raising young men and women to be independent and thinkers meant they would someday be independent and thinkers. That included, most importantly, independence from him.

None of them were immune to the stupidity of youth. Underage John snuck out the family car and hit a tree, and during his third semester in college he dropped all of his classes to work as a deckhand on a Florida shrimp boat. True to form, he took twenty-one hours the next three semesters to make up for it. Hannah, for all of her pragmatism, saved money through school and upon graduation, left for France for three months. What her parents didn't know was that she went with her boyfriend and returned pregnant. He'd stayed there to complete the trip; she'd returned to have an abortion.

Now a successful mother of four and hard-working claims adjuster, first-edition book collector, and church treasurer, Hannah's anguish over ending that pregnancy never left her. She would never tell a soul, not even Grace. This is one of her secrets, a cross perhaps too heavy to bear alone, but she did anyway.

The only lie she ever tells is to the doctor when she goes for checkups. How many children? Four. How many pregnancies? Four.

That secret was a shame she felt she owned, and no confession beyond God would help. What she gained in it, however, was a prideless unwillingness to judge people. "Judge not," she had stamped upon her soul, "lest ye be judged." For this she had sympathy. For this she had compassion. For this, the anguish of her lost baby, she embraced humanity with love and honor in a way that was fully committed to forgiveness in the unending hope she could forgive herself.

As the phone began to ring, John thought he might hang up; might keep his concern over his father to himself, at least until he knew more, but Grace answered too quickly.

"Hey, Johnny-boy!" Grace answered with excitement, "How's it hangin'?"

This made John laugh because she always made him laugh. She was always so glad to answer his calls, a fact that made John feel better about being in the world. "I guess it's hanging well, Sis, how's it hanging for you?"

"John," said Grace condescendingly, "you don't ask a woman how it's hanging. But things are good, business is good, we have a new litter of Goldens. What's up?"

"Oh, Dad's missing. I'm sure it's nothing but he's not answering his phone, so I thought I'd run out and check on him."

Grace paused, sizing up the level of concern in John's voice, which didn't square with his willingness to drive three hours just to check. "How long has it been since you talked with him?" she asked.

John measured his delivery, "Well, I talked with him day before yesterday and he was great, working in the garage. Hannah called a while ago and has been trying to get him for a few hours, so I thought I'd go check."

Grace, who couldn't imagine a future without her father and, in fact, hadn't even noticed he was old, was confused. He'd been a paragon of vigor and energy her entire life, seeing her through every hard time, every trial, every triumph. The very idea John and Hannah were worried alarmed her, as John knew it would, making her feel as though she'd missed something or was irresponsible for not fretting.

"That man is fine, Johnny. No telling what he's doing," convincing herself, "but whatever it is, it isn't moping and dying. He probably can't hear the phone over the chainsaws he's juggling!"

John laughed, assured she was right. "Lord knows he's stubborn, probably working on that Volvo or a motorcycle. I honestly pray he never gets one of those running, Gracy."

"You know he will, and you know he'll ride it," she answered, "but that's just Dad. He's fine. But let me know when you see him, okay?"

"I will," he said and hung up.

There really was no telling what Tom was doing. No telling.

PART II

Ain't new to me, it's sad an true.

Been down a hundred times; down one more 'gain.

—*Blind Sampson Burrow*

Tom gazed up through the trees, past the limbs, past the branches, past the leaves to the warming sky. If he listened intently and the wind was at a lull, he could hear logging trucks heading north or south from a quarter mile away until they passed through the tree line in a blur. The caffeine and sugar made him feel better and a bit more alert. Saving half for later, more from habit than any sense of survival, Tom recapped the Thermos and lay there quietly.

Interestingly, the pain had abated entirely until the waves of arbitrary agony came upon him, which, while still excruciating, became more manageable through their predictability. Still too early for infection, too early for gangrene, Tom knew two things: 1) the current waves of pain were his body's neurological alarm, and 2) if infection set in, it would get far worse. Fever, inflammation, and death, if exposure didn't get him first. As it was, the pain would begin in his hip, radiating outward as Tom would start to inhale. Exhaling and fanning his arms and leg, it would wash over him, spilling the lesson of existential hubris out onto the forest floor around him. He loathed every wave, not just for the pain, but for the reminder of his own humanity.

He began to personify it, Pain, as he had done with most everything since he was a boy. It had given him something to respect or love or defeat; a challenger he could engage. He would not give Pain more respect than he gave a messenger, a mere informant telling him he was broken. He would not listen to Pain, in the way he would not listen to Worry, or to Doubt, or to Pity's gnawing whispers for fatherless children or wounded men. So as was his habit, he focused on Pain, and while not actively cursing it, picked up the gauntlet in defiance. And in that defiance, separated himself from it until it was time again to fight.

He lay there in the quiet. The forest, now fully awake in the warming sun, had settled into the day in the way it had every day since the beginning. On this day, Tom was integrated, not as an observer or outsider, but embedded into the day in the way only immobility can embed a person. On this day, Tom was an ornament, affixed to the ground by a 1969 Triumph motorcycle only feet from the road, but somehow less anonymous there than his years in the prison camp.

Somehow, almost welcomed by the surrounding trees and earth and animals and crushed by the weight of the machine and of his hubris, Tom felt more hopeful than he had young and alive in a South Korean prison camp. He had personified the Pain, and angrily embraced it. Had he grown to accept life's surprises? Had he grown to accept not coincidence, but the lack thereof? What is it, he thought, that could make a man hopeful against the practical obvious? Against the impractical obvious? Against the glaring odds?

Peering up into the blue, he watched as the spring gusts pushed the limbs and branches like brushes back and forth, painting the sky with the light green leaves of rebirth over an undulating blue eternity. The magnolia over his right shoulder was in bloom, pink blossoms already turning a deep, rich, pure, endless white. So white, in fact, Tom thought the blossoms defined the very word, and found himself wondering which God had created first, the blossom that informed the word, or the word to describe the blossom. When the breeze picked up to paint the April sky, likewise the magnolia's aroma bathed him, that sweet, pungent smell of lemon and vanilla and honeysuckle and heaven.

So, there he lay, coffee's memory on his breath, the now-cool motorcycle upon him, the clean, unassuming innocence of spring holding him quietly in its palm. Indeed, Tom personified the forest, while somehow, he knew the forest likewise personified him.

Leaning on his good hip, he pulled the Pentax box over to him and opened it, toppling out the oranges and cigars and lighter and pocketknife. He had completely forgotten about the ibuprofen! His heart leapt, as the thought of reducing the swelling, thereby reducing the pain, gave him a jolt of hope he hadn't realized he'd lost. With more excitement than he should have had, he popped the film canister open with his teeth and quickly downed four tablets with his last half of coffee. Then, satisfied he had driven Pain backward, pulled his watch from his breast pocket to mark the time in his notebook.

He hadn't opened the notebook in three years because he hadn't ridden in three years; and because the two had gone hand in hand, the journal sat with the bike. In fact, it had remained strapped to the back of the seat until Tom took it off to restore it, so for him it was a time capsule of sorts. The notebook was bought as a journal, as was fashionable for artists and thinkers and graduating med students at the University of Texas Medical Branch in the early 1960s. It had been accompanied by a sterling silver Cross mechanical pencil, engraved plainly, "Dr. Thomas Welton."

The pencil and journal had been a gift from his sister, Ruby, who didn't know what else to give him, and while the journal had been Tom's for nearly fifty years, he'd misplaced the Cross pencil shortly after graduation. He'd never told Ruby he'd lost it, because he never truly thought of it as lost, as is the case with many lost things. A person is simply certain they still have something and expect it to turn up at some point. In Tom's mind the pencil was simply unfound.

How could Ruby have known what to give him? How can anyone know what to give anyone? She was forever grateful to have her brother—without fanfare—returned to her three years after the war ended but would lie awake at night praying for him to be comfortable in his own skin.

"Father," she would pray, "please watch over Tommy. He's a good man and needs your comfort. Thank you for bringing him home, for giving me such a wonderful brother, and thank you for our closeness, but please settle his soul."

Over time her prayers were answered in Roseanne, Tom's ethereal bride and deliverer from himself. Roseanne worked in the admissions office at the school, helping veterans with their GI Bill applications. Roseanne Maria Hernandez Garza, carrying two surnames as was the tradition, had more of his mother's characteristics than he would ever know, let alone admit. Short, black hair, black eyes and fair, she'd abandoned herself to him soon after their meeting, as he abandoned himself to her.

He'd pretended to struggle with the paperwork more than was true, and she pretended to believe he was struggling. She saw in him a stalwart intellect and boyish charm, a kindness unencumbered by fear; his attention to her unfeigned and unaffected by insecurity. She saw in him a magnanimity independent of instruction or rearing, instead simply born within him. Many years later she would tell her daughters she had also sensed a struggle in him, where the world was a poor fit for him, and while he hid it well with his charm and humor, somehow knew he needed her to hold his hand in it.

Charming, funny and sincere, she would come to know him as courageous and driven, smart and thoughtful, everything she knew she wanted in a man and many more things she didn't. While she had come to slowly accept herself and her intellect, her insight and understanding, she had not yet embraced what that would mean in finding someone to spend her life with.

Through study and introspection and the support of her parents she had grown wise early, chasing wisdom through reading and writing and earnestly pursuing an understanding of people. Without knowing, she had come to want more than an average man. As it was on that first day, and the second, and the third, she found herself drawn into him like a magnet, like gravity, like two bodies in orbit. Soon, this orbit would no longer be good enough and beyond resistance anyway.

Until Tom, Roseanne expected to meet a man, expected to get married, expected to have children, but using her parents' marriage and her friends' parents' marriages and the marriages she'd witnessed as models, expected to meet and marry a man who would be moral, Christ-focused, caring, and devoted. She had not, however, dreamed of a partner. She couldn't have, because she didn't know of such a thing. Tom, on the other hand, had never expected anything, as was his way. Instead, what they had found in one another was much deeper than duty and honor and commitment. They had found the missing pieces of themselves.

From a middle-class family in a middle-class neighborhood, Roseanne's Spanish paled compared to Tom's, even though she'd come by it naturally. This went over well with her Abuela if not her parents, who had actively and purposefully spoken English as she grew up in the house. Tom, as was also his way, would sit on the porch with her ancient grandmother, hearing and speaking in Spanish hour after hour. Soon Roseanne and Tom were inseparable, including Sunday mornings whereupon he would attend Roseanne's Lutheran service to his mother's Baptist chagrin.

He'd simply fallen into the cadence he missed most, a level of comfort born in familiarity, and although he struggled with Christian concepts and salvation as a message, he believed in God, or something like it.

Mostly, however, he believed in Roseanne and in short order would think of her as his savior.

Within the year they were married, followed ten months later by Jonathan, the delight of his mother, sister and in-laws. Her father's name was Juan, Tom's father's David, so the baby was called Jonathan David in honor of them both. Now a family, the three of them lived with her parents in a back room of the house, as was often the case with young Mexican families then.

More than just an invitation, Tom came to understand it was an expectation because it would show respect and commitment to the family, not just the bride, and since these relationships and all relationships were paramount to Tom, he accepted. There, he was quickly woven into the fabric of the family, becoming resident mechanic, resident doctor, resident son and brother and friend. In time, what he'd first felt as acquiescence became a gift to him, embracing Roseanne's parents and siblings as his own as they embraced him.

In answer to Ruby's prayer, Tom found Roseanne and, becoming more and more comfortable within his own skin, ultimately settled into a cadence and world view that was uniquely his, as world views are like fingerprints. In all of it Tom would never stop being Ruby's hero, if not for watching over her when they were children, if not for surviving five years of Korean concrete, if not for going to medical school, if not for the life he'd built and the family he'd raised, then for the feeling of security he had given her in the world. "If you hadn't come back," she would say as they grew older, "I don't know what I would have done."

And come back he had, parts missing, parts left there, and parts that would eventually grow again like the phantom tail of a salamander. These parts, the unseen damage and unseen absences, were simply added to the list of damage and absence he'd left the country with anyway. Gaunt, haunted, teeth and pieces of his face simply missing, he had scars on his ankles and legs from infected, untreated insect bites, and scars on his back and shoulders, the result of beatings at the hands of his guards. Because the wounds to his face and back had healed without treatment, the scarring was bulbous and red, grotesque cross-stitching over fresh, young Army skin.

In Ruby's eyes, however, Tom was a handsome war hero, a doctor, a provider, a friend to all who knew him, a solid, upright Christian man with a moral compass imparted to him from God. For Ruby, all Tom had to do was draw breath.

So in those days, harried and joyous, rich and full, while his classmates read the fashionable "smart" books like Kerouac's *On The Road* and *Book of Dreams*, or Maslow's *Toward a Psychology of Being*, Tom was reading Kierkegaard and Nietzsche and the Bible in an attempt to rationalize moral philosophy with experiential and existential reality.

Roseanne, exhausted from work and pregnancy, would sleep early with Tom in bed beside her, while he read and studied and wrote in the margins. That isn't to say he didn't fit in, exactly, because he did, or appeared to have. He saw *Rio Bravo* and *Psycho* with the rest of America, but when it came to understanding his place in the world, Tom would rather find it than be led.

More importantly, he would rather find it than be led by writers whose charisma trumped their insight; whose celebrity cloistered their insecurity. For Tom, the idea these popular writers were so readily accessible and understood in the first place meant, to him, they didn't matter as much. Mostly though, he'd felt like he fit exactly where he was: in bed beside Roseanne. And when it came to a diary, or journaling, Tom's notes were written in the margins of the books he read, and predictably, in the margins of his psyche.

To that end, Ruby's gift went unused until Tom began his sometimes sojourns, which, of course, began with those motorcycles.

PART III

I got what I need to make my soul right,
I got what I need to make my soul right,
If I stay off my knees and out of the light,
Got no one to blame but me.

—*ELWOOD JOHNSON*

Tom and Johnny had finished the Triumph in late summer 1971. Obsessed with shortcomings and unrealized potential, he'd stripped the salvaged motorcycle to nuts and bolts after first wrecking it in a ditch. In the spring of that year he'd owned both a 1968 Honda CL450 and the Bonny, but as his favorite, he rode the Triumph almost exclusively. Late one night in early April he was on the way home from evening rounds at the hospital, taking a road less travelled to avoid the traffic. On a straightaway

Tom saw a farmer's truck in the lane up ahead, but because the lights were on, didn't realize the farmer had stopped to open the gate to his property while leaving the truck parked and idling in the center of the road.

Tired and not paying attention, Tom was on top of the idling truck before he realized it wasn't moving, bearing down on two tons of Ford that weren't going to budge. In reflex, he veered off the road and put the bike down sideways in the culvert at 45 miles an hour. The bike spun away from him with the front wheel plowing into the culvert, cracking the frame at the neck and bending the wheel rim and front forks. Tom, skinned from ankle to hip and in rabbit-like wounding, set that motorcycle up and limped it home.

Embarrassed and injured, Tom entered the house and went to the bedroom where Roseanne slept. He turned the light on to wake her, and to assess his injuries. Gasping awake, she leapt from the bed and instinctively put her arm under him. Tom had no risk of falling, having been through much more, but her desire to hold him up reached out from semiotic allegory to practice, wherein she scooped him and held him tall.

"Oh God! Tom, what happened?" she asked, already knowing the answer.

They walked into the bathroom, where she pulled his belt off and scissored his pants from waist to hem.

"I put the bike down," he said meekly, "My own fault. I wasn't paying attention."

She was breathing heavily through her nostrils, working. Scraped from his ankle to his knee, the scratches turned to gouges up through his hip.

"This might need stitches," she said aloud, but to herself. Blood was running from the deepest spots: three- and four-inch claw marks an eighth-inch wide and quarter-inch deep. "Where else are you hurt?"

Tom hadn't even thought about that. He took his jacket off, the very jacket he now wore, to look at his elbows and arms and wrist.

"That's all, I think, baby," he answered sheepishly.

She looked up at him from where she knelt to look at the wound. "You know I have to clean this, right?"

His sock was wet with blood, though the stream had already slowed with coagulation. Tom threw his leg over the edge of the tub, followed with the other and sat on the rim. The tub was cool, porcelain, cast iron, claw foot and deep. She got in the tub to pull off his socks and shoes, then ran the water hot and fast.

"Get in, mi cielo. Get in," she said, overwhelmed with what could have happened.

Trading places with him, she pulled his tie off, unbuttoned his dress shirt, pulling his undershirt off with them. She saw her naked husband every day, but on this day—midnight and newly awake—the stark contrast between his old scars and new wounds was overwhelming. She understood the wounds and the torture and the healing, of course. She understood the dynamics of what he'd been through, the facts. But until this night she hadn't understood what it meant to have someone nurse him. Until this night she didn't understand exactly what she meant to him.

She saw him, eighteen years old, on the concrete floor of a cell, injured with no one there to help. She began to tear, grateful for him and for the opportunity to take care of him in this way but put her head down so Tom wouldn't see her. Grabbing a washcloth and bar soap, she rubbed the two together and began to gently bathe the wound as the tub filled. Tom's reaction was to sweat.

Draining the blood and filth, Roseanne blotted at the wound until she could see the damage. It was starting to run again, but not as badly. Tom watched as she pressed and dried his leg, ashamed for having done this to her.

"Well," she said, "maybe we can bandage it up. Can you get a penicillin shot at work?" It was 1971, so of course he could.

She then covered the entire wound, from hip to ankle, in monkey blood, the southern colloquialism for the antiseptic Mercurochrome, now long since disowned. She may as well have been applying fire for the way it burned, which, in fact, was worse than the scrape in the first place. Finally taping bandages over the length of the damage, she felt good about the amateur nursing. Pulling him up from the tub, his wife looked at him through her worry and concern, feeling him and what he was thinking; feeling him put a part of himself away for her.

"Tommy, listen to me. You are not to stop riding motorcycles. You fix that motorcycle and you ride it."

He got into the bed and raised his leg slowly, saying "Rosie, I don't deserve you."

"We don't deserve each other," she answered, "we're gifts to one another. God's gifts to one another. I love you very much."

"I love you very much," he answered as she lay down next to him.

Wide awake with the rush of surprise, Roseanne lay there for five minutes, quiet. "Do you remember my cat, Paco?" she asked in the darkness.

Tom did indeed. The cat had been dead for years but used to live under the front porch of the house. With thick, short white hair, the cat's face and shoulders were scarred from fighting, but he was as sweet and loving as any cat he'd ever known.

"Sure," he answered, as he'd spent many hours petting the purring cat while talking with her grandmother.

"When I was little the neighbor down the street gave me the kitten," she began. "Momma loves animals, so that was easy, but I had to beg Papi to let me keep him. When he couldn't stand it anymore, he said yes."

Tom knew this and chuckled, but she was building something.

"Momma and I wanted the cat to live in the house. Papi wasn't having it. I just thought he was hard-hearted and didn't want Paco in the house because he would make a mess or thought I wouldn't take care of him. Every morning I would get up and race outside to make sure he was okay and pet him and love on him. After a week I wanted to try again, asking mi abuela to talk with Papi about it. I remember I was crying."

Tom instinctively pulled her closer, his arm under her shoulders.

"'Gorda,' she told me, 'some people have a cat or a dog in the house, like Mrs. Garcia across the street. The house is safe and warm, and the cat sleeps many hours a day. The cat sits in the window and looks outside where it is raining or cold or hot or there may be dogs or owls. Mrs. Garcia loves that cat and feeds it and takes care of it, but the cat isn't really a cat.'"

Tom had loved that old woman and was glad to hear a story he hadn't heard.

Roseanne continued, "She said, 'A cat is outside, doing what a cat does. It's cold sometimes and wet sometimes and dangerous sometimes, but when it isn't, Gorda, it is a wonderful life. And listen, it is a wonderful life—a sweet and wonderful life—only because it is sometimes cold and wet and scary.'"

Roseanne sat on her elbow and kissed her husband, "You are an outside cat, mi amor."

Tom would limp for a week and ride the Honda until his Triumph was redeemed, newly-adorned with a necklace and Columbanus of Bobbio pendant—the patron saint of motorcyclists—from Roseanne. Because you can take the girl from Catholicism, but you cannot take Catholicism from the girl.

The wreck gave him the opportunity to rebuild the bike the way he wanted it, dissatisfied with the please-everyone hope of the factory. He'd welded frame gussets for rigidity and relocated the rear suspension brackets to allow more controlled travel. He fabricated a new neck that would accept tapered bearings and reduce rake, ensuring greater control from a modified front-end, which he'd taken and improved from a wrecked Norton Commando. He bought new wheels and hubs developed by Honda for the innovative CB750, which gave him a powerful front disc brake in a world where disc brakes were new, using the Honda fork tubes as well.

He sent the frame to be nickel plated, and while out, rebuilt the engine. He bored the cylinders to give him over 720ccs, enlarging the valves at the same time. He changed valve springs and pistons, switched carburetor needles, and enlarged the jets. He ported and polished the head, changed the pipes, cut the fenders, lowered the new handlebars, and installed braided brake and fuel lines.

He removed everything that was unnecessary to reduce weight, bordering on the illegal, which included cutting down the frame hoop, removal of turn signals and reflectors, and the installation of a miniscule brake light and small, bar-end mirrors. When it was all done, every component on the bike had been modified in some way to suit Tom's fancy. At last, in August of 1971, Tom and Johnny finished the bike and Tom had the motorcycle he'd always wanted.

Most important in these modifications, or at least most practical, was the entire replacement of the electrical system. Lucas, a huge British electrical component manufacturer started by Joe Lucas, had enormous contracts with auto and motorcycle companies and to this day no one understands it. The components were low quality, rarely worked as intended, and became the quirky evil every Triumph rider had to study or, in Tom's case, replace.

Having struggled with Lucas components on his 1945 BSA, Tom wanted no part of diagnosing and repairing factory defects. Ranging from mysteriously drained batteries to seemingly haunted lighting to poor recharge and intermittent function, the Lucas factory junk components were terrible enough to spawn a litany of frustrated inside jokes about their automobile and motorcycle parts.

These all became grand bonding moments for Triumph owners' groups, engendering cottage industries of "workaround" parts, T-shirts, replacement rebuild kits, bumper stickers. and myriad other efforts to take the sting out of their misery. Tom loved the jokes, especially after replacing the electrical system meant they no longer pertained to him, including:

- The Lucas Motto: get home before dark
- Lucas is the patent holder for the short circuit
- Lucas: inventor of the first intermittent wiper
- Lucas: why use lights when you have reflectors?
- Lucas: inventor of the self-dimming headlamp
- The three-position Lucas switch: dim, flicker and off

And Tom's personal favorite:

- Lucas: Prince of Darkness

During his rebuild, Tom bought a schematic for a German BMW R75 and set about replacing everything English Lucas with everything German Bosch. Only in this absolute 100% replacement could he be certain the bike would function as intended and that he would never be left in the darkness. By the end, Tom effectively touched and modified nearly everything the motorcycle was.

Then, and without actually planning it, announcing it, or even scheduling it, he began to ride out past the city limits without telling anyone he was going. He'd had many motorcycles before and would have many after, but this bike inspired a freedom, and more importantly a reliability, that allowed him to run off at length. Tom wasn't discourteous, and the last person he would intentionally worry was Roseanne, nonetheless, at times he would be gone for hours. This wasn't something she had to get used to or tolerate. From the very first day, truly, from the moment they'd met, Roseanne recognized a restlessness in Tom she knew had to be left alone.

This restlessness wasn't to be repaired or erased; it wasn't to be healed or even discussed. This restlessness was indelible, and while she may never have fully understood it, she did understand it was his. His colleagues would take weekday afternoons to golf or hire fishing guides to take them out to deep water. Not Tom. He would leave straight from work in his dress clothes and ride late into the evening, or before sunup on Saturday and be gone half the day. The motorcycle only had room enough for him and a skinny 12-year old boy, so as Jonathan grew older and got bigger, the bike was Tom's alone.

Early on he would snap the throttle and throw the bike in and out of lanes, screaming past traffic like it was parked. Accelerating hard from a red light, he would roll on the gas until the front wheel began to leave the pavement, then lean in to bring it down. He stopped this in short order as he knew where it would end, but he was so enthralled with the horsepower and performance of the bike, the initial couple of months had been dangerous.

Reserved or racing, that simple joy cleared his mind and allowed him the peace that his depth and imprisonment and anxiety and mourning had stolen from him. He didn't have to be a boy, didn't have to be a man, didn't have to be a doctor or husband or anything other than part of that machine, another moving part. In the Zen of shifting gears and braking, leaning, banking, breathing, Tom could almost stop being human altogether.

One Saturday morning, getting ready to head out with Johnny on a newly acquired Honda CB350, his son wanted to take paper and pens so he would have something to do if his dad wanted to stop and "think about things." This was how the traveling journal was born.

The first few pages were sketches John had drawn as a boy—doodles, which became the beginning of a lifelong hobby for him. In his son's twelve-year-old hand were written notes about where they'd been and what they had for lunch, along with rough drawings of buildings and bridges, trees, and woodland. The seeds of the notebook had been planted by John, growing fully for Tom into an anthology of meandering thought, reminders, photographs, logs. Now thick with notes and magazine clippings and pictures and the occasional pressed leaf, the stout, cracked leather binding and cover was more beautiful with age than it had been new. It was so thick, in fact, Tom had taken to tying it closed with a length of twine.

"For Tommy," read the inscription, "I hope some of what's in you finds its way to these pages. Much love, Ruby."

In those days, few people, at least few southerners, actually said fully, "I love you" but would instead sign off with "Love" or "Much love" and expected their actions speak louder than words. Not so with Ruby.

She'd then followed with a quote from Sophocles: "One word frees us of all the weight and pain of life: That word is love. I love you, Dr. Tommy. Congratulations!"

Now fumbling one-handed for his glasses, Tom managed to open the journal, flipping through almost the entire book to the first empty page. There he scribbled the time, along with "four (4) 200mg ibuprofen: 800mg ttl" as he had on countless charts for countless patients over the years. Then, fearful he could be unconscious when rescued but wanting the EMTs to know, he tore the page from its binding and stuffed it between his shirt and jacket, behind his watch. He'd been pinned down before and lived through it, after all, and wanted to increase his odds. Then, with no choice but to languish upon the cool earth, pungent magnolia filling his head, his mind drifted to patients long gone.

Tom was drawn to old people, their reflective wisdom and stories and experience, having grown up doing the odd jobs they could no longer do. He would spend as much time talking with them as it took to perform the task, and as he'd grown older came to understand the talking was at least as important as the job, sometimes more so. After delivering his mother's eggs, he would often mow or paint or fix and repair whatever needed done, riding his motorcycle when he didn't need tools; walking pulling a wagon when he did. Besides his sister, he'd spent more time with adults than he did with friends, first from necessity and then from desire. Most important, however, was the way in which he saw his mother. She had gone from young, vibrant married bride to broken-hearted widow overnight, and while twelve years-old was too young to witness that, it was too old to forget it, too.

When it came time to declare his medical specialty, Tom had no other wish than geriatric medicine. Five years older and one hundred years wiser than his college classmates, he saw in older people not just a way to give meaning to their twilight, but through engaging them and knowing them perhaps glimpse the meaning of his own life as well. In treating them and knowing them and devouring whatever it was they could share, he'd hoped to know the ways we are bound together.

Among his classmates, he was alone in this desire. Most would chase the glamour or the money of some specialty or the security of a local general practice, but Tom saw a need and wanted to fill it. His friends would ask what compelled him, but because it took him the better part of fifty years to know himself, he couldn't quite articulate it except to say, "Old people need doctors too."

This explanation always seemed to work, even with his professors, because they'd come to know Tom as intense and introspective. Convinced any conclusion he'd come to must be well thought-out, they were right, and given his army service and confinement as a POW, assumed his distance a function of torture and what was called, in 1963, "shell shock." They had no way of knowing this was his nature.

That berth also included dispensation for his beard, as Tom was allowed facial hair in medical school when no one else was. Unbeknownst to them, he'd been warned by the dean his first week of school that facial hair was not permitted. Upon seeing him two days later, clean shaven, the dean understood Tom's need. The red, monstrous puncture wound on one side of his jaw was nothing compared to the overlapping white and silver scar tissue of the other. The teeth had been replaced, but the scars would never be. His beard, while spotty when short, had grown to effectively cover the scars.

The dean, kind and embarrassed for his insistence, stopped him in the courtyard. "I think a beard can make a doctor look distinguished," he said softly. Then, "I couldn't see the scars, young man. I'll allow it."

That week was the only week in his adult life Tom was clean shaven, which also happened to be the week he'd met Roseanne.

Now on his back in the Big Thicket, mindlessly stroking that beard as was his habit, Tom drifted.

"Whut kin'a name is Welton?"

It was 1965. Tom was attending to his then-oldest patient, ninety-seven-year-old Buttercup Moses Lincoln DuBois. It was a Friday, where he gave his afternoons to St. Mary's Hospital for the Poor in Galveston. While there was no official segregation, black patients were separated by floor from white patients, who were separated by floor from Mexican patients. While President Johnson was making sweeping changes in segregation legislation, the transition was slower in practice.

In those days, bigotry was far more insidious than a word, instead embodying a stratum that wasn't social or economic at all, but rather the market value given someone based on skin color. Almost as though skin color carried with it varying degrees of right-to-life, if for no other reason than the level of treatment each race received, except in some places like St. Mary's Hospital for the Poor. Buttercup was as dark as molasses, her black skin shiny enough to give a reflection, with milky yellowed eyes and short, white, sparse hair. Tom, like a lot of people he knew, had no place in his heart for racial nonsense and saw in her an astounding beauty he only saw in old people.

"Movin' rail for chicken feed," he'd heard gandy dancers chant, "negro make his poor hands bleed." Holding her wrist for a pulse, her skin was thin and non-elastic. The palms of her hands felt like cool, buttery suede.

Tom answered, "It's German, Ms. Buttercup. It's an old family name. Started out as Weltanschauung when my people got here in the 1800s."

Buttercup raised her eyebrows, "Ooh, Lort, dat's too tuff, no way. Welton is much bettah. Un wats yore Christian name, Dr. Welton?" she asked, squinting both eyes and nose.

Tom replied, "Thomas Elias Welton, Ms. Buttercup," and upon seeing her struggle to hear it, he repeated loudly, "Thomas Elias Welton, Ms. Buttercup."

"You like ta fish, Dr. Welton? Cuz Thomas was a fisherman. Doubt'n Thomas was a fisherman, mmm hmmmm. Nat'ral born."

Tom grinned, replying while counting the beats, "I have fished, but don't do it much. Do you fish, Ms. Buttercup?"

Buttercup Moses Lincoln DuBois chuckled a phlegmy chuckle, "Jes take a look at me, suh! I ain't helt no fishin' pole fo thirty year now! But I use ta likes it, Lort knows I used ta."

She looked past Tom, seeing her hands on a pole a time long ago. "My daddy use ta strip cane 'n let it dry under the house ovuh wintah. Come spring end pull tat cane out 'n put a string an' hook on it fo me. Sometime he'd have a cork 'n put that on it fo me too. I wut snatch up my sistah an we't spent all day long, I means all day, down't ta creek un come wif a mess 'o lil' perches 'n sunfishes 'n whatsnot. My momma wut grease ta pan 'n fry 'em up wit buttah an conemeal, Lort, Lort, Lort. My daddy love't that frite fish."

Then laughing again, "I nevuh dit know if'n my daddy mate dem cane poles fo us o' fo him!"

"My momma did the same thing," Tom replied, "only we lived in Corpus so I could get shrimp and grouper and sea bass and sometimes shark at the marina."

"Sharks!" she exclaimed, "I ain't nevuh seen no shark but sho as I'm breavin' I ain't eatin' one! I et a lot 'o things: squirrels 'n possums 'n ev'n nutra, but no kina way is I eat'n sumpin' wanna eat me!"

They both laughed at her refusal and squeamishness over the shark. "Any ol' how, Missuh Welton, I's glad yo name's not Weltonshong."

"Well, Ms. Buttercup, I'm glad you like Welton," Tom answered.

"Oh, gootness, mmmm, mmm. I didn't says I lik'd it. I jes says it bettah dun Waltonshong!"

She laughed with the liberty of age, chuckling with a gravel phlegm and toothless grin. Then, bluntly, "You believe in God, Missuh Waltonshong?"

The question took him off guard, but Tom had grown accustomed to old peoples' renewal in faith. Because he was a geriatric doctor, his friends jokingly called his practice "God's waiting room," and in God's waiting room, faith and death and eternity come up often.

"Why do you ask, Ms. Buttercup?" Tom asked in return.

"Mmmm," she answered, "'cuz I wants t' see you 'gin in Gloreh, dats why."

"I suppose I do, Ms. Buttercup. God or something like it," Tom answered.

Ms. Buttercup DuBois opened her eyes wide and leaned in, "Lort, Lort, Lort, boy! God or something like it?! It?!?! Mmmm, mmm, mmm, you bettah watch out, Dr. Tom, fo fear lightnin' strike you."

She'd been born Moses Lincoln Johnson, the surname "DuBois" adopted in marriage, which had, in turn, been taken from her husband's parents' former owner. The given names had come after her father's appreciation for liberators of slaves. She'd come into the world three years after the Civil War ended, poor, with conflicting stories about life prewar. Her mother and father, like many mothers and many fathers of any color, would tell her often how lucky she was, and how she didn't know what it was to have a hard life.

Other adults had told her they missed their pre-war life, because at least they knew they'd have a roof over their heads and food to eat. Called "Buttercup" by everyone, she was fourteen before she could read, having been taught by her Sunday school teacher with the sole purpose of reading the Bible. She was a mother at sixteen, again at seventeen, again at eighteen, again at twenty, and had outlived all of her children.

"Don't worry, Ms. Buttercup, I won't let it strike you," Tom said smiling.

"Ain't me I'm worri't 'bout, Baby," Buttercup said earnestly, "Ima only be here 'nother lil' while 'fore I go home. You betta come 'round les'n I fear fo' ya."

"And why would you fear for me, Ms. Buttercup?" Tom asked, her hand now sandwiched between both of his. The attending nurse, who had grown deaf to idle conversation, finished her bed check and left the room without understanding this was not idle conversation.

Tom knew the answer, having grown up sitting in a pew beside his mother. His church had been a fire-and-brimstone church, where the sheer terror of a lake of fire and an eternal bath in that lake was bellowed from the pulpit. His church minister, the preacher, Brother Bill Jackson, had attended seminary in Montgomery, Alabama, and had moved to Corpus Christi when the Southern Baptist Convention built a church there. Brother Bill had been the only preacher, starting twenty years before Tom was even born. As a child he'd been terrified to hear of this place, this Hell, where torment was physical and excruciating and everlasting.

As he grew, the notion of eternity began to look suspect altogether, let alone the notion of eternal misery, with two distinct lines in young Tom's reasoning. First, it seemed to him, no matter what someone did or does in this life, eternal punishment seemed too much. How could that be right, after all, to pay for all eternity against crimes committed during a single person's short lifetime?

Second, that damnation would include people he loved, and he simply couldn't bear the thought of that. He began to see this admonition as fear-based propaganda and in that clarity, dismissed it as manipulation by the church and by the politics of kings.

His suspicions were supported in much of what he was reading and, gravitating to work and to authors and to thinkers that resonated with his suspicions, Tom was emboldened to dig deeper. In digging deeper his curiosity was ratified, which in turn made him feel smart, which in turn compelled him to continue down his road of suspicion. Having inherited his father's library, at sixteen he'd read Marcus Aurelius' *Meditations*. While heralded as a great stoic philosopher and thinker of the ages, current wisdom struggled with Aurelius' brilliance on the one hand, but persecution of belief on the other.

It was obvious to young Tom, however, that the philosophy was simply a platform in support of Aurelius' own selfish political desires and had nothing to do with thoughtful liberation. The people read Aurelius' thoughts on the social construct as reasoned logic, where Tom read it as brilliant propaganda.

This propaganda, conveniently, built a case to keep the political system intact and Aurelius' lineage in power, giving license to the persecution of Christians. Christians, by the way, threatened the system and the power of his lineage. In reading this, Tom began to see all systems, all entities of power, leverage the fear of the listener and the listener's desire to feel purposeful in an effort to have their way, and to perpetuate a system or legacy that endorsed the power of the very people in charge. That "way" might be temporal wealth or control but might be as simple as validation through convincing other people you're right.

Within the confines of this definition, Tom squarely placed lakes of fire and salvation itself. Further and ironically conversely, this desire for pleasure and fear of pain were antithetical to stoic philosophy to begin with. The church was simply ensuring their position by promising eternal safety.

Comparing notes with his Catholic friends, he was confused to discover the disparity in how heaven is attained, what with confession and sacraments and transubstantiation and Hail Marys. He began to recognize some of the differences in a strictly faith-based religion and in a works-based religion, where the goodness is external and it is the participant's job to gather it up, versus accepting the goodness through Christ and changing from within. It felt very much like two paths to the same destination, and it occurred to him neither path was the wrong path.

This notion, he knew, sounded less confrontational and more forgiving, sharing these ideas with his mother. What he didn't share, however, was what he believed and that is: neither path was the right path as well.

He concluded the God-centric parts of our legacy and lineage, our brains and our inheritance, simply sought a version that worked for our individual make-up. For some people, accepting forgiveness and blossoming from the inside was sweet and final. For others who found it difficult to believe salvation was this easy, the rigors of sacrament and Hail Marys and attendance and rules rang more true. Then, as he secluded himself into the night with his mail-order books and theologies, he saw humanity's desire for a god was global and insistent. He saw it in caves and canyons and codex. He saw it in Pamplona and pyramids and papyrus. He saw it in hieroglyph and legend and lore. He saw it in the face of his mother and sister, in the faces of Sunday-morning attendees, and in the faces of patients in God's waiting room.

On the other hand, he was at least fascinated in the continuity of the eternal damnation message, with variations in nearly every world religion including Buddhism, Hinduism, Islam, Judaism, Egyptian, Tibetan, and Greek Mythology. That message is this: if you are not forgiven of your transgressions, you go to hell. So yes, he knew why Ms. Buttercup feared for him.

As he grew still, he began to build a case against this nonsense, including the idea that lakes of fire are only relevant from a physical perspective, and without a body, meaningless. At ten years old he was savvy enough to ask his father what all of that meant, desperately hoping his dad could make sense of it for him.

"Dad," he'd opened, "How can a lake of fire burn you if you don't have a body? How can anything hurt you if you don't have a body?"

They were sitting in the front seat of a 1940 Chevy Business Coupe, windows down and driving the fresh asphalt between Corpus and the new Naval Air Station a few miles away. The road was flat and flawless, built specifically for this commute. Tom's father was the closest thing to God he knew. Thirty-one years old, hair cut high and tight, khaki pants and white t-shirt, with his crisp white uniform blowing on the hanger in the back seat.

"That's a big question for a little man, Tommy Boy," he answered, "Some people read that and think it's a real lake and a real fire, and simply believe it somehow works like that. I think it's a metaphor."

Tom was reading Yeats and Shakespeare at eight, as his father had read to him his entire life. He knew what metaphor was.

"I believe," he continued, "Hell is an eternal agony for the sins of this life, because the only thing you take with you is who you are, including the bad stuff. It is a burning of sorts but not a literal fire. Your soul is tormented by the things you've done to people and to God. But we don't have to worry about it as Christians."

"Why not?" Tom had asked. His father looked at him quizzically, as this is the kind of thing a Christian doesn't ask.

"Tommy," his father said, "Christ died for the sins of humanity. He took all of that on him and died in your place, died in my place. He was perfect as the Son of God, and in that perfection, was willing to sacrifice himself on the cross; was willing to die for crimes he didn't commit, along with all of yours."

Tom couldn't really think of any crimes he had committed, but for some meanness to his sister once in a while and he'd said he was sorry. His mind was racing, searching for sins and wondering if accidentally seeing Mrs. Perkins through her bedroom window was a sin. She was topless in a girdle, putting a bra on as he rode his bike past.

"He took the sins of all humanity to the grave with him, and all anyone has to do is let him, and thank him, and accept that gift. Understand?"

Tommy nodded because he could tell it was important to his dad. That's the only reason he'd nodded, because in that conversation it occurred to him his father wasn't answering his question. This sounded too tidy to young Tom. Too easy, and more than Christ's sacrifice, sounded as though he, himself was being asked to sacrifice his reasoning. He was to shut up and stop asking questions. He was to pay no attention to the puppeteer's hands; willingly turn a blind eye to the things that don't make sense. This hadn't made Tom feel any better and in fact, had made him feel worse.

Ms. Buttercup sat up and pulled Tom close, the clouds in her corneas serving as a scrim between her iris and her view of the world. He saw for the first time her eyes had been blue, those deep azure jewels hidden by her ninety-seven years.

"Why Doctor, you gots to know this life ain't all dey is. You knows dat too, wiffout me sayin' a wort, amen? You feels it likes we all feels it."

Tom didn't want to upset an old woman but couldn't lie to her either. "I believe that part, Ms. Buttercup. I just don't know how any of that works. I believe in a higher power, but I don't know how any of that works."

"Higher power? Data's sum lazy ass no-sense; don' mean nuffin'. Dat takes no courage. Ain't nobody know how it work, Baby, I just know dat it do. You got to beliedat. You got to trust on Jesus dyin fo' you, sho do."

Not knowing wasn't good enough for Tom. It had to be knowable. It had to be understandable. If it was not knowable, not understandable, too mysterious to be believed, then he felt he wasn't to believe it. The gaps in understanding were filled by propaganda and manipulation. And as much as he appreciated Ms. Buttercup Moses Lincoln Dubois's effort, her blind faith was simply not good enough for him. He was glad she had it, as he was glad his mother and sister had it, as he would come to be glad Roseanne and his children had it, but he couldn't have it himself. In fact, if he judged people at all, it wasn't for skin color or education or intellect or social standing. It wasn't for prosperity or lack, it wasn't for beauty or lack, charm or lack, manners or couth or kindness or lack.

If he judged people at all it was for this blind, unexplainable, senseless faith that served as a warm blanket against the cold of the unknown, but nothing more. He judged them while wanting to be them. He wanted the warm blanket but would not take it in fear. He would not have fear drive his conviction. He refused to take refuge from the unexplainable.

Peering into her blue abyss, past the clouds and into her fathomless, blind depths, Tom asked, "What if I'm a good man, Ms. Buttercup? What if I treat people kindly and do good work and help people? Shouldn't that be good enough?"

Buttercup now had her second hand on top of his. With quiet earnest, "Baby, dey is no 'goot 'nuff' doncha know? Dey is no goot 'nuff. Like dey is no goot people o' bat people. Dey is only fuhgiv'n and unfuhgiv'n, and all you gotsta do is aks fo' it."

Then, staring through the fog of ninety-seven years, she said, "Yo gonna need somebody on yor bond, mmm, mmmm."

He lingered for a long time, then gently pulled his hands from hers, that soft, buttery velvet suede of her hands sliding over the tops and bottoms of his own.

When he turned to leave, she said, "Hell ain't what dey says it is, Dr. Tom Welton. Dat burnin'ain't fire; dat burnin' ain't even sumptin' what is, but is sumptin' what ain't. Dat burnin' is da pain of no God. Is da pain of no gootness. I don't wants dat fuh you, amen? Mmmm, mmmm, mmmm. No suh, praise Jesus."

Chapter 4

PART I

If you come o'er my house
And can't find me in or out,
I'm gone with boogie in my feets, lettin' it on out.
Lettin' the boogie on out my feets,
Lord, Lord, lettin' the boogie on out my feets.

—*Cornbread Curtis Zant*

JOHN AND DIANNE PULLED into his father's one-hundred-yard driveway on his seventy-three acres mid-afternoon, gravel crackling under the tires. The garage door was open, which was true from dawn to dusk every day, regardless of whether Tom and Roseanne were home.

"Aren't you afraid somebody will steal something, Dad?" John would ask.

"Well, Johnny," Tom had always said, "not out here. Plus, when I fret too much over what I own, it begins to own me."

The house was small, tiny in fact, at just over 900 square feet, with an additional bunk house built for guests on the other side of the driveway. Tom had no need to insist on a small house as Roseanne wanted it too. The kids were grown and neither wanted much to maintain. Besides, the small house allowed retirement earlier than they'd planned, where they could spend their days together "piddling."

With all the acreage, Tom could hunt if he liked, or take target practice alone in the woods. Because guns were machines, he liked these too, marveling in the simplicity and cooperation of very powerful moving parts. They could hike, take pictures, and Roseanne could bring kids out from the church to spend the day running through the woods. Mostly, however, he and Roseanne spent their days gardening and talking, reading, cooking, thinking. They had their kids and grandchildren in the house and staying as often as they could get them but spent most of their days simply together. He would work on cars and motorcycles and she would paint, and on Wednesdays when she volunteered as the church secretary, he would ride off into the countryside on one of his motorcycles.

John walked through the front door hurriedly, straight through the little den to the bedroom, then the bathroom and sleeping porch. Coming through the kitchen he noticed a steak in the sink, thawing but still hard. Dianne met him as he walked through the door into the garage.

"The motorcycle is gone, hon," she said with relief, "He's just out riding."

John quickly scanned the large, one-car garage. All tools hung and in their proper places; the shop lights off and gently swaying over the workbench with the incoming breeze. There were two other motorcycles sitting unused and silent: John's later model Honda 650 Hawk, which he'd bought to ride with his father but hadn't ridden in years, and Tom's project bike, a 1978 Moto Guzzi 850T. Tom's Toyota was parked in the driveway and another project, a 1967 Volvo wagon, was parked under a tree with Roseanne's cat atop it. It was quieter than John had hoped. On the bench was an empty cup of coffee, still wet in the bottom and beside it, his father's cell phone.

"Well, crap," John muttered, partly because he disapproved and partly because he felt he may have wasted his day driving out for no reason.

He put his arm around Diane and walked out to the edge of the garage, surveying the grounds and listening, as though intensity may give him some insight. The cat, who may or may not have recognized them, dropped from the roof of the Volvo to the hood and stretched, tongue curled. He then lazily leapt to the ground and sauntered over to rub his head and ears against Dianne's leg. The cat was scarred from fighting, with an ear tip missing. Now purring, Dianne crouched to pick it up, scratching under its jawline, over its ears, its neck and head.

"You worried?" she asked, not worried herself.

"At what point do I worry?" he answered, "The man is pushing eighty years old and you can't tell him anything about anything. I don't even like him living here alone, much less riding a motorcycle! A motorcycle, Dianne!" His love and worry and anger were filling him.

"Honey," Dianne said calmly, "Loving and respecting and honoring your dad is beautiful. Being mad at him for being himself, and for doing the things he has done his whole life, which by the way, make him the very man you love and respect, is not your job or even for you to say."

John looked at her and knew she was right. It wasn't his business, but he dreaded a world without his father in it. She was right, but his long-held hope that his dad would never get the Triumph finished vanished when he saw it missing and was replaced by the anxiety of understanding his will would not be answered. She was right, but his need to impose what he deemed wisdom on the man that helped give him wisdom in the first place compelled him to anger. She was right, but he was mad at his father for worrying him.

He pulled her in close and kissed her on her closed eye, whispering in feigned mocking, "It must be exhausting to be right all the time."

Dianne smiled, "Don't worry, being old doesn't mean he doesn't know what he's doing. And we'd better get used to it. Now that he fixed it, he may do this every day. We have a much better chance of talking him into taking his cell phone than we do talking him out of riding. We'll just wait."

John turned to walk back in and do just that, as Dianne set the cat back down. Hoping there were more steaks, John looked through the freezer in the kitchen before heading out to the "ice box" in a shed in the yard. Finding none inside, he walked across the yard to an outbuilding John had built for the sole purpose of housing a big freezer, where he kept the deer and wild boar he'd hunted, along with anything that wouldn't fit in the kitchen freezer. Half-full of meat wrapped in freezer paper and then in Ziploc bags, the labels were written and dated in his mother's hand: back strap; pork loin; cabrito. She had dutifully dated them as well, some as many as six or eight years ago. John paused.

When his mother wrapped and marked the meat, John was still in Houston, still working at the hospital, still married to his first wife with kids at home. Both his mom and dad lived in this house in the country, having built a life as retirees that didn't include him or his sisters, where he hunted deer and she put up tomatoes and cabbage and corn and beans. His father, Dr. Thomas Welton, wasn't even a practicing doctor anymore and had been living a life John had never known.

It struck him to realize he hadn't lived with them many more years than he had, having had a life of his own while his mother wrapped bacon and put it in the freezer. The older meat now, too old to use and worthless, waited in the cold dark until the day came it would be thrown out. A waste, which of course no one knew or believed when the meat first went into the dark. That cold flesh, waiting to emerge; waiting to be brought out into the light, becoming what it was meant to be. What it was born to be but would never happen.

Pulling two new steaks from the freezer, John walked back to the house and placed them in the sink beside Tom's while Dianne went to the car to retrieve her knitting and book.

Feeling better, John decided he would just surprise his father with their visit and only talk about the motorcycle as an accomplishment.

"Beautiful!" he would say, then take it for a spin himself up and down the Big Thicket blacktop. He would suggest his dad go to work on the Moto Guzzi or the Volvo or even his own Honda, knowing every hour spent restoring these machines would be an hour he wasn't on his Triumph.

His Honda, John's Honda, sat dusty and unused. He hadn't ridden it since one of the earlier visits to see his mother. The house had been loud with siblings and nieces and nephews and activity and John, claustrophobic and weighted with the knowledge of his mother's coming death, lit out on the bike south to Woodville.

Woodville was the destination, not a coincidence, as he could think of nothing he wanted more than chicken and dumplings and peach cobbler. There is a place there—an old place—called The Pickett House, serving chicken and catfish and greens the way his southern memory served them. He and Dianne would take his parents there when they visited, driving the 25 minutes south as a treat.

His father would always say, "This place reminds me of Ms. Flo and her bakery" and while the restaurant was actually nothing like the hardware-store-bakery, the smell of baking bread and cobbler was. The place wasn't really decorated, as a restaurant might be expected to be, as much as it was simply authentic and a place for the owner to hang his collection of vintage circus posters. Picnic tables, gingham cloth, and circus posters, the way it had been since the 1940s, with a gravel parking lot and the sometimes-deafening sound of crickets and locusts in the close woods.

John had gotten to The Pickett House late afternoon, riding back to his parent's in the dark, flanked by the twinkling of lightning bugs in the coal black darkness of the forest. When he'd walked into his parents' house no one asked a thing. No one wondered where he'd been for three hours because they all knew. John, like is father, went his own way.

He walked into a living room of conversation and ice cream, with Big Bill Broonzy spinning on the record player. Dianne moved to make a spot for him on the couch beside her, holding his hand as he sat down, and while he joined the conversation and laughed and told stories, he could not shake the allure of that dark forest, lit up in magic and lightning bugs.

The very forest holding his father in that space between the ground and a 1969 Triumph. A crushing squeeze; a relentless grip unwilling to let the old man go, all while John rummaged through Tom's pantry and refrigerator.

He made a mental note of what else he would cook for dinner, glad for the chance to do this for his dad and stacking the spices and condiments together on the countertop. Alone in the kitchen, he felt an attachment to knives and pots and a stand mixer his mother had used his entire boyhood. He could see her hands on them, the way she moved and held them. He could see her cut potatoes and onions and carrots and apples. He could see her stir.

He could see his father now too, chopping what she needed chopped; washing what she needed washed, and always, always, talking with him and his sisters, loving them, teaching them. He grew up watching his father wait on his mother, with an adoration and gratitude that, counterintuitively, made him the strongest man John had ever known.

Likewise, he witnessed his mother wait on his father. John, Hannah, and Grace had come of age witnessing partnership and a vision of what a marriage should be. This model became the goal and now, divorced and remarried, John had it too, in Dianne.

He closed his eyes there, standing in the small kitchen, the soft, faint memory of his dad's blues collection playing grainy on the stereo in the living room, as it had played when he'd walked in that night. Blind Willie Johnson, Robert Johnson, Etta James, Howlin' Wolf, Elan Vital, Lightnin' Hopkins, B.B. King.

Hundreds Tom bought, and hundreds more given him on Ms. Flo's passing. John's mother, pitch perfect and unabashed, would sing Bessie Smith and John Lee Hooker like she'd lived it, and *Stormy Weather* like she wrote it, seeing Etta James as her back-up singer. Her soft Spanish accent lost in the vocals, she'd fallen in love with the music because she'd fallen in love with Tom and in both, was all in.

John and his sisters had grown up with rock of the 1960s and 1970s, but unlike their contemporaries knew where the music had come from. Without the blues there would be no Led Zeppelin; their entire catalog covered 1930s and 1940s blues artists. There would be no Credence, there would be no Bad Company, there would be no Yardbirds, or Eric

Clapton. They knew who copied Leadbelly and Blind Lemon. When they heard *Midnight Special* and *Black Betty* and *House of the Rising Sun* covered by musicians in the 1960s and 1970s, they understood where the music came from.

Overwhelmed with gratitude, John prayed thanks; thanks for his mother, thanks for his father, thanks for his children and his wife and even his trials. Spontaneous and fervent, he leaned against the kitchen counter with eyes closed, grateful for the life he had, grateful for the peace of salvation and eternity. John prayed for his father, his father's loneliness and solitude, his father's health and his safe return from his ride. He prayed thanks for his father's influence and example, his mother's kindness and insistence he become the very man he was.

He prayed thanks for Dianne, for the forgiveness afforded him, and for the love and guidance of his Listener. In this prayer, as in his life, John's relief and willingness to turn over his fears was accompanied by a humility that is part and parcel in exchange for the peace of grace. This peace was the peace John's father wanted, the peace John thought his father had as he lay dying in the east Texas Big Thicket.

PART II

Wavin' my stavin' pole, won't you say my name,
Just swingin' my stavin' pole, somebody shake my hand,
Can't thump a man with a stick, expect him to be your friend,
Pride is a skinny path, an here I go again.

—*CLARKESDALE RAINEY*

Tom felt better. The ibuprofen was working to a degree and the swelling was down, as was the overall pain. He was itching as his skin had stretched and relaxed but knew better than to scratch what was broken and bruised. Looking down the length of his body, his right leg and hip filled his pant leg better than his left leg did, his right thigh snug against the woven cotton khakis. There were spots of blood soaking through his pants in places, but nothing that would indicate a gaping, open wound, at least as far as he could tell.

About mid-shin his leg disappeared beneath the bike, buried under the swing-arm and engine cradle, but he could see the top half of his bare foot poking out from beyond the bike. The impact had been great enough for him to lose his shoe and even his sock, his bulbous foot and bloated toes almost alien to him. He was warm enough, dry, protected from direct morning sunlight and had a bit of food, and in this, was confident he could last a day or maybe even two.

Reaching above him, Tom pulled the helmet back under his head to prop himself up. The notebook, substantial and heavy and worn, had become a keepsake over the years, stuffed with drawings and notes and ideas and photographs. Tom again opened the book at the beginning. The first few pages were pencil drawings John had drawn. They'd stopped at a rest stop north of Woodville, built in the 1930s when traveling by car was a feat. With mossy stone and mortar picnic tables built among the pines, there was a spring that fed a large, shallow, concrete pool for people and horses alike. John was twelve and at two hours there and two hours home, the boy needed a rest between coming and going.

"What are you drawing?" Tom asked, while spreading pimento cheese on white bread. He left it on a napkin with an apple.

"It's a picture of me and you," the boy replied with no self-consciousness. "But don't look till I'm finished."

Tom stepped away from the boy and crossed the drive to another empty table, ate his sandwich, and lit a cigar. The image of Johnny, his boy, studiously drawing under the trees, would be burned into his memory forever. So much so, in fact, that every time he had thumbed through the notebook he started there—with that page—and every time not only saw the picture drawn but the picture of his boy in his head as well.

"What are you thinking about, Dad?" Johnny looked up to ask.

"Thinking about you," he answered, "and how quickly you're growing up."

Erasing something and starting again, Johnny asked, "When do you think I'll have a beard?"

Tom laughed, "Well, let's not rush it. I mean, just yesterday you were in diapers and now you want a beard?"

"How old were you when you had a beard?" he pushed.

Shaving was one thing, and a beard something else entirely. Tom started shaving when a young man starts shaving but hadn't grown a beard until he was in a Korean cell.

"I started shaving when I was fifteen or sixteen, and had a beard when I was nineteen," he answered, not wanting to go any further. He had flashbacks of picking scabs from his whiskers.

"I hope I have a beard when I'm twelve," Johnny said, then, "Did your daddy have a beard?"

Tom remembered his father's face, square jawline and heavy brow. He could see his clean cheeks and lip and didn't know whether he remembered it firsthand or from pictures. He could hear the sound his father's razor made as he cut his whiskers.

"No, he was in the Navy, remember, and they wouldn't let him have a beard on base."

"Why not?" Johnny asked as he drew.

Tom had never thought about it. "Well, I don't know. Maybe they thought it wasn't hygienic or maybe just because it didn't look clean."

Johnny closed the notebook and took a bite of his sandwich. "That's dumb. I think everyone should have a beard."

Tom, preparing himself to be complimented, asked, "Everyone? Why's that?"

"Jesus had a beard. Everyone should have a beard."

Tom laughed, as Johnny spent many hours—hundreds if not thousands—at his grandparent's house in south Houston. In every room hung a picture of Jesus, light-skinned, backlit, hands clasped, looking upward, and bearded.

They spent the afternoon at the rest stop, wading in the clear pool and throwing rocks at floating pinecones. While Johnny put his socks and shoes on, Tom checked the oil and the tension on the chain, squeezed the tires to check pressure, straddled and shook the motorcycle to listen to how much gas was in the tank.

"Can I look at your picture now?" he asked his son.

Now self-conscious, Johnny opened the newly designated notebook, the binding still fresh and stiff.

"I might color it when we get home," he offered, turning the book so his dad could see.

It was perfect. The two of them standing beside one another with the motorcycle next to them. The tank said "trumph." There were pine trees and cars on the farm road behind them. There were birds. They both wore smiles too large for their faces, and both of them had beards.

"Hey!" Tom exclaimed when he noticed, "I think you added something here!"

Delighted he'd snuck this into the picture, Johnny giggled the way only innocence can giggle. "It's a joke! I'm gonna erase it!"

Tom kissed the top of his head. "Leave it alone, I think it's terrific."

Johnny shrugged, embarrassed. "You know," his dad said, "you may not have a beard now, but you seem like the kind of guy who would have a beard, so I think you should leave it."

Tom looked back down at his aching hip, aware the wave of pain was late. Moving to try and get weight off of his cheek and hip, he slid a handful of pine needles under the edge of his khakis as a cushion. He tried to remember whether he'd ever seen road crews or linemen or prison crews working this road, hitchhikers, bicyclists, or horses. Past his foot and front wheel, he could see the hurdled fence and knew he was on private property. For the first time, he noticed he had clipped the top strand of the barbed wire fence, pulling it from the posts where it lay tangled in the front rim of the bike like a steel vine with steel thorns. Maybe the owner walks the property, maybe the owner comes out this way.

Trying not to worry he held the book over his chest and flipped through it as he had many times before. This time, however, the book was inverted and out poured leaves and a handful of Polaroid pictures. He had inserted the leaves between the pages where he had marked oil changes and repairs, giving him an easy way of finding the maintenance records. He'd had a strange prohibition against dog-earing pages, a holdover from his librarian's admonishing as a boy, and instead used leaves as bookmarks. Mostly brittle and crumbling, they came spilling out in the breeze, some nearly powder having waited so long between the pages. Free they now were, returned to the woods they'd come from as they wafted away in the cool zephyr.

The few pictures were of times long gone, of motorcycles long gone, taken with a Polaroid camera long gone. One of Johnny sitting on a 1974 Kawasaki KZ900, a brutally fast rocket of the day. He was sixteen in the picture, tall enough but not man enough to ride it. Skinny outstretched arms holding the grips, and insistent on no smile, Johnny looked every bit as hopeful and eager as his father had at that age. Tom remembered taking the picture, remembered how frightened he was over John riding a motorcycle, not knowing at the time he needn't have worried. John had never developed that same burning desire, never had the same image of freedom or escape, never wanted to know how machines worked. Instead he was absorbed by the clarinet, then the guitar, then jazz, then rock music; a truth that was both relief and disappointment to Tom.

A second picture of Hannah standing on the seat of a 1965 Moto Guzzi Falcone, she wore a Casper costume in August without the mask, a plastic tiara and held a baton. She was only five or six and Johnny had taken the photograph, the two of them giving him the picture as a present over supper. While Tom would never allow the kids to use the motorcycles as a jungle gym, more for their safety than the motorcycle's, he cherished the picture and had kept it all these years tucked within the journal.

Then there was a picture of Grace at fifteen, sitting atop Tom's 1980 model Honda XL500. He'd taken the picture on a Sunday after teaching her to ride it, soon smudging the top with his own greasy thumbprint. Three days after he'd taken the picture, she would sneak the bike out to see Sonny Terry and Brownie McGhee at the Pavilion in downtown Houston. He and Roseanne were in Boston at a convention and while they had strict rules and both John and Hannah were to keep an eye on her, Grace couldn't resist.

She pushed the bike from the garage, down the driveway and a half block downhill, where she kick-started it and took off. After picking up her best friend, Claire Deigh, the two girls rode the access roads to the center of town, through downtown traffic and concert congestion, where they parked to see the duo perform live. Her parents wouldn't know for twenty years, when she laughingly confessed over dinner.

Among the pictures there was an image of Tom and Tom-Tom, Grace's boy. She and her son lived with Roseanne and Tom after her husband had passed, blessed with a place of safety and love during a time she felt there was little safety and little love. The Polaroid had been titled in blue ink, scrawled across the white bottom band, "Two Toms." Grandfather and grandson sat on Tom's restored 1948 Knucklehead, the two-year-old sitting between Tom and the tank, his diapered bottom and bare legs straight out toward the headlight. The toddler leaned forward slapping the tank, the blur of his movement captured in the image. Tom had his arm around him, holding him against any fall and looking down on the baby in his innocence.

The picture had been taken late afternoon facing west so there was a lot of glare in the background and looking, Tom noticed someone standing in the yard beyond the driveway. He'd never noticed that before and couldn't identify the person because of the glare, but thought it must have been a neighbor or maybe one of his sons-in-law.

The next picture was a picture of the two of them, Tom and Roseanne, a few months after Johnny had been born. Her parents volunteered to babysit so they could go to the beach, taking this picture of them just before leaving. His bride, his wide-eyed optimist, sat behind him in the picture, her young arms wrapped around his young waist. She wore a scarf over her hair and large black rimmed sunglasses, because every woman wore Jackie-O sunglasses. She wore canvas boat shoes and no socks, her ankles revealed by her rolled pants. Tom wore an undershirt and jeans, loafers and Ray Bans. They were on his 1957 Harley Sportster he'd bought second-hand to ride back and forth to school.

Staring at the Kodachrome image, softened by the grain in the color and the age of the photo, Tom wondered, as he always had, what she'd seen in him.

To Roseanne, Tom was Sampson. Rather, what Sampson would have been had he had a good woman. Strong and fearless, protective and loving, she would groom and support him rather than betray him and his secrets. She groomed him, his hair, the brown then gray then white locks, combing and preening and washing and brushing until his brown then gray then white locks were one foot, two foot, ten feet long. Together they stood in growing piles of his hair, like purging pillows of silken flame up around them, guarding them, holding the world at bay. And when they had children, she'd known somehow, these brown then gray then white mountains would protect them all. And in this recognition and growing of his abilities and confidence, Roseanne had been the strength all the while.

He had only known her to be so at peace, so full of love and of charity, that a goodness seemed to emanate from her. Her laugh was infectious, her smile captivating, her manner irresistible in the best of ways. People, men and women both, would gravitate to her because she was special, making them feel good simply by being in the room with her. She was kind, good-natured, and gave all of that credit to God and to her salvation, where Tom gave all of that credit to her and to her parents and to her inherent nature.

For her kindness she was sometimes taken advantage of, and while she knew it, she didn't let that keep her from doing what she thought she was called to do. Tom was so grateful for the place she gave him in the world that he'd never mustered the wherewithal to tell her he didn't believe what she believed. That he thought of God as a benevolent observer, not an active participant in his life or the world.

That day, the day the picture had been taken, they'd gone south to where the highway ended on the seawall, then west, out past Galveston to the desolate Galveston State Park, choosing a spot under a stand of mangrove trees. There they spent the day swimming and sunbathing, laughing and eating and sleeping in solitude. They'd made love in the afternoon, lying together afterward to talk about the future and the day and how much he loved her. In the evening breeze Tom was reading Hermann Hesse's *Der Steppenwolf*, Roseanne C.S. Lewis' autobiography, *Surprised by Joy*.

In his mind's eye, he could see her feet and her naked body, the soft crease where her legs met her backside, while she put her bathing suit back on to swim one more time before leaving. One more time before leaving. Just one more time. He, her absence unbearable, had gotten up to swim too.

PART III

I'm halfway between the light,
and I can't sleep a wink.
I call on your telephone,
but the bell just keep on ringin'.

—*MISSISSIPPI MAMA RAY*

Grace walked up the stairs carrying clean bedding, still warm from the dryer. Passing Eric on the landing she stopped long enough to kiss him and moved on, preparing for the coming guests. She was an early riser, most days beating the sun, where she would have coffee with her husband before he left for the restaurant. Then she would mind the silence, sitting in her comfortable, worn leather club chair under the light of a French industrial table lamp. When it was cold, she would wrap her slender shoulders in a blanket; when it was hot, she would turn on an eighty-year old Hunter fan, the tired electric hum covering the silence like her blanket covered her shoulders. She would take an hour to linger with her coffee, reading everything from Poe to *People* magazine, or simply sit in the darkness and pray while the sun rose. Many days, however, she would read her Bible.

Certainly, she didn't want to be a person whose only point of reference was a book of scripture that was only relevant to Christians and to seekers and to academics, but this book, this Word, was a source of physical and psychological comfort like her chair was, like her blanket was, like her fan was. When she was younger, she would study it, comparing analysis and interpretation, but those days had long since passed. Instead, simply reading it made her feel as though she had dropped a hook in fathomless water, and more than something to catch and pull up, she had instead hooked the ocean itself.

The bed and breakfast inn, an 1890s "Sunday house" had just four guest rooms, which stayed booked more weekends than not. Cut limestone blocks and a tin roof, the house had an addition on the back to accommodate a living room and kitchen, with a detached garage in the rear. Tommy had grown up in this house, having recently moved to a trailer in Kerrville, but assumed he would work there until he inherited it. At twenty years old, he had his future planned. They had a chicken yard with Cherry Eggers, Indian River and Leghorn chickens for the fresh eggs, and honeybee hives behind the garage for the honey. They always had fresh eggs for the guests' breakfasts, and honey for their biscuits.

Eric ran the family restaurant on Main Street, a traditional German affair open for breakfast and lunch only, after which he was home and helping Grace. On Sundays, they left fruit and bagels out for the guests, as they were at church, afterward giving their departing guests gift baskets of honey, local produce and logo-embroidered hand towels. In the evening, she would paint or watch television with her two men, seemingly having managed to squeeze the sensuality and good stuff from every day. Sometimes Tommy's friends would come over to make an impromptu band, three to four boys playing steel and three-string cigar box guitars, singing Willie Dixon or Junior Kimbrough or Leadbelly, their only musical aspiration to just remember the lyrics. It was a quiet life, it was a peaceful life, it was the good life.

This day, Tommy had the shutters off the back of the house and across sawhorses in the yard, repainting them a creamy yellow to match the budding brown-eyed daisies in the beds around the trees. In the garage sat his Ducati Monster, the bike he would ride home after work. He called Eric "Dad." He was articulate, smart, and well-read. He liked to work outside. He loved his momma. He hummed while he worked. He needed a shave.

Grace, heavy mobile phone in her pocket, had just talked with John about their father. Where was that man? Unworried but needful, she sat on the unmade bed and prayed quickly for her father's safekeeping. Her prayers were not words into the ether. Her prayers were not simply a means of expressing her concerns. Her prayers were not a way to expel her fears. Her prayers were not a ruse, sold to her by tradition or her psychology. Her prayers were not her self-imposed therapy. No, her prayers were entreaty and gratitude to an omniscient, omnipotent God of the universe, whom, she knew, loved her. More than that, the God of the universe who heard her, embraced her, and by virtue of her embracing Him back, saw her as pure.

She desperately wished the uninitiated could feel the truth in this and the peace it gave her, working hard to that end in seen and unseen ways. Each of the four guest rooms had Bibles in them, and each Bible had a bookmark reading, "If you don't have a Bible, take this one!"

One could look at Grace and think of many reasons she should be discouraged or trenchant, which is true of most of us. In many respects she'd had a hard life, enduring much, having seen a lot of heartache and struggle, and it would have been understandable if she'd given up in some way. Bitterness and fear and sorrow would have been understandable indeed, if not an expectation by some.

She was an artist and had a tender heart, after all, and life is harder for tender hearts and artists, but she had something else, too. Believing Jesus Christ was the Son of God, and embracing His death as the path to purity, to peace, Grace was infused with the "Godness," that is, the part of God that resides in people who believe it. This transcendent residence, a foreign or peculiar or naïve or desperate idea to anyone without it, turned her into something she wasn't, and couldn't be, by herself. It turned her into something greater, made her a part of something greater, something sublime, something abstract.

Indeed, she'd become a new creature, one no longer bound by the tyranny of humanity or of time. She had become part of the very depths she'd plumbed. She was not the hook in the water but was part of the ocean itself; not a kite, but the sky. Eternity was never the question, as she believed everyone eternal. The defining question, for Grace, was whether she or anyone else would enter the eternal light or eternal darkness.

In fact, if she had sorrow at all, it was sorrow in understanding the people who haven't embraced the truth have no idea what she felt or was even talking about, and in fact, thought of her as silly if not delusional. Simple for her, really, but the everlasting influence of the love of God and what that meant to everyone's healing and forgiveness, and what healing and forgiveness meant to her husband and son was her driving force. Basically, the legacy of living a life in Christ, and how much more robust and fulfilling it is than in what would have been her bleak, hopeless future as a non-believer.

She simply could not imagine a life wherein the Spirit of God did not impact her view of the world, her view of existence, her view of her place in the timeline of beginning and ending. She had long since, and gladly, turned over the notion she was the center of the world to a God whose Son was, in fact, the center of the world. She could not imagine atheism, flying in the face of all physical and existential evidence everywhere she looked, noting it took more energy to disbelieve in a Creator than to believe—an unending effort to keep the door of truth closed despite the pounding to get in. So, where an atheist may have seen her as weak and frightened, she would see an atheist as a child lost.

She mourned for these lost children, for insecure pseudo-intellectuals for whom phrenic acrobatics cloistered the obvious; where self-delusion was enough to satisfy their pride and their longing for meaning. She mourned for the people who insisted goodness of heart and righteous intent would give them a pass. She mourned, and she prayed for the lost children. And lo these many years, Grace had no idea she prayed for her father.

PART IV

Mississippi water took my people down,
Lord, Mississippi water done took my people down,
Woke up early mornin' and all my people gone,
Woke up early mornin' and all my people gone.

—*BLIND HENRY BISHOP*

Tom's hip and leg throbbed, but the pain had become a dull constant rather than intermittently sharp. He couldn't feel his foot any longer, as the swelling kept the nerves from reporting back to Tom's brain. His body's mutiny had begun, the retreat, beginning with abandoning the sensation in his foot and toes. While he would have been alarmed if it was happening in a patient, he was glad to be relieved of it. Keen on the wound, he knew the pain would come in phases. The initial injury and sharpest pain, followed by a dulled throbbing, followed by fever and localized heat, and then a guess as to whether his seventy-seven and one-half year-old organs would begin giving up, or he would last long enough to become septic and suffer through the agony of systemic inflammation. He hoped not. He'd only seen it untreated and run its natural course once. Not seen so much as heard.

While in the Korean prison cell he heard septicemia take over another prisoner. Low groaning for hours, followed by crying out, then screaming, then begging in a language Tom didn't know, though begging sounds the same in every language. The prisoner had been Korean himself and while Tom never knew what he had done to be there, he'd only seen him once when he was dragged past his cell with horrible, bloody ankles and feet. The guards were ordered to let the sepsis go, allowing the prisoner Tom had never met to die in the most agonizing way.

He flipped over the picture he held of himself and Roseanne to reread a poem he had written, having taped it to the back. He'd written it for Roseanne the afternoon at the beach, one of many over the years, and while he'd buried her with the original and a full box of the rest, this poem he had copied and kept with the picture:

> Happy, early youth, spring and rain and heat,
> Tender, hoping (or understanding), grow.
> Happy the young, only unjaded,
> Me—I—gleefully honoring the love, I keep everything true hidden.
> I, stonewalling, eager and steadfast, take every relief, every grief,
> God, how I'd die in never-ending gallows for obeisance, reverence, you.
> Our understanding is love; oblately, verily, everything,
> Young, O! Unblemished, vernal, everlasting ramparts yell "Magic!"
> Undulating, constant, hope.

He read the poem again, aloud, and a third time, finally stuffing all the pictures in the breast pocket with his watch. Roseanne had been their photographer, the recorder, the sentimental keeper of their history and while she took many pictures and created many photo albums, Tom was convinced there would be nothing if it had been left up to him. After she had gotten too sick to be home, Tom had taken the albums to the hospital, where the two of them would go through them to reminisce about the life they'd had together.

Despite having had a career treating older patients and despite knowing better, Tom was convinced she would beat the cancer until the last days she'd lived. Roseanne, on the other hand, felt her end coming after the first round of chemo, enduring the treatments just for the extra time with her husband and children and grandchildren. In the beginning, when Roseanne could feel it, she would try to talk with Tom about it.

"What will you do when I'm gone, Love?" she would ask.

She didn't ask in self-importance, but in compassionate curiosity; in the worry of a woman who loved her husband. She wanted to know he would be busy, occupied, and okay without her.

Tom, whose inclination was to joke his way around the conversation, couldn't. "I don't have to figure that out, Rosie. You aren't going anywhere."

As their kids filtered in and out with more frequent visits and phone calls, their mother would pull them aside to have candid conversations. They denied the reality at first, then began to pretend to deny the reality, feeling somehow obligated to show unrealistic hope to their mother. They came around sooner, however, than their father did because he had, over the years, begun to see their marriage as a single thing, a single entity, a Siamese whereby one would not live without the other. A shared heart and shared mind. After fifty years of marriage he still looked forward to seeing her, still enjoyed her company, still wanted her opinion, still adored her.

To the world and to his children, Tom was stalwart and strong, wise with an understanding of what to do and the courage to do it. His points of reference were equal parts intuition, experience, and the fervent pursuit of wisdom and philosophy. He was gracious and gentle but not because his demeanor demanded it. He gave his patients and his family and his friends and his neighbors the best parts of himself, and while violent only a few times in his life, he kept his violence close by in case he needed it, using it judiciously as he believed every man should. He was afraid of nothing, including death, but tempered this hot fearlessness in the cool oil of kindness.

"Kindness is the greatest portion of strength," his mother would say, and Tom believed it because he had no father to ask.

When it came to Rosie, however, she knew him for all of these things and a hundred more. She knew he sometimes woke himself up shouting and sweaty. She knew he changed the television channel if he stumbled across footage of Pearl Harbor or Korea. She knew he cried when the kids moved away to college. She knew he would sit with ailing patients long after his shift was over, and when he lost one, send flowers to the grieving families. She knew he would sometimes stand in the backyard for hours, hands in pockets in the middle of the night. She knew to not interrupt it. She could see him there in the moonlight, stocking feet, hands shoved deep into the pockets of his khakis, the white scars on his back catching the moonlight. She couldn't read his mind, but knew it was racing.

She knew he wrote copious notes and missives and journal entries the world would never see because it was for his understanding and her understanding of him, not the world. She was the only one to read them. She knew he knew things he would never share in pride but would always share in sympathy or empathy or to benefit someone else. She knew things about him he didn't know about himself.

She was grateful for this intimacy, this picture of marriage, this privilege to spend a lifetime with her husband. He had once told her he'd like to die while he still looked like trouble, and even though that time was long gone now, Roseanne had always seen him as her lion. While his elbows sometimes ached with arthritis and his shoulders had narrowed and thinned, while his beard was gray and his hands were specked, she still saw him as her warrior, her protector, her man. And he was.

Likewise, Tom had completely exposed himself to her and the thought of her passing was more than just denial, it was blasphemy. He simply could not reconcile his coming grief against his present opportunity, denying her illness rather than accepting it. Her hair had been thick and black, heavy even, each strand thick enough to roll between his thumb and index finger. Her ponytails were densely trellised bunches, woven together as hibiscus shoots are sometimes woven, and when she wore it straight behind her he imagined her royalty, he imagined her other-worldly, he imagined her magic.

As she aged, her hair remained thick, those heavy hibiscus shoots turning an earned mix of black and white, while the face her hair framed became seraphic, almost holy. As she lost her hair in alarming drain-clogging clumps and within the bristles of her treasonous brushes, her face became framed not by the yin and yang of her hair, but by the glowing, virginal skin beneath. She became more angelic, more holy, with a look of destiny that both amazed and terrified Tom.

My hands are so cold," she would say as she got closer, "Hold my hand, baby."

Tom would put both of her hands between his, rubbing one atop the other facing her. He would wrap her in a blanket and stare at them—her hands—remembering them as they'd knitted, as they'd cooked, as they'd written, as they'd held babies, and held him.

His children would visit, sometimes for the day, sometimes for days, praying for her with earnest. Tom would hold hands and bow his head, hoping the universe or the higher power would intercede, but angry with it, nonetheless. He'd had enough for one lifetime and had no patience for his wife's suffering. Likewise, he felt put upon himself. Hadn't he seen enough? Hadn't there been enough? Hadn't he paid his share in grief and blood and loss? Hadn't he helped enough and done enough to earn some kind of favor?

"Please God," he found himself saying as she slept, praying as a beggar.

Finally, in the last month, she told the family to stop pretending. The children were there for the day, grilling hamburgers and doing their best to feign normalcy. Grace, who had begun calling her mother Aunt Jemima on account of her head scarf, wheeled her mother from the bedroom to the patio. Weak and bald with radiation, Roseanne told them their patronizing was silly and embarrassing for her, and she would much rather spend her remaining time in honesty than in pretending.

"That isn't faith," she said, "that is selfishness. I know where I am going, and you know where I am going, so let's stop pretending I am not going."

While John, Hannah and Grace heard that with relief, Tom heard it as revelation, for he hadn't been pretending.

"What will you do when I'm gone, Tommy?" she would ask again that night.

"I have no idea, baby," he answered. "I can't imagine."

She would have suggested he move back to Houston if she thought there was a chance of it. Instead, "No moping, Love, understand? I don't want you to be that old man who sits in a chair waiting to die himself."

Tom was never much of a sitter, but he was certain that's what would happen. She continued, "I want you to go see Tommy Boy. Spend some time with Grace in Fredericksburg. Spend time in Houston with Hannah and the kids or Galveston. There's no reason you should just sit here."

He listened but was numb. It didn't matter whether he agreed or disagreed. It didn't matter what he said he would or wouldn't do. He knew within a short time what he did wouldn't matter at all.

"Go buy a new motorcycle and ride it all over creation," she said, "go fast and far and see the world."

Tom chuckled, "Baby, you know I don't like new motorcycles," then feeling more tired than he could remember feeling, Tom said, "Rosie, I'm not a young man anymore," almost as a confession; as news to her. Maybe even as news to himself.

Roseanne laughed, "Baby, you were never a young man. You were 500 years old when I first met you." Tom, weary, laughed with her.

Roseanne continued, "Missing me is one thing, Tommy, but staying out here by yourself? With nothing to do? That would be a terrible idea. You aren't twenty, but you aren't ninety either and you're in great shape. There are forty-year -olds who can't keep up with you. You have too much to offer to just dry up."

Tom wondered how many times this conversation played out every day across the world. The last goodbyes. The advice and wisdom. What was left to learn? What was left to pass along? What, exactly, had they learned? What, exactly, had they given to future generations that distinguished them from any generation before them? How had humanity changed by the coming and going of good people? He couldn't answer that but knew how he had changed by the coming and going of a good person.

"It just went by so fast, Rosie," Tom said, tearing up in the dark as he pulled her closer to him.

"We did pretty well, though, didn't we?" she asked rhetorically. "The kids and grandkids; our friends and all the people we've touched and been able to help?"

The next morning, she started vomiting and couldn't keep the promethazine down, so Tom drove her into Houston for the last time.

Chapter 5

PART I

I drink coffee in the mornin', eat molasses biscuits too,
I drink coffee in the mornin', eat molasses biscuits too,
Can't no man grind my coffee half as good as you.

—*LUCY FLOWER*

DIANNE MADE A POT of coffee using Tom's percolator. As it bubbled, she strolled along the short walls of the living room as she had when she'd first met Tom and Roseanne, remembering the initial family tour. These pictures, these paintings, this artwork, these interests were not just a way to know her in-laws and relate to Roseanne but were a way to know her own husband's history. The combination of crosses, grandchildrens' handiwork, "home is where the heart is" needlepoints and dozens of photos created a mosaic that became more meaningful as they talked. There was no chronological order, what with the photographs a myriad mix of people, decades, accomplishments, and simple days, requiring countless conversations between Dianne and Roseanne. They had become very close in the short time they'd had with one another, prompted in their mutual love of John and of God.

"Who is this?" she would ask, leading her mother-in-law along the wall.

"Ha!" she answered, "That is your husband! He was five at the time and thought crawfish would make better pets than dinner."

Rosie would take the reins and instead of being asked, went from picture to picture. "This is Hannah and the kids, and that's her husband, Wayne." Then, "This is Grace and our grandson Tommy, named after my Tom. And this is Tommy's father, Todd. He passed when Tommy was a baby."

"John told me," Dianne said, "but she found and married a great guy, right?"

Roseanne pointed to another picture, "Yes, he's a wonderful man named Eric. You'll meet him. He's good to her and Tommy-Boy."

"And who is this?" Dianne asked, working her way down the wall. The yellowed picture had been cut from a magazine but matted and framed as had all the rest. It was a picture of a near-naked man lying prone on a speeding motorcycle, feet pointed, hands outstretched.

Roseanne laughed. "Tom cut that picture out of a magazine when he was a teenager. It's a man named Rollie Free, who broke the land speed record in 1948 by taking his clothes off. One hundred-fifty miles an hour lying down like that."

Then, understanding again how strange this would seem to someone new, followed with, "Tom is a little odd, if John hasn't mentioned it."

The wall covered from almost the ceiling to knee-high, Dianne spotted a black-and-white photo of her beaming young father-in-law, twelve years old standing beside a Whizzer motorbike. Within the same frame was a magazine advertisement featuring Santa Claus riding the same Whizzer, captioned, "If Santa rides a Whizzer/ with all he has to do/ chances are a Whizzer/ is just the thing for you." The wall hosted pictures of parents, children and grandkids, notes and awards and documents, along with framed artwork her children had done along the way. This included crayon drawings as well as a couple of oil paintings Grace had given them as housewarming presents. Their whole lives were on display.

"This is wonderful," Dianne said, marveling at the history, "Who is this?" She pointed to a young Navy officer.

The man was handsome, in a stark white undershirt, formidable looking. There was an intriguing kindness about him, broad-shouldered and athletic. His arms were hairy. He stood on the deck of a ship with the ocean in whitecaps behind him.

"That's Tom's father." Through the kitchen window Roseanne protectively checked for Tom and could make him out sitting with John in lawn chairs facing the forest. They were smoking cigars and laughing. "He was killed at Pearl Harbor when Tom was nine."

Dianne faltered. Standing in a small living room in east Texas, under the cool pine trees dotted with pink redbuds, Pearl Harbor went from American history to family history.

"Nine, Lord. John hasn't mentioned that," she said, prompting.

"Well," Rosie answered, "he may not talk about it because Tom doesn't talk about it. Funny, no one ever said, 'Don't talk about that' but that's just the way it's been. Tom has a sweet younger sister and the four of them were living in Corpus where Tom's dad was stationed at the Navy base. He was transferred to Hawaii in the summer of 1941, and Pearl Harbor was bombed in December."

"And she raised those kids by herself?" Dianne asked, because her curiosity went to the things of women. To sympathy, to respect, to awe.

Roseanne looked at her as women look at one another when they know the struggle. "She never remarried, never dated. She told me she'd decided she would rather raise the kids alone that have a lesser man be their father. Her parents lived in Refugio, which is pretty close, and her in-laws lived in Rockport, so they both helped some."

Then, pointing at the picture of Tom and his Whizzer, "He bought this when he was twelve because his mother couldn't drive, and he wanted to help her."

"In a lot of ways," Roseanne continued, "Tom raised himself while raising his sister and helping his mother, spending most of his boyhood alone. He's still alone some days. At times, I'm afraid he'll leave the ground and drift away." She smiled at Dianne weakly.

"What do you do on those days?" Dianne asked in a somber whisper.

"I hold his hand to keep him down," she said. "That isn't to say his childhood wasn't great, as he tells it. He enjoyed the responsibility and growing up at the beach. He spent countless hours fishing and swimming and riding that Whizzer. Tom and John are alike in many ways, and one of those ways is in their chipperness! Tom is most always in a good mood. Most always has a joke or quip or story to tell. So, while he's had tragic things happen to him, we can all say the same."

Dianne thought for a moment, "I suppose that's true. For me, I would be lost without the Holy Spirit and the peace of that."

Roseanne nodded, grateful for a daughter-in-law who felt the way she did. "It's funny. I find as I get older, I am grateful for the hard times. Not that I want more of them, Lord knows, but my, how terrible it would be to only know an easy life. How much more I appreciate the good things because of the bad."

They'd spent the afternoon walking that wall and with each story Dianne knew more about her man, knew more about his family, knew more about the ways in which influence is permanent. She saw the best parts of

Tom in John, believing and knowing John and his sisters flourished because their parents loved them, as her parents had loved her. By the time she'd stepped out of the house and into the yard, Dianne felt the need to call her parents, siblings, and her own children to tell them she loved them.

She put her arm around her husband, bent and said, "I love you" in his ear.

Now these few years later, with John outside going through the freezer, Dianne stood in the room alone waiting for coffee.

The house quiet and empty, she stepped down the hallway and into Tom and Roseanne's bedroom. The bedside window was half open. She could smell the history, the upholstery, the aging books, the faint odor of illness close and fainter distant spring magnolia as she peered through the open window. A dogwood twenty feet from the window stretched its white spring blossoms over a broken and breaking and fading trellis, held up only by Tom's unkept grape vines and weeds.

Pushing off of the sill, barrister bookcases lining the wall beneath the windows, she read title after title of books she knew and books she didn't. Many had paper bits sticking out from between the pages. Curious, with one hand she grabbed a random three to flip through them. The first, *Breakfast of Champions*, Dianne had read herself. His copy, Tom's copy, however, had a folded piece of notepaper separating the pages. To her surprise, Dianne opened it to find a hand-written letter, as follows:

> August 22, 1974
>
> Dear Tom (if I may be so informal as this is both my way and I haven't the wherewithal for formality),
>
> Thank you for your note, which I read with great interest. "Great" may be too strong a word, but perhaps not. After all, how would I know what weight you give to such a word? It could be too weak or perhaps exactly right. You'll have to decide for yourself. In answer, while I have sometimes felt as though all are robots except me, I never truly believed it. I can't imagine robots that would elect to spend time with me, which has been the primary motive behind my disbelief. I am tempted to think, however, that some of us are robots, and some are not. I suspect by your note you are one of the humans.
>
> Best wishes,
>
> Kurt Vonnegut

Dianne laughed, knowing a handwritten note from Kurt Vonnegut is exactly the kind of thing she wouldn't know about, because likely, no one did. Perhaps not even Roseanne. Inside, written on the front jacket, was another note from someone named Steven Gilbert: "Thought of you when I read this, Tom. Hope you like it. P.S. Always serve corn."

She tucked the note back between the pages to look at the second book, *Black Elk Speaks* by John Neihardt. Having no real interest herself, she flipped through the third, *Sailboat Living, a Beginner's Guide to Full-Time Life on a Boat*. She thumbed through the washed-out Kodachrome pictures of sailboats and sailboat interiors labeled with reminders to bring camp fuel and signal flares. The men wore white denim jeans rolled up at the cuff and canvas sneakers; the women cotton pants and striped shirts tied just above the naval. The color pictures were all in the center of the book, where the remaining pages were peppered with black and white images of the men looking over maps and the women talking to Coast Guard agents. About five pages in there was an impromptu piece of Christmas wrapping paper used as a bookmark, making Dianne think that's as far as Tom had gotten one Christmas morning.

The books ranged from the esoteric, running between philosophy and theology, then fields of study including everything from architecture to firearms to semiotics to American folk art, to more mundane topics like cookbooks and how-tos and Texas gardening. The majority of the books, however, were fiction dating back to 1944 and all in hardback; all stuffed with bits of scrap paper and bookmarks and notecards.

Finally, there was a full four feet of shelf space occupied by nothing but motorcycle and automotive manuals. Alphabetical from Arial to Zundapp, she wondered where on earth someone might acquire these manuals, much less need them. Randomly pulling the book sandwiched between Vespa and Yamaha to find *How to Keep Your Volkswagen Alive*, a repair manual by John Muir, she flipped pages in idle curiosity. In it were receipts for VW parts, a couple of parts lists on folded notebook paper, and a page with what appeared to be a few drops of blood.

When she pulled the manual from the shelf, she pulled with it folded sheets of paper and a Polaroid. Opening the note, she discovered her interruption of some long-ago dialogue between Tom and someone else, one seemingly unfinished. All she held was an interruption, an overhearing, a morsel of what had to have been a years-long conversation. She had long suspected and was occasionally proved right, her father-in-law had no secrets, but many—perhaps an immeasurable number of—things he hadn't told anyone. She had come to know his interests were varied and abounding, forever fascinated by his curiosities and capacity for understanding.

John often told her his father was only a doctor because he chose to be a doctor, but could have been an engineer or a chef or a horse breeder as easily, and while all of it was true, the only thing he'd ever said he would have enjoyed more than being a physician was in being a blues slide guitar player.

The top sheet of paper was a penciled illustration of the solar system, beneath which was a cutaway drawing of Earth, poorly done over lined notebook paper. Then below that was a drawing of a generator. The second sheet was typed. Lost in her discovery she read,

> June 21, 1993
>
> Denny, I got your message today and while thinking about it thought I should begin articulating my thoughts on paper. Regarding the four universal forces (Gravity, Electromagnetism, Strong, and Weak forces):
>
> The first component is really my attempt to understand gravity, how it works, and more importantly, how it is generated in a way that explains solar systems "hanging" in a void. Electromagnetism and gravity are two of the four fundamental forces of nature, but my hypothesis says electromagnetism and gravity are the same thing.
>
> It is tough to imagine nothingness, but that's basically what space is—vastness void of everything except the occasional hydrogen atom. This is interesting and important, because only in a gravity-less void can I explain perpetual motion. Verlinde's hypothesis of gravity suggests gravity is NOT a fundamental force of nature, but rather an emergent phenomenon. I think he's right and believe this word "gravity" is simply magic cloistered by electromagnetism, which is, in fact, the emergent phenomenon. Gravity is simply electrochemical engineering. Like the old guy behind the curtain in The Wizard of Oz, gravity is the grand magic wizard—the awe-inspiring thing we witness—and electromagnetism is the old guy throwing switches. So to start:
>
> 1. Remember the picture I drew of an electric motor? Think of the Earth's poles as the end of a shaft that runs through the center of the planet. Think of the planet's molten iron core

as the spinning armature of that motor. Magnetite, which is Fe3o4, is an oxide of iron and can be permanently magnetized. So you have this molten iron mass inside the Earth. Next is the lower mantle, which is silicate perovskite, made up of magnesium, iron, silicon, and oxygen. When silicone is alloyed with iron, it increases the resistance to changing the shape of material as it undergoes magnetization. I do not believe this is an accident.

2. In short, the molten core spins within an internal pocket, serving as an armature and rotor coils with zero tolerance against the interior mantle. The planet, for all intents and purposes, is a giant electromagnet. It is also not an accident that Venus, which is about the size of Earth, spins in the opposite direction. Likewise, Uranus, which is many times larger than Earth, spins in the opposite direction.

3. This picture of a series of electromagnets spinning around the sun, in turn create a larger electromagnet called the solar system. Then there are over 500 solar systems in the Milky Way Galaxy, each spinning as would an electromagnet.

4. So my theory says this: In a perfect void, a perfect symbiosis of magnets could be arranged in such a way that the very push/pull of positive and negative forces would keep them in place. They would simply hover in the void—the same void that makes perpetual motion possible. The absence of friction enables the motion, which is the very motion generating positive and negative magnetism. Each of these electromagnets are held in place by the positive and negative forces acting upon and against it, generated by the other electromagnets—the other planets.

5. This is a fantastic metaphor for existence too. Light and dark, positive and negative, push and pull, stagnation and motion.

The picture is simply a macro version of a subatomic particle spinning around neurons protons, electrons, which in turn comprise atoms, which spin around one another. It should come as no surprise that the fundamental level of existence mirrors the cosmic version of spinning relationships.

Note: there is a thing called the "Higgs boson" that I need to study more. For now, it looks like the most fundamental of elements—the basic thing—that does not spin, has no charge and exists unto itself. First theorized in the 1960s. Interestingly, they called it the God Particle. I suspect the Higgs boson is the center pole, around which all of existence spins. Each subatomic particle spins around the Higgs boson, creating its own electromagnetic "gravity" which in turn attracts only those subatomic particles whose electromagnetic gravity keeps them in perfect equidistance of the core. This unit (atom) likewise attracts only those atoms for which their electromagnetic gravity responds perfectly—not too much, not too little.

Do you remember the golden section or golden ratio? Fundamentally, it is the mathematical relationship of natural elements that produce the same geometric shape. Examples would be a seashell, a tornado, the swirl in a toilet, some flowers, etc. Now think of a picture of the galaxy. Guess what? It's a golden section. As something spins, its outermost perimeter is affected by centrifugal force, right? The closer to the center, the less centrifugal force so the concentric circles are tighter. Out on the edge, however, the trailing edge begins to swing out because the centrifugal force is greater than the electromagnetic force, creating this cone of spiraling circles, forever tighter toward the center.

Interestingly, the physics Standard Model of elementary particles is a widely accepted model for understanding everything in the known universe—except, that is, gravity! Anyway, that's my theory of how gravity works. I don't know what I'll ever do with it but hope to make a much more solid argument and submit it at some point.

Now for theoretical physics and time/space theory. Always remember this, Denny: theory is not owned by scientists. All you have to do is back it up. It doesn't matter if you're a janitor or fry cook or Nobel Prize winner. Just be smart, do your homework, and come to the table with facts.

Not too tough, at least for smart guys like you, Dennis. Anyway, I'll be relieved when you're back. I hope to finish the BMW this weekend and can't wait to ride it myself. I'll try not to wear it out before you get home.

We'll talk more when you get back. Above all be safe!

Tom

Dianne read the letter twice, no less lost after the second than she had been the first. She made a mental note to ask John who Dennis was and what Tom may have been writing about. Unlike most people she'd ever known, Tom didn't talk about what interested him unless there was a point. Unless he was asking for feedback or needed to vocalize his thoughts in order to sort them out. He certainly would have told her his father had been killed at Pearl Harbor if she'd asked but wouldn't blurt it out if it had never come up. And why would something like that ever come up? It was exactly those kinds of things she wanted to know. How can you ask someone to tell you their secrets, when they aren't holding any? When you haven't asked many questions, and never the right ones? A secret, after all, is not a secret if the truth would be given freely but is just never offered up unsolicited.

Roseanne once told Dianne her husband's wheels were always turning and that over the years she came to understand there were parts of him she would never know, maybe because of his years in prison but maybe because he had endured so much as a child. Maybe, even, just because he was smart. She'd said there was something in him making the wheels turn, and neither of them knew what it was.

The Polaroid, completely unrelated to magnetism and physics, was of Roseanne sitting in a shiny white Volkswagen Karman Ghia, with a pre-teen Grace balancing on the front bumper. Dianne's first thought was to hold the photo to show John but was suddenly embarrassed for going through Tom's things and put the book, letter and photo back where she'd found them.

The automotive manuals made Dianne smile, as it reminded her of the bookshelves she shared with John in Galveston, where he'd collected books about cooking and travel and birds of North America, but more than anything else, books about guitars and music. His books, John's books, were dog-eared and book-marked, with writing in the margins much the same way Tom's books were book-marked with writing in the margins. But that was in Galveston, where Hambone Happy Cheese waited under the picnic table for their return.

Walking a fine line between nosy and curious, she opened their closet doors wanting nothing more than insight. Pulling the door wide, she was met with a rush of Roseanne's perfume, her soap, her scent. Tom had changed nothing, it seemed, done nothing to disturb his wife's things and it occurred to Dianne the rush of Roseanne's scent was a daily reminder for him. She'd been gone almost two years, but her closet looked as though she may return any second. There was a nylon slip on the floor. On the inside of one of the doors hung a First National Bank of Houston calendar, long out of date, but with a Bible verse printed for January 1968. Everyone believed in God in 1968, before Babylon and meaninglessness, before the wet pride of arrogant enlightenment doused the light of faith.

In that faithless feigned wisdom comes a misery that excludes hope, skews a moral compass, festers into ulcerous boils of bitterness, makes kindness a judgment call, and inflates nothing in the human spirit but the buoy of pride. A buoy untethered and adrift, but solid enough to make the doubter cling to it like salvation. On the calendar was printed Romans 8:28—*And we know that all things work together for good to them that love God, to them who are called according to His purpose.* On the same hook as the calendar hung a cross woven in yarn around a popsicle stick frame.

Beneath the cross was a type-written poem, on what looked like a tenth-generation copy machine sheet of paper; pinned to the door with a white thumbtack, corners curled toward the center with the weight of age:

Tree by Its Fruit

I am the broken stock, wind-worn and desperate, curling tendrils anxious for that earth hidden beneath the weeds, spread along the fence line,
    on a forgotten slope in a forgotten wood.
I am gangly and spotted, leaves burned by the sun and eaten by the locust.
I am the monstrous, the headstrong, the frantic, the frenzied
    suffering the trials of spring thunder and summer drought, of fall
    cold and winter's wrath.
I am the sufferer, the forlorn, the eager and afraid,
I am the proud and resistant, my leaves tattered and partial, my vine brown and green and gray.
I am the grape, the muscadine, solidly rooted in purposeful dirt,
    judged as a tree by its fruit.
I am bruised and plucked and crushed and bled; bled to be what I am.
I am the wine. I am the wine. I am the wine.

–Anon

In the back of the closet was a gray steel gun safe and in seeing it, Dianne could see in her mind's eye the folded, lined sheet of paper she had in her kitchen junk drawer with the combination written on it, along with an inventory of the contents. She remembered little of the list except that there were many rifles and many handguns, and beside each Tom had written the value of each of them along with anything he thought important. The only two she could remember had notes next to them. One said, "Like James Bond!" and the other said, "Like Jesse James— original and working. I promised this to Tommy Boy." Taped to the front of the safe was a Morris Bishop poem Tom had torn from a magazine and attached. It was an entire page from *The New Yorker*, October 1946.

$E=MC2$

> What was our trust, we trust not,
>   What was our faith, we doubt;
> Whether we must or must not
>   We may debate about,
> The soul, perhaps, is a gust of gas
>   And wrong is a form of right-
> But we know that Energy equals Mass
>   By the Square of the Speed of Light.
>
> What we have known, we know not,
> What we have proved, abjure.
> Life is a tangled bowknot,
>   But one thing still is sure.
> Come, little lad; come, little lass,
>   Your docile creed recite:
> "We know that Energy equals Mass
>   By the Square of the Speed of Light."

On top of the safe was an opened envelope with a letter inside. The front was written in Roseanne's hand, and said, "To My Love." Dianne wanted to read the letter, but felt she would be violating not just Tom, but her friend as well. Still, standing alone there in the bedroom, Dianne held the letter. She could feel the intimate nature of its contents and in her desire to reaffirm what she believed to be true of them, it was everything she could do not to open it. She put her thumb and forefinger within the scissored fold, but before she could pull it out, she slapped it back down onto the safe. On the floor beneath the clothes were Tom's shoes and upon recognizing them, she felt strange not seeing them on Tom. Elastic gore slip-ons in two colors, blue and tan; a single pair of black dress shoes, hunting boots, brown loafers, never-worn 1970s dingo boots with steel rings on the sides. His Clarke's desert boots were missing.

He'd worn Clarke's almost exclusively since the late 1960s, drawn by their unassuming simplicity and forever surprised by their comfort. For a doctor making rounds, this was important. He'd stayed with John and

Dianne in Galveston when Roseanne was in the hospital, as did the girls when Roseanne was nearing the end. In the evenings, he would come back exhausted—sometimes alone and sometimes with the kids—having sat with Roseanne all day in what would come to be known as hospice. The three of them would sit out on the balcony with plates of fried fish or baked chicken or bowls of beans and rice.

"Thank you," he would say sincerely, crossing his feet before him in oiled leather Clarke's with gum rubber soles and mismatched laces.

"She won't be long now," he'd whisper like air being let out of a tire.

Dianne had never seen Tom as frail or as old, but that day, with him sitting on the balcony of their Galveston beach house and defeat escaping his lips in undeniable resignation, he'd seemed to have aged forty years. Hunched over a tired paper plate in a tired tweed sport coat and tired oiled leather Clarke's with mismatched laces, staring out over cold chicken, the balcony rail and breakers, over the muddy Texas gulf, past the calm, past the twinkling lights of the deep-water rigs, Tom was flagging.

Just five miles west and fifty years behind him, Tom and Roseanne had made love on the dunes, where there was now a T-shirt shop, where 1957 Harley Davidson Sportsers and baby blue beach towels only lived in memories and faded pictures. Dianne had reached over and held his hand, for fear he might drift away.

PART II

Can't ride no blinds from my lowering hole,
Can't jump the fence past Peter,
Gotta stand tall in forgiv'n shoes,
With Jesus on my bond.
Gotta stand tall in forgiv'n shoes,
With Jesus on my bond.

—*TECUMSEH GRAVES*

The funeral, her funeral, had been a beautiful affair. As is tradition, the visitation had been the afternoon and evening before, whereby mourners could pay their respects by telling Tom and John and Hannah and Grace what a wonderful friend Roseanne had been. Relatives not seen in years and Tom's former colleagues shuffled about the room. An endless procession of well-meaning old people and church members and people Roseanne had helped seemed to maunder through the room like ants, each with their own similar version of condolence and mourning. Eleanor Dobson, their former housekeeper was there, crying quietly in the back. The hugs would transition to arms and shoulders held, often with a funny story.

"God bless ya'll," they would say, "God bless you."

Then, "We really need to do better about seeing one another, you know? It's a shame we only see one another other at funerals."

Everyone would agree they would keep in better touch, then, "We love ya'll," and it would be the next person's turn.

Dianne sat in the front pew next to John, who sat next to his father. Roseanne's casket was open as is the southern way, and from Dianne's vantage point, she lay in silent, absent repose with the midday sun filling the room. Both families and extended families filled the rows, with many of the couples' former Houston neighbors and Tom's friends in the rear. Gray men and women marking time by funerals and holidays and the birthdays of grandchildren, instead of by date or appointments to keep. Even John's ex-wife attended, having had a love and respect for Roseanne that transcended their marriage. The minister spoke of her kindness, her devotion to family, his certainty of her salvation. With emotion and earnest, having known her and Tom personally for many years, he gathered himself and going off script, Pastor Gene spoke of her.

"Hmmm, mmm." He started to choke and laughed, "Well who's gonna make King Ranch casserole for potluck now?" Everyone laughed, happy for the relief. "Lord Jesus, Lord Jesus, You have her now," he said, addressing God, His son, the Holy Spirit. Then, "Listen, she's better today than she was last week, or any day before that, amen?"

In and among the congregation you could hear soft "amens" and one "glory" in agreement. Everyone there knew the person who said "glory" went to a different church. A two-year old pulled from his mother, slipped through her grip and sprinted for the door laughing. Stained glass windows lined the walls, the gothic peaks in a Bible church remnants of the building's Lutheran intent. The molding was missing from the bottom edge of the pulpit, where the raw pine stood in contrast to the mahogany stain. The deacon's bench was empty. The door leading to the choir's seats—where four quartets sat on Sunday mornings—was cracked slightly open, with the light from a hallway window squeezing through the gap and dissecting the pulpit in waves of violet, orange, red, and blue.

One person was wishing they'd gone to the bathroom before they sat down; one of John's former RNs, who'd had a crush on him thirty years prior, regretted not knowing Roseanne personally as she dug through her purse for tissue. Grace's friend and neighbor hoped the ice chest had kept her potato salad cool enough on the drive from Fredericksburg, chastising herself for forgetting napkins. A man in the back didn't know anyone but Tom, but had read of Roseanne in the obituaries and felt compelled to attend because of his respect and admiration of him. Later, he would eat Grace's neighbor's potato salad. His name was Daniel.

"Listen," Pastor Gene continued, "I'm gonna read you a poem Roseanne wrote a while back. A long while, forty years maybe, working on her degree in literature. It was the 1960s, and everyone wrote poetry." The room chuckled. "I bet Nixon was writing poetry." More laughs. "Maybe not Nixon."

"I didn't know her then, maybe some of you did. If you did, I'm glad for you, because you had more time with her spirit and generosity than many of us." He looked at Tom as he spoke.

"Anyway, her daughter, Hannah here, was kind enough to share this with me. It's a poem about a young woman coming to Christ, an assignment in a college course."

Then restively, "Salvation wasn't the assignment. The poem was."

The room collectively smiled in forgiveness of his nervousness, exuding that low noise that is less than laughter, more than silence.

Continuing, he said, "In her illness she was going through her things—her mementos and memories and photo albums—and came across this poem and, Hannah tells me, saw it in a different way. She said in hindsight it is about her own salvation; her own rescue from the darkness."

Pastor Gene opened a bi-fold sheet of paper and put his glasses on. Looking over the bridge he said to the attendees, "I hope I can get through this, because it is a poem about me, too."

Beautiful Marie

In darkness sinks her body free
Into the depths whomever she
The Blackness grows and shouts to tell
"Her name, her name is Mary Bell"
The Philistine's cold fingers cling
Her garment and her sacred ring
Drag her down to depth and yell
"She is ours, sweet Mary Bell!"

The Merciless, the Evils say,
"We celebrate her icy grave!
We celebrate the unsave-a-bell!
Her name, we call her Mary Bell"
But wait! Across the bow be heard
A cannon shot! Commanding word!
A loaf of bread, quicksilver-filled
A cry, salvation, love fulfilled
The body, mine, rises true
From black depth, green, a white-blue hue
The blinding light from hopeless grasps
My nape, my body, my spiny gasp
My depth, my cold, my lost salvation
Again to rise this sweet carnation
And in it all, this ne'er-do-well
My name! My name is Maribelle
Into the light!
Into the glory!
Into the blinding expiatory!
Thwarting me and thwarting hell!
My name! My name! Is MARIBELLE!

Taking his glasses off, he paused. "Sometimes," Pastor Gene confessed, "sometimes I am asked to perform a service for someone I didn't know at all. As in all things you do again and again, I got better at knowing what to say and find myself on those occasions bearing witness to my savior. I witness to the congregation on those days, in the hope a seed will be planted."

A murmur of "amens" softly filled the room.

"But Roseanne was no stranger," he choked, "not just because she knew no strangers, but because she and Tom are members of the church and the community. Most everyone in this church knew and loved them both and I will miss her dearly."

"But know this," he softened. "We don't mourn for her, we mourn for ourselves and for our missing of her. She is with the Lord now, and as her salvation through Christ saved her, so will salvation through Christ save you."

He looked to the family pew as if to confirm they would be with her by and by. Hannah, on Tom's right, sobbed. "I'm going to miss her so much."

"Jesus," Dianne softly prayed for Tom, "Jesus, please help him. He's a good man and needs your help."

Tom would never go to church again.

PART III

Standin' side that track, jus waitin' for that train to pass,
Standin' side that track, jus waitin' for that train to pass,
Ain't but four peoples ever loved me,
My grandmother, my mother,
My sister and my wife.

—*BLIND STUMP MCBRIDE*

Tom woke with a start, jerking his broken wrist from his chest with a grind where the broken bone scraped jagged pieces, one unto the other. The jolt was blinding, causing him to cry out, dropping the photos and notebook to his side where the oranges and cigars lay. His fingers, swollen to bursting like sausages in a skillet, covered most of his fingernails. He tasted blood, not knowing whether it had come up or he'd bitten something, but it was slight, so he just swallowed.

Taking a deep breath, then another and a third, he lifted his head to survey his leg. Alarmed, he saw his right pant leg straining against the swelling. "How can this be?" he asked aloud, then wondered how long he'd been out. The sun was warm now. Pulling his watch from his pocket, found it was after 11:00 a.m. Grateful he'd woken up at all and vowing to stay conscious, Tom leaned onto his left elbow to see better. He would have prescribed elevation and ice packs along with morphine, but he was at a slight angle, feet downhill and certainly had no ice or morphine. His pants were tight to the knee, where he lost sight of his leg under the engine cradle and frame. He saw his bare foot standing up from the other side, toes swollen almost as badly as his fingers and alarmingly dark, a dark he had seen before. Seen it in wounded soldiers, in diabetics' extremities, in frostbite; it was the darkness of a dying appendage. The toes and top of his foot were foreign to Tom, looking as though they belonged to someone else.

For a brief moment, he wondered whose foot that was and how it came to be in the forest with him. In that entranced instant, he'd convinced himself there were more of him; more wounded waiting for evacuation, more wreckage, more desperation. They were coming, surely, whomever they were, as rescue parties always come, as cavalry always comes, as saviors always come. He watched the toes move, then suddenly realized he was moving them, as it was his foot after all, but he could not feel it.

Tom lay back down, finding gratitude for his pants and in his oranges. The pants for restraining the swelling; the oranges for what mouthful of joy he still had. Reaching without looking, he pulled the two oranges to his chest and felt around for his knife. He opened the knife with his good hand and teeth, biting down hard on the staghorn handle while pulling the blade from its hinged pivot. The knife was old, having been made when steel was softer and prone to rust. It had belonged to his father and was given to Tom when he turned twelve almost as a rite of passage. His poor mother only knew to love him, but having no experience with being a boy herself, tended to fail when it came to masculine milestones.

"What does a boy want? What does a boy need?" she would ask herself. "Lord," she would pray, "please help me. Please help me raise a righteous man, Lord."

She only knew to love him, to dress him, to feed him, and tell him he was loved.

His mother relied upon him in ways she couldn't bear to acknowledge, to include his help with the chickens and the garden, and delivering preserves and with watching his sister, but also in helping her feel grounded in the world. Esoterically and theologically she was affirmed, certainly, in her belief God would provide for them and that her salvation was eternal. Her faith kept her focused and alive, and while she was a widow, she knew, her temporal identity was that of Mother, of Momma, of Mom.

Her faith helped drive her maternity and the responsibility she accepted to teach her children Christian tenets and the joy of salvation. She was funny and engaging and smart, pushing her children to learn, to do well in school, to dream, all while knowing she only had a few years to impart everything unto her children a man and woman both would normally impart. Both children learned to cook, both children learned to garden, both children learned to raise chickens, both children learned to manage money, both children learned everything she knew. And in all of it she did her best to infuse an insatiable curiosity and desire to learn.

She did not, on the other hand, know or even question what it was to be a twelve-year-old boy, what it was to feel the wanderlust of a young man, what it was to feel the gravity of the world, desperate to separate what it meant to be a good boy from what it meant to be a good man. She praised him and loved him for his willingness to help, with no pause to witness the heaviness of the world carried by her boy, nor his desperation to escape it. At twelve he was lost in a world he only pretended to know, his panicked searching for the right path finding him only with his books, and with the daily affirmation of his doing the right thing by way of Ms. Flo's pies and his mother's hug.

"You're a good boy, Tommy," Ms. Flo would say, and while she would never know it, her words saved him.

No, his mother couldn't have known, and couldn't have fixed it if she did. No masculine guidance. No prodding. No conversation of empathy or example. No one to ask but his mother or a wonderfully plump baker.

So, on his twelfth birthday his mother wrapped his father's pock-etknife in one of her husband's handkerchiefs, then in a pasteboard box and ribbon, and with as much ceremony as she thought appropriate, said, "Tommy, this was your father's. You're old enough now to carry a knife and he would want you to have it."

A boxed Case brand with two blades, Tom had carried the knife every day between his twelfth birthday and boot camp, and almost every day since he was released from capture. And every time—every time he opened the knife—he felt the exhilaration of passage, of trust, of rite. He sought out reasons to use the knife, to get done what simply could not be done without just such a tool.

On one beautiful early summer afternoon, Tom sat four dozen eggs on the counter at Springs Hardware while Ms. Flo blended flour and bak-ing powder and butter and peaches. Sugar was war-rationed, even for bakeries, so she'd become good at using other fruit sweeteners and some-times honey. In July and August, she would press ripe figs, extracting the nectar for pastries and jams, and would do the same with countless varieties of citrus grown in deep south Texas.

But being on a port meant access, and every June and November throughout the war and for years thereafter, Ms. Flo could get raw sugar cane brought up from Mexico—in large quantities if she let the ship's captain know ahead of time. These long stalks of cane she would cut up and boil, drawing the raw sugar from each segment. The pulp would float, so she would skim it as the water churned, eventually leaving just an inch of brown sugar-mud in the pot. Afterward she would set the pot outside covered in cheesecloth, letting evaporation do the rest, followed by grinding the root-beer-colored crystals into a dry brown sugar.

Ms. Flo would often cut a segment of the cane, naturally capped by the fibrous diaphragm between the segments, and give it to Tom. "You share this with Ruby, hear?"

Tom would carry the hard cane home where he broke it open with a rock and cut the brown pulp from the center with his shiny new Case jackknife, as they were wont to call them in 1945. After dinner, he and his sister and his mother would sit on the porch chewing to crush the pulp and suck the sugar until there was no sweetness left to draw.

"Lord, Lord," his mother would say, "Lord, thank you for this sweet cane." She would smile and spit the pulp to the side of the porch, asking, "Ruby, what's your favorite part of eating sugar cane?"

Ruby, indignant, would shout, "Sugar. Momma!"

His mother had a way about her. Many ways, actually, in raising her kids. She would ask them questions to make them think, whereupon they came to understand there wasn't always a right answer. More important than the answer was their thinking about the answer, the thinking itself serving as the solution. For Tom, this was his beautiful motivator.

"And Tom," his mother would ask, "What's your favorite part?"

As he grew older, she could look at him and see her husband; his pensive brow, his heavy dark hair. At night she would look in on him, enormously proud of the man he was becoming, while mourning his growing up all the while.

"What's your favorite part, baby?"

At thirteen, Tom knew the answer must be more substantial than sugar, not for her sake but for his. Still, he could not tell her what he thought. He could not tell her he was smart because he did not yet know himself. He had only been Tom for thirteen years, and what with that singular perspective, he'd not yet considered his view of the world being specific to him, let alone expansive. He could not tell her his approach to reflecting upon and deconstructing sugar cane was his approach to understanding everything he'd ever known.

Self-conscious, even with his mother, he could not tell her he saw sugar cane as a metaphor, and as is true with the best metaphors, an allegory. An allegory for people and for humanity and for life. He was thirteen, and simply loved her too much to embarrass her with an interpretation she hadn't considered herself. The cane, for him, was a metaphor embodying existence and what it could mean to be human. Tough and hard and uniform on the outside; a shell impervious to nearly everything, but a shell to crack in order to reveal its purpose. Or of life, the sweet inner pulp is to be chewed, exhausted, wrung out to ensure not just his satisfaction, but the very purpose of the sugar cane's existence.

The pulp is work, but the pulp is worth it and only in devouring the pulp does the sugar cane become its namesake.

Or perhaps the cane was the way he saw his mother: smooth and dark and beautiful and stoic on the outside, but the sweetest, most tender heart within. Sometimes the cane was life, sometimes the cane was his mother, sometimes the cane was a sweet treat to share with his sister, sometimes the sugarcane was simply cane like a windbreak on the local ponds and brine channels, where red wing blackbirds gathered in mass, noisily singing to rats and to king snakes and to young boys who'd stopped by on their Whizzers to skinny dip in solitude. Then sometimes the cane wasn't anything at all, rather a metaphor in a dream on a warm night, when the sea breeze mixed with honey and fat arms hugged him and Ruby had kittens in her apron, and he could see through a screened window his father smiling at him from the yard.

"I guess my favorite part is this," Tom would answer grinning. "Sitting on the porch with you and Ruby and talking."

"You're a good boy, Tommy, and a smart one too," his mom glowed. Then added, "It also makes me thankful for Flo," she reminded, "and what she means to you and to the family."

He'd never opened the jackknife with his mouth, and while he had broken the tip of one blade trying to pry a can open (a mistake he never stopped mourning); had sharpened and honed both blades so many times they were two-thirds their original width; had cut countless strings, sugar cane, vacuum hoses, fuel lines and cigar tips; had cleaned fingernails, opened packages, scraped splinters out, and whittled sticks, he had never tasted the knife. Cool, with a slight odor of oil, the knife tasted like steel and sweat, iron and age, the dirt from the ground beside him. It tasted like his twelfth birthday. It tasted like legend. His thumbnail found the divot in the blade and snapped it open.

Then, holding an orange to the blade and dragging it across the sharp edge, Tom sliced the peel, put the knife down, held the orange to his mouth and pulled the bright orange zest and bitter pith off with his teeth. He then ate the orange like an apple, the sweet juice popping and running over his beard and neck.

"You're making a mess," he heard his mother say.

Tom replied aloud to his imagination. "I know, mom, but I hurt my arm and can't eat it any other way."

He lay there in the quiet, opening the second orange the same way, but not before dropping eight more ibuprofens into his mouth to swallow with the juice.

The sharp waves of pain had stopped, but not on the lull side. Instead it was emanating from his wrist and hip and thigh as an excruciating noun instead of a nebulous, amateurish number between one and ten. It was an object, a mass, a living entity Tom had no option but to bear. It was in him and of him, a parasitic throb pushing from the inside to get out, even if it meant destroying its host. It was alive, vengeful, wicked, and furiously gleeful, eager to punish an old man for his temerity. He likened it to purging, to pride, to destruction, and impatience. He felt it as penance, this pain, visited upon him as an indiscriminate, alien worm eating him, one nerve ending at a time.

In his agony he thought to cut his own throat, to turn his sharpened blade to his own neck, leaking his life out into the pine needles and loam of the Thicket. In his mind's eye he could see the glistening of the opened artery spill out thick, rich streams of red as it chugged from his whiskered neck to the ground below, sinking into the dirt with everything he had ever been. Drained, he would be; reduced to self-induced mulch. He thought of the ease and the peace, and in his pride held fast to the notion his life was still his own, and he still had decisions to make. Still, he refused for three reasons. While he believed time was not on his side, he did believe he could be rescued at any moment, wherein he still had a chance. Second, if this was to be his final act, he would not have it be one of capitulation, of resignation, of defeat. Finally, and maybe most important, he would not have his demise be reported as anything less than what his children and neighbors and friends expected. That is, to fight to the end.

"God, God please," he exhaled into the air above him. A breath like any other; a breath of exasperation and meaninglessness. An entreaty more to hear a voice, even his own, than anything else, as there was no hope the forest held ears for the sound to fall upon.

"Please what?" he heard from the trees beyond his head. He was certain he'd heard it and as his heart leapt, he arched his back and rolled his head backward to see who it was.

"Please what?" the voice said again, this time on his left, twenty feet away on the other side of a thick, lightless bramble.

His brain told him he must be wrong about where he'd first heard it, but was certain he had indeed heard it, and turning to the bramble shouted, "Who is it?!" No answer. "Who is it?!" he cried out again.

From his feet he heard it again. Maybe from under the motorcycle. "Please what?" the voice asked.

Tom could see his motorcycle and could see his leg, could see his blackening foot and the open distance between the bike and the bank rising up to the road. He saw a broken mirror on the slope from the road's shoulder and a truck rushing by at what seemed like light speed. A breeze gusted high up, pulling three magnolia petals from their flower and carried them to the ground, while Tom searched for the voice. Was his liver failing? Was this infection-induced paracusia?

Then in his right ear, close and hard, demanding even, but still a loud whisper, "Please what?!"

Startled, but his body too exhausted to flinch, Tom responded, "Get me out of here. Please get me out of here."

"To do what?" the voice asked, "To live? You can live, Tom."

Tom had witnessed patients having hallucinations many times and had always wondered what it was like. Convinced he was answering his own questions, Tom chuckled through his phlegm, then simply saying what he felt, "I don't want it to end like this. Alone, alone and my kids don't even know where I am."

Now, the voice came from over his head once more where his helmet lay on its side; maybe from inside his helmet. Definitely from inside his helmet.

On the ground two feet beyond his head, the voice echoed from within, "Are you afraid to say "die" Tom? Are you afraid to die alone? You will do two things alone, Tom, that is all. You will believe alone, and you will die alone."

Where had he heard that? Had he heard that? He must have heard that, as the auditory hallucinations reached back into his psyche to pull some latent quote from his memory.

"Platitudes, platitudes, platitudes," Tom whispered with another self-deprecating chuckle, his phlegm tasting like blood and salt and oranges, ashamed his own imagination could do no better than a vague verse or slogan or bumper sticker.

"Think!" he shouted to himself, "Think!" Surely he could remember something more profound than an enigmatic quote. "What do I want to be?" he asked drifting. "How do I do this? I don't know how to do this!"

His mind racing in fear, Tom felt it necessary to remember people and historical figures and philosophers and writers and laureates who had said something he could still cling to. Some bit of wisdom that still held meaning. Something he'd embraced over seventy-seven and one-half years. The words and the vision and the quotes he found worthy of memorizing but struggled to recall now. A Taoist's Tzu crumb or artist's insight; the earned wisdom of Alexander or a Sioux reflection. Chanakya's advice; a proverb.

Drifting away on an untethered tangent, with difficulty finishing a thought, the only thing he could remember he said aloud, "Home is where the heart is," and wrapped his thoughts around it like a cleat on a pier. Was that right? "Home is where the hard is." Maybe a bumper sticker or framed needlepoint. Is it heart or hard? Maybe it's both. Sometimes it's both.

He thought of Ms. Flo, as old as he'd ever known her and plump in a flour-specked apron, sitting with her feet up on a crate and working a needlepoint frame. Home Is Where The Heart Is, surrounded by cotton-threaded brown-eyed susans and multi-colored woven lemon grass. There was an unfinished white farmhouse in the middle, with incomplete wisps of gray rising from the unfinished chimney. Pulled tight in a two-piece nickel frame, the working needle and thread punched through her pattern and back down again as she worked. Too young for broken blood vessels in her swollen ankles, Ms. Flo had them still.

"A mondegreen, Tommy, is a misheard word the listener turns into something else," she said. "Sometimes people call it a malapropism. It can be funny, too. I heard on the Jack Benny hour about a town in Kentucky called Weiwichuah, an Indian word meaning across the river. At Christmastime they hang banners in town that say Weiwichuah Merry Christmas. That Jack Benny makes me laugh every time."

She sat her work down on the counter, taking the eggs from the hurried boy. "What's the rush?" she asked. In his remembrance he could hear Louis Jordan's "Caldonia" in the background and see the needlepoint on the countertop, the needle dangling from the counter's edge on the thread. The song was skipping, likely due to a scratch: ". . . head so hard, head so hard, head so hard, head so hard."

He was again in Spring's Hardware rushing to drop off eggs. He skidded to a stop, respectfully mindful of the adult asking him a question, as young people were in 1949. "I have to make hay while the sun is shinin', Ms. Flo!"

"Make hay but not haste, baby," she said. "Hay, but not haste." Then, "Will you go put a penny on the arm, baby, and come right back?"

Tom hurried to the back room, performing the job by rote. When the needle was skipping, he could place a penny, sometimes two, on the big end of the record player's arm, adding just enough weight to stop the skip.

Flo continued, "Tom, will you go somewhere with me tomorrow when you come by, if you can tear yourself away from your motorbike for a couple of hours? I have a surprise for you."

Tom would have been insulted had anyone but Ms. Flo called his motorcycle a "motorbike," for now it was 1949 and at seventeen years old he'd graduated from his Whizzer to a used 1945 BSA. Green and chrome with black fenders, he'd paid seventy-three dollars of the one hundred and ten dollars he'd saved, having plenty left over for the BSA high-performance kit along with a leather helmet and goggles. Bought from a sailor who was shipping out, Tom had seen the motorcycle around town and had even been given the chance to sit on it when he'd seen it parked at the Pig Stand on weekends. Capable of nearly eighty miles an hour, Tom would take to the tarmac between Corpus and the base just to open it up. He would tuck his knees and elbows, crouch behind the speedometer—an extra five dollars when the bike was new—and watch the needle sweep the dial until it would go no further.

He would imagine Rollie Free, flat as a board in his underwear at nearly twice the speed. He was a daredevil, a man, an adventurer, and he rode a British-made BSA motorcycle. A company which, incidentally, made guns too. And because Great Britain was an ally, he was still supporting America somehow in his mind. Tom would talk about that motorcycle the rest of his life, lamenting the day he sold it and always ending the conversation with, "I was so proud of that bike."

He kept his pride to himself, however, as he did everything else. And because Tom would have done most anything Ms. Flo wanted, in that truth he said he would go with her.

"And here, baby," she said, tossing him a quarter. "Put some gas in that thing."

The next day Tom delivered eggs and preserves to everyone else first, giving the rest of his day over to Ms. Flo. It was early June and with this, his last summer before graduating high school, Tom wanted to make the most of it. That meant saving what money he could, working as much as he could, fishing, swimming in the beach and local ponds, playing baseball on the school field with classmates, and maybe—hopefully—spending time with a pretty girl at the Pig Stand on the weekends.

Dotty Lindquist she was; a beautiful ray of sunshine with slender, freckled alabaster legs and copper-colored hair. She bought a pie every Saturday from Ms. Flo and had sat at the front of Tom's mathematics class two years in a row. Her parents were wealthy, at least by Tom's standards, her father owned a Ford dealership and forty acres of citrus in the valley.

Dotty had become a preoccupation for Tom, and while he was busy reading Shakespeare's tragedies over the summer, he still found himself drawn to the idea of a girlfriend. A girl, his girl, Dottie Lindquist, the thrust of 10,000 years of history, of Shelley and Wordsworth and Keats and Byron, of hormones and springtime. He wanted her to ride on the back of his wonderful BSA, hair tied up for the wind. He wanted to go, to grow up, to leave Corpus on some grand adventure with his new pretty girlfriend and never come back. He wanted to head west where California called him, riding up the National Auto Trail into Oregon. He wanted to head east, where high up, the salt air came in off the open ocean in cold gusts, covering eastern seaboard accents and hoagies and magical things he'd only read of. He wanted to ride south, over the Rio Grande into Mexico and through the Chihuahuan desert, racing with his girl to faraway Bolivian adventures or sleepy fishing villages. Or north, through a million miles of corn rows, past mountains and prairies and into Canada to the tip of Nova Scotia, just he and his girl, where the gritty earth ended, and they would stare off into the North Atlantic.

Each of these dreams began on a whim, whereby he and his girl would ride hell for leather, racing as fast as the motorcycle would take them. Each of these dreams ended with the two of them together, kissing and holding hands in a place they'd never been and a place no one would ever find them.

But in June of 1949, Tom had only spoken to Dottie twice: once to say, "you're welcome" after she thanked him for opening a door, and once to say "yes" when she asked, "You buy that motorcycle from the squidy?" followed by, "It's definitely on the beam."

And while he was serious in his desire to whisk her away, Tom had only been to Hawaii as a child, Refugio, Rockport, and once to San Antonio on a church trip to the Alamo.

On that trip, the Alamo trip, Tom would walk where Travis and Bowie and Crockett had walked, bear witness to the walls of this little sanctuary that had been part of a larger fort. He would revel in the atmosphere of men who stood for something, if only their own refusal to back down, and died for it. He likened these men to his father and by osmosis, to himself, if he would ever have the chance to prove it.

In 1940s Texas, only one hundred years after the battle, no one asked whether the Alamo fight was a righteous fight. No one asked whether they should have been there in the first place. These questions were asked fifty years later by un-calloused, unscarred men in air-conditioned university classes, who knew nothing of taking a punch, much less firing shoulder to shoulder at an enemy outnumbering you by fifteen-to-one. You were there, as was your enemy, and regardless of personal moral or cosmic trajectory, regardless of the circumstances that put you there, the only thing left to do was the fight. Often, in fact, the only thing left to do is the fight. The fight is the thing. You cannot account for or amend history. The only thing left is the fight.

Today, however, this day, was promised to Ms. Flo. "Where are we headed, Ms. Flo?" Tom asked.

Ms. Flo, in baggy men's jeans and a baker's long-sleeve shirt, grinned and said knowingly, "We're gonna go see some dancers!"

Tom, not at all keen on seeing dancers and knowing she knew this about him, played along, "I'll go see dancers if you'll ride on the back of my motorcycle to get there."

"You're on!" she shouted and throwing her heavy leg over the back of the seat the two took off toward the outskirts of town. With Flo directing him, Tom rode out past the last warehouse on the west end, past his pond, and down a dirt road where the railroad tracks crossed overhead in a low trellis.

"Right here, Tommy," Flo said, tapping his shoulder excitedly.

Tom pulled over in the shade of the bridge and switched the motorcycle off. The engine pinged and popped as it started to cool. "I believe it's here," Flo said, thinking aloud. "I believe they're up here."

She began to climb the embankment beside the road, up the few feet to the railroad track. Her thick feet made poor time in the granite gravel, giving up underfoot as she pressed toward the top of the rise. Every third step she would slip and drop to one knee or the other, the scrapes and bruising slowing her down not a whit. Tom, following, crested the top and could see workmen a hundred yards down the line.

"Halleluiah!" she wheezed, "There they are! These are the dancers, Tommy!"

She started walking hurriedly down the tracks, an awkward gait as she tried to step on the railroad ties. The ties weren't spaced as stepping-stones, too close for most steps and too far apart to skip one, so every step was a new experiment in timing. As they got closer to the men, Tom could hear why they had come.

"These are the dancers, Tom. These are what they call gandy dancers," she said panting and pointing. She put her hands on her hips and raised her shoulders high to breath. "These men straighten the tracks with pry bars and teamwork, sweatin' out here in the full sun to keep the rails spaced perfectly. Listen."

From fifty yards Tom could hear. "I don't know but I been told, Susie got a jelly roll." When they all ended on "roll," the dozen men would heave on steel prybars, moving the heavy tracks an inch or two over the railroad ties beneath.

These section crews replaced track and ties when needed but mostly aligned the two, manually ensuring the train's safety.

"Susie, Susie don't you know, I can make your belly grow," and on "grow" the team pried again. Half chant, half song, there was no mystery why Flo wanted to see and hear this. She'd read in the paper there would be a section crew coming through the area and knowing a little bit about it from stories and from an interview she'd read of Ethal Waters, she couldn't miss it. And as important, couldn't let Tom miss it.

> "Ten thousand biscuit in my hand
> On my way to the promised land," heave,
> "On my way to the promised land," heave,
> "On my way to the promised land," heave,
> "On my way to the promised land."

Flo clapped in time, grateful for this opportunity and grateful for these men. Then,

> "Moses stood on the red sea shore,
> Smote that water with a two by four" heave,
> "Smote that water with a two by four," heave,
> "Smote that water with a two by four."

These were happy times, as many times were happy times. In fact, over the years, most times were happy times because Tom made the effort. This begat his reputation as a good man and prompted him to believe in his goodness himself. He worked to create an environment of peace and happiness, and through his Judeo-Christian upbringing put the interests of the people he loved mostly ahead of his own. To add to his burgeoning reputation, Tom was competitive and keenly interested in satisfying his broken mother and by extension, the seaside town of Corpus Christi, Texas, compelling in him an admirable effort to protect and take care of her, while glad to be besting others who fell short.

Secretly, he judged others' failures while likewise condemning his own, satisfied in being better than the arbitrary competition if for no other reason than giving his mother something to brag about. These victories add up, and for Tom added up quickly, becoming the paragon of child and young adult virtue all parents wished their children would become. Between the accolades and expectations, Tom rejoiced in doing the right thing, collecting these small wins and compliments and grades and certificates and championships and trophies and knowledge and understanding in a way he was certain would make his father proud. This collection, these jewels, the shining nuggets of satisfaction created the mosaic steppingstones with which he paved his road to happiness, interrupted only by five years in a Korean prison.

Early on, over the course of his young life, Tom found himself stringing together moments of bliss, found mostly in works for others like Ms. Flo, working diligently to close the gaps between blissful instances in a way to construct a general happiness. Tom saw it as metaphor, almost, each blissful moment a steppingstone. And while there were times in his life he leapt from stone to stone in a grand stretch—as in all lives— he came to build enough stones and close enough gaps that his general path was paved with what he perceived to be happiness.

Through diligence, wisdom, study, pursuit, and struggle, Tom paved an existence that was as close to happiness as he could imagine. Then, because humans are humans, we reflect on our histories through the glasses of hindsight, making nearly everything look like happy times; everything look like beautiful mosaic steppingstones leading to this very moment. This, he thought, is what Abraham Lincoln meant when he said, "Most folks are as happy as they make up their minds to be." In the wake of his father's death, Tom had made up his mind to be happy, while never knowing peace.

So, the two stood on the tracks mesmerized while the crew worked their way toward them, until the stench of labor and the unbathed reached them. With undershirts wet with sweat and straw hats stained brown at the band and brim, the men moved toward them until they were no longer distant observers but were among them. Ms. Flo and Tom moved off the tracks like ghosts, unseen and unheard and unbothered by these men who had work to do.

Tom would think of these men, these gandy dancers, often in boot camp, the work song cadence-calls of trotting young men sounding off between the barracks:

> Close your eyes and hang your head
> We are marching by the dead
> Dress it right and cover down
> Forty inches all around.

"Tom, Tom, Tom," Ms. Flo said earnestly, "focus, boy." There was a tone of reprimand, out of character for Florence.

Confused, Tom could smell the creosote hot on the railroad ties, sticky under his foot like the orange juice in his beard.

"Focus," he parroted, trying to understand what she meant, while the voice from inside his helmet said simultaneously, "Focus."

PART IV

I been in many cities and country places too,
Played in many countries from Spain to Kathmandu,
Been all over t'world from the south to north pole,
Ain't nobody tell me what is a man's soul.

—COUNTRY JOHN BASTIAN

"Focus, Thomas! Look alive!" his father shouted from the front porch, Tom hearing the voice as he had as a boy. Behind his father's voice, somehow juxtaposed, Tom could hear Ernie recite his altered prayer. Ernie, gone now sixty years, but not his prayer. *Now I lay me down to sleep I pray The Lord my soul to keep if I should die before the morn let it be in courage born with gun in hand and in the breach between the wicked and the weak in triumph, Lord if I should perish the honor I forever cherish.*

Tom's father pulled his arm back to rifle a fastball as Tom woke with a start, yanking his bloated hip and leg with a jolt. The pain was excruciating, driving him upright on his buttock for the first time since the crash, his abdominal muscles and back snapping him vertical in spasm.

He wept, not over the pain, but over the clarity with which he had heard his father's voice. He wept over what he thought might be rescue. Wept over the rescue he'd been waiting for his entire life. He could feel the pulse pound in his neck. Perched on what felt like pillows, he was hot, the fever coming over him so fully it felt like sun, while the lingering echo of his father's voice left him. The sun, that ball, that light, that globe, welcomed for seventy-seven and one-half years was high now—noon at least and likely after—and had begun cooking him as the sun will do.

He could hear the ocean. He could smell bait fish rotting on a pier. He could see a puppy pulling on a bathing suit in a Coppertone poster hanging on a beachside icehouse wall.

He could feel the pink burning of his forehead and nose, the tops of his hands and cheek bones. He could feel it on his eyelids and on his ears, on the sides of his neck where they peeked out from under the shadow of his matted beard. He could feel it below his Adam's apple, where the course short white whiskers below his shave line collapsed within the wrinkles of his neck, scratching his now-sensitive derma. He could feel it on his lips, the burn lifting the top layer in blistering pustules filled with sweat. He'd been asleep, falling away in exhaustion as the sun had risen above him. That light sneaking up on him in a way he simply could not escape, as he was trapped beneath it. That light had found him, beaming through the damp loblolly pine, bald cypress, redbud, white oak, and magnolia, finding the soft spots in him seldom exposed to light long enough for him to notice.

"How long has it been?" Tom gasped aloud. "How long has it been since I've been sunburned?"

Tom sat panting, catching breath he'd lost between the sound and the fury, the weeping and the pain, and even the memory signifying nothing. Hunched over his near-octogenarian paunch, Tom surveyed his body as best he could without lifting his drooping head. The fingers extending past his broken arm were almost comically huge now, but still with the color of living extremities. Purple and red and flesh-tone digits, plump and hard against his new sunburn, the skin had begun to split at the fingertips and beds of his fingernails. The leaching plasma and seeping blood had dried in the heat and the sun, making his fingers look as though they'd been dipped in something dark like chocolate or varnish or motor oil. The splintered bone protruded unchanged, but for several flies rubbing legs and vomiting and laying eggs on the exposed marrow. The swelling in his leg had actually come down just a bit, his pants looking less like a sausage casing but still without slack.

As near as Tom could tell, the pain had abated a bit as well, quelled against the screeching of the universe, almost to the point of bearing. His foot, on the other hand—that errant appendage separate on the other side of the motorcycle frame—was ghastly. Through the haze of sweat and dehydration, the blackened flesh seemed to undulate in the midday light, seemingly moving his toes through no intention of his own. Tom could no more move the foot than he could move the motorcycle itself, having lost all feeling, and certain the foot would be lost with the weight of the swingarm pressed upon his leg like a tourniquet. Still, he strained hard to understand what he was looking at when it hit him. His foot was covered in ants! Hundreds of thousands of fire ants, whose name, Solenopsis invicta, means invincible fire.

The ants were at work, having discovered the rotten flesh of his heel and ankle, treating this living man no differently than they would treat a dead rodent, a dead locust, a dead cat. The ants did only what ants do, which is to devour the fallen. Ants are not in the fight nor know victory. Their role, as cowards of the wild, is to clean up. Tom would have panicked had he more energy, but instead marveled at their work and at his inability to feel it. So covered was his foot he couldn't make out the skin from the army of deconstruction, crawling in and around and over one another in a manic frenzy while the weather and the quarry and the time permitted.

They were in a hurry as ants always are, rushing against a pronounced end they could only sense, as though their frenetic pace and single-mindedness held more meaning than simply feeding the mound; as though their machinations held some relevance beyond simply existing to dismantle a memory, to clean things up. Their frenzy and seeming chaos spawned by a fear their treasure would be taken from them, or their offspring would starve, or some manner of evil would befall them, so they struggle against time and weather and the day with an end coming to it bearing no more reason than an end coming to everything. The good of the colony, the good of the queen, the assurance of perpetuation in a future that held no more for them and their offspring than finding more decay to devour, more labor, more frenzy. A future devoid of everything but eating the dead, while still a future they desperately wanted.

Curious and with his mind wandering, afraid to move for the pain, Tom forgot his predicament and watched the ants eat him. He pulled the notebook onto his lap, turning the pages slowly with his good hand. He turned a folded corner to find several sheets of lined spiral notebook paper folded and stuffed between pages, along with a typed letter and photograph. Opening them, he took a minute to remember a diagram in his own hand, drawn of planets, each with crescents emanating from the poles and labeled +/- beneath which he had written "electromagnet," and beside which was written a shopping list of hardware store items. The letter was wrapped around the photograph, and opening it, he rediscovered it had been written by Eleanor Dobson, their housekeeper many years prior.

"How long ago?" he asked himself, and because people used to date letters, saw it was written in the early summer of 1992, ten years after she'd moved away with her son, Dennis. She had worked for them for the five years prior to the two moving away, so it occurred to Tom he had known Eleanor many more years of his adult life than he hadn't. The picture the letter held was a snapshot of the two of them, with Dennis in his high school cap and gown, grinning widely.

Dear Roseanne and Tom,

I hope you are both well, but first want to apologize for having fallen out of touch. I think it's been at least four years since we talked! Tampa is far from Houston, but not too far for the U.S. postal service, so for that I am sorry. I've planned to write this letter for some time, as I think of you both often and have no doubt my life, and Dennis' life would have wound up remarkably different had you not taken us under your wing when we needed it.

He is such a great young man, full of hope and promise, and has plans for a future he simply would not have if you two hadn't convinced him how capable and smart he is. He's been accepted to the University of Central Florida and Florida State, but is holding out for the University of Florida before committing. He's studying mechanical engineering and wants to spend some time working in third-world countries helping with infrastructure before settling down. He has a great head on his shoulders, and I am very proud of him.

I am remarried to a wonderful, hard-working Christian man named Lincoln Moore, so my name is now Eleanor Moore. We own a plumbing business here in Tampa and I work with him managing the office. He had a daughter when we married, Amber, three years younger than Dennis, and we had a baby together two years ago. His name is Scott after Lincoln's father. We call him "Beanie".

Anyway, we would love to call you to catch up and Dennis tells me all the time he wants to get to know you guys again.

Sincerely,

Eleanor

Tom smiled when he looked at the photo of a beaming eighteen-year-old boy, glad to have helped him. "El" had come to work for them when Roseanne's women's Bible study leader let the class know she knew of a young woman who needed help. Her husband was in prison for assault and battery, and this woman was out of work with her young son. She had no family who would take her in so without a job she was in real trouble. Roseanne was doing so much work with the church herself she jumped at the chance to help, giving El a job as all-round housekeeper and errand-runner and allowing her to bring Denny in the summers and when there was no school.

Over the next couple of years, they had all become very close, with Tom taking time with Denny as he had his own children. No structure, really, just time as he worked on motorcycles and cars, landscaped, grilled, went target shooting, and fishing, engaging the boy in his curiosities and questions as a mentor. Sometimes during the week, the two of them would stay for dinner, after which Roseanne would help El with all manner of paperwork and life coaching or help Dennis with his homework. Over this time El's secrets emerged, as happens with secrets, divulging the nature of her life, her husband Steven, and her fear of his coming release. He had been a violent, intimidating drinker, who would Jekyl-and-Hyde with no warning whatsoever, but that's what she had known. As a result, he would hit her and had begun hitting their boy just a month before he was arrested.

This abuse was repulsive to Tom, as was any abuse of children. How could this man, the father of this boy, destroy the only innocence left on earth? How did the helpless become the hopeless? How did the pure become a reasonable target for the rage and darkness in a man's heart? Evil is drawn to purity, not to become better, but because only in the destruction of purity does wickedness alleviate the contrast. Purity is a reminder of the wicked's own impurity. Only in tainting innocence can evil rationalize its existence. Pedophilia is worse, in Tom's understanding, as the damage is irrecoverable and there is but one countermeasure. He called it "the fifteen-cent solution" because that was what he paid for each .38 caliber shell.

Tom, like many men, was violent under the right circumstances, though the "right" circumstance rarely presents itself; in fact, not once since Korea. Often, women don't want to know this, and men play it down if they aren't denying it themselves, but it's in them as it has been since the beginning of time. Dormant, roiling, like a pacing tiger forever caged. The world never saw it because Tom never showed it to them, wrongly assuming it wasn't there if it hadn't been seen. Roseanne knew, because she knew about everything a woman can know about a man.

The night they came to understand Dennis had been beaten and likely would be again, Tom saw red. Roseanne was his balance and rightly so, as that balance in a marriage is paramount. He was not a balanced man without her; fearing what he might do. Most men go to their graves pretending to be peaceful, when any peace they have is a result of self-control, not desire, because a man's desire is to eliminate anything that threatens what he loves or cares about. He had killed men in Korea, after all, and believed some men needed killing. If pedophiles didn't have it coming, no one did, and while, as a civilized man, he was willing and insistent to have the law take care of the abuser, he likewise lost no sleep over the death of evil men. This unwavering drive to eliminate threats was likely—without any of them knowing it—why he never knew of Grace's rape in college.

"I grew up in a violent, alcoholic house," Eleanor said, "and I just so wanted to move away from home I guess I thought I loved him, marrying a man just like my own father. Now things are so good for Dennis and me I'm afraid of him getting out."

Eleanor had come to Christ, through witnessing the peace in Roseanne's life and through Roseanne actively encouraging her to read the Bible and attend church with them. In that acceptance, El and Dennis both had reached a peace of mind and hope for their future she had never known, surrendering her prideful floundering to good will, kindness, and honor in a way that made her abandon any attachment to a life in the world and to the men and women in it who would love nothing more than her failure. So, she shook the dust from her feet and entered a new life with many strangers, all of whom loved and welcomed her as family.

"Why," Tom wondered, "would anyone spite her for her faith? Whether you think Christianity is silly or poorly informed or somehow too dubious to be believed, why would you wish a return to misery for a woman and child simply because one may find believing too difficult?"

He marveled at people who would rather a person be miserable and hopeless if it meant otherwise supporting beliefs that contradicted their own "enlightened" ones.

Their un-enlightened "enlightenment" also attached beliefs to Christians that aren't true, having no understanding, no study, no true evaluation outside of what they've seen of television evangelists or witnessed in Christian hypocrisy. They didn't understand nor care whether the hypocrisy is not part of the Christian ethic, but is instead part of humanity, Christians being a subset of that. Their selfishness insisted someone who didn't fall in line with their cynicism cannot live blissfully happy and content believing something the cynic deemed silly.

Beyond that, Tom knew he could always count on a Christian to be motivated by a moral imperative, and while sometimes failing the imperative, your chances with a Christian in any dealing were better than with a non-Christian. This made Tom trust Eleanor more in his house and with access to his belongings, eventually trusting her with house and car keys. Tom knew, even in his own doubt, a moral imperative and an ethic that superseded a person's desires or rationalized need—a morality that exists independent of its adherents—drove behavior that simply does not exist when the ethic is circumstantial, or morality is subjective. When Tom was shopping for another car or motorcycle project, he was always more likely to believe the claims of a man selling a machine if he thought the man was a Christian. That isn't to say others can't be trusted, simply that their perspective wasn't necessarily eternal, and in some cases, felt either no real harm in ripping someone off, or simply believed there would be no reckoning. It is also not to say Christians are perfect, because they can be liars like the rest of us. It only means the odds are better of finding a good man when drawing from a pool of people who live by a moral imperative independent of themselves and independent of rationalization or generational, temporal morality.

Are there good people? Are there good men? People certainly do good things and can live in a way whereby the good outweighs the bad. Tom was thought of as a good man, a good boy, a good son, a good student, a good soldier, a good doctor, a good friend, a good citizen, a good father, a good husband, a good brother, a good neighbor, a good motorcyclist, a good man, a good man a good man a good man a good man a good man a good man a good man.

"I'm a good man, right?" Tom muttered, staring at the photograph of El and Dennis, "right?"

He could feel the pain of it as he asked himself, convinced he was only as good as people thought he was, and knowing El and Denny thought he was a good man, he implored the photo for an answer.

"Perception is real. Perception is real. If they believe me to be a good man, and I do the things good men do, I must be a good man. I must be." Even as he said it aloud, he felt it a lie.

"What is a good man? What does a good man do?" he mumbled weakly. "Is a good man defined by good deeds? Or does good only mean he doesn't do those things deemed bad?" Because all of the good men he knew, including himself, had done bad deeds as well.

Broken by injury and heat and dehydration, his psyche simply had no energy to defend him from the angst of his rationalization.

"By your friends' standard? By your standard?" asked the voice from within his helmet. Tom jerked with surprise but didn't turn, as his gaze was focused on Dennis and El and the ants eating his foot.

"The world doesn't know what's in your heart, Tom. Some men are perceived good because they are too afraid to break any rules; they are afraid of the world, they are afraid of what people think, they are cowards," the voice continued. "These men sell their cowardice as goodness. Some men are perceived good because they have never been exposed. Some men are perceived good because they never perpetrated an evil they could not rationalize. Some men are perceived good because the mores of their generation set a low bar on goodness. Some men are perceived good because that's the way their wives and children present them, in prideful defense of their own lives."

The voice went on, "Some men are perceived good only because the world has no idea what is in their hearts and in their minds, but I do. Goodness is seen to be a collection of good things, such as charity and kindness and listening to people and making people laugh and helping those in need. A gathering of deeds to be presented as your legacy; a monument to the way you want to be remembered; honor badges you hope will hide a darkness from the world or measured in terms of what love a man has for people. But goodness is not an attachment or a perception. Goodness is a wellspring from which these things—charity and kindness and help—flow. Real goodness is righteousness, is purity, and there is only one way to become pure again."

The voice went silent, and Tom began drifting, faint in the heat and the pain, drifting between visions of a .38 caliber Smith & Wesson model 32 in the jaws of his bench vice, held tight while he ground the serial number off the butt with a file, and a second memory of a theology professor he'd had in college. A man he thought of often as his wisdom and kindness made an impression on everyone he'd touched. This day, this lecture, however, had been different and had stuck in Tom's mind like a tick. Now, in burgeoning septic shock, dehydration and delirium, Tom recalled the man's intensity with near-present clarity.

"Subjective morality is a trap," insisted Dr. Daniels, pacing with both hands in twill khaki pockets. "And an ideology put forth by people who need to believe human beings are basically good, flying in the face of 10,000 years of recorded history and countless world theologies that condemn human behavior."

Then shouting, "Just look around! Time after time after time I am confronted with well-meaning students who have much more esteem for their own wisdom than they do for actual philosophical deduction or in the wisdom of women and men who made understanding their life's work. They make no effort to understand but claim wisdom by virtue of Kerouac poetry and Gertrude Stein quotes."

Tom and the entire graduating class would later discover Daniels had been served divorce papers that very morning, and like every man of that age, would not think of leaving work or showing weakness. His wife had been seeing their neighbor for a year or more, a shock to the professor's psyche to be sure, but more than that, a shock to his sense of righteousness.

This had been an impassioned speech, an out-of-character soliloquy that stuck with Tom for a long time. "Song lyrics, maybe?" Daniels continued, "Their favorite movie star? And it gets worse every semester! Blind leading the blind! They remind me of tapeworms, each proglottid sexually mature and capable of reproduction, but brainless worms, nonetheless. Only these particular worms are possessed by a delusion that convinces them they know something."

Tom remembered the room, looking around him to find thirty-five students in their second semester of philosophy—the very people he was railing against. They were sitting all around him now, in rows amongst the trees, while in his lap sat a bench vice and a .38 pistol. Strikingly, he saw and remembered the clothes they wore, the books they carried, the shoes and the watches and the hair bows. He and Daniels were the only two with beards.

Then Daniels, in almost a whisper, said, "Left to our own devices, we are cruel and selfish and egregious; thieves and liars all of us." He was pacing casually between the magnolia tree and the bent rim of the motorcycle's rear wheel.

Continuing the lecture, Daniels said, "We prove it time and again by the flaccid wickedness within us that seldom demonstrates the force and violence of what we deem heinous, but often demonstrates those lesser crimes; those manipulations to get your way; that selfish administration of language and behavior and facial expression and body language that allows our getting what we want at the expense of others, then with that same wickedness rationalize our behavior so we can sleep at night."

Then, "How many people in this room have lied about something this week? How many people have stolen? How many people are sleeping with their neighbor's wife or wishing they could?" On that he stammered, barking a short cry followed by a deep breath.

A hand went up on Tom's right. It was nineteen-year-old Dorothy Swanson. Confused, she asked without being called, "Will this be on the test?"

Ignoring her, Daniels continued, "Yet proponents of subjective morality insist people are good at heart. We are not, class. We are not. The only goodness is by grace. The only purity is by grace. The only life is by grace."

Tom looked down to find the revolver tight in the vice and on his good thigh, the serial number missing from the bottom of the butt, replaced by rough scoring where the file had done its work.

Dr. Daniels let the room rest in silence for what seemed like several minutes but was likely much less.

"How do I know?" he asked. "I was one of the unwashed, unclean, filthy-ragged philistines. I was living a life that made you beatniks look like amateurs. But my desire for goodness was satisfied in Christ. That desire is actualized through the forgiveness of our own innate and subjective amorality and our complete inability to be true. This is why the Bible says we become new. We are new creatures through Christ. We are forgiven, as we forgive those who trespass against us."

He then absentmindedly said again in a whisper, "As we forgive those who trespass against us."

Dr. Daniels began to quietly weep. The students had stopped taking notes and sat silently. Two young women were crying with him, as was Tom. Taking a deep breath, Dr. Daniels spoke, quietly burdened, "Listen, Protagoras said truth is relative, but that is a flawed theory from a flawed man. The idea you don't feel badly, remorseful or guilty has nothing to do with whether an act is a transgression. While feeling badly or regretful or remorseful—guilt—is often used as our indicator for whether we've done something wrong, but these feelings are unreliable and liars. Guilty feelings are simply not the litmus test for transgression. Because whether you feel guilty is often relative to the social construct, but whether something is wrong is never relative to the social construct. Wrong-ness, like righteous-ness is a constant."

Tom thought, "I hope I'm not filing while this thing's loaded," looking down at his gun. "I wouldn't do that, would I?" Then, with a vague memory of removing the cylinder and only having the frame in the vice, he wondered how the entire revolver wound up there. He never would have put a loaded revolver in a vice, but there it was. He could see the brass feet of the loaded ammunition and the primers.

By this time the hour was up, and the hall was filling with the next class' students. Tom's entire class, however, seemed to know staying was important, so no one got up to leave.

Daniels continued speaking. "You see," he said, "it isn't the guilt or the darkness or even whether the offended forgave you. As the offended—as you are and will be—forgiveness is paramount and in itself a gift from God. The power to forgive someone is liberating and true, and difficult at times. The very idea you have consciousness makes you aware of your own selfishness and, if you're honest with yourself, aware of the things you've done to satisfy your own longing, whatever that longing may be. And oftentimes, maybe most often, satisfying that longing comes at the expense of someone else."

Daniels paused, taking in a deep breath. "It is this impurity that keeps you from entering a pure eternity. Don't you see?" he asked. "The impurity keeps you out, and the only way to be redeemed is through the sacrifice of the only one requiring no redemption. For only that purity can pay the price for you. Only that. Only that gift; accept it."

Tom, in his haze, recalled thinking that day in class, "Why do I have to accept this gift, this Christ?"

And in answer from behind him—from inside the helmet—he heard, "Because that acceptance includes the humble acknowledgement of your need for salvation. It is a submission of self, a humility and understanding that not only are you unworthy, but you can never be worthy on your own. You simply cannot donate enough time, or be kind enough to strangers, or apologize enough, because there is no cosmic scale to teeter you into the purity-zone."

"And in fact," Dr. Daniels continued, "it has nothing to do with whether you are a good person, (whatever that's supposed to mean) because there is no good person. That's hard to hear for a non-believer; the idea that there are no good people in the truest sense of the word."

"Even if that's true," Tom interrupted aloud, sitting sunburned on the floor of the east Texas Big Thicket, "I've known plenty of people, myself included, that don't deserve eternal damnation."

Leaves crackled under Daniels' feet as he stopped to lean over to within a foot of Tom's face, adding matter-of-factly, "The irony of your statement proves my point, as it assumes you—or whomever might say this—get to decide what constitutes a transgression worthy of damnation."

Looking directly into Tom's eyes, Daniels continued, "This is your comment on subjective morality, Mr. Weltanschauung. In your judgment, you are the arbiter of all things right and wrong. In that statement you take on the presumption you are somehow qualified to rank sin, to judge, when in fact you are no more qualified than any of the rest of the world is or has been."

"Look, Thomas," Dr. Daniels explained, "whether it is one minor transgression, a series of reprehensible behaviors, or simple evil, we're only talking about degrees. Any and all of it keeps us from entering a place of purity, where no sin abides, because the sin abides in you. Your acceptance of that fact is not a judgment of others or your condemnation of them, but is instead a judgment of self and a fearful, sprawling run to a place of light and salvation, where making sense of everything is as unimportant as it is unattainable."

The professor had strength now, and conviction, standing beneath the oak and magnolia, dappled in the light of a tired day. Wise and seemingly past his classroom, past his time, past his body and his pain and his need to endure. His face appeared less weary, now holy, now glowing. His resolve, planted in commitment to truth, found a home in his voice bouncing between tree trunks and embankments and rocks and wreckage.

On Tom's left came a second voice, Dorothy Swanson, somehow sitting beside Tom in the pine needles and flowering spikenard with her legs crossed. She wore blue sailcloth pants, cat-eye glasses, and a head scarf. Her hand was on Tom's forehead.

Kindly and coolly she spoke to him, "Tom, Christ's taking on the mantle of sin was truly taking on the mantle of filth, abandoning His own purity to save our eternity, whereby He became the crucible. He is the vessel, Tom. He is the smelting pot. Only purity could have taken that on, free of selfishness and manipulation; free of regret or harm to others; free of greed and hate and lust and violence. Only purity, only Love could take on the sins of the world as a sacrifice in penance and homage. Only His son could atone, because you and I certainly can't, and in that atonement, you become pure yourself. Suddenly and forever worthy of entering a place of purity only through the acceptance of this gift of Jesus Christ, who died and suffered for your transgressions. It is acceptance of the gift and faith."

Tom now held the revolver in his hand, pulling the hammer back to rotate the cylinder; letting it down with his thumb. There was a turn ring on the cylinder; rotation marks showed signs of use.

Then from inside his helmet, Daniels spoke again. "The torment of Hell is not something God is doing to you, Tom. It isn't even completely about punishment, but rather is about consequence. You have simply given up the right to exist in a place of purity and light, because allowing your entry would mean it is no longer a place of purity and light. Hell is banishment, and banishment is a burning, chaotic mass of agony. It is an eternity of you and your transgressions, because none of your seeming goodness is there either."

Tom glanced up from his pistol, knowing it wasn't there anyway, looking around on the empty forest, knowing his classmates weren't there anyway, as Dr. Daniels wasn't there, as Dorothy wasn't there. Tired and angry over the lecture, Tom understood the argument for acceptance. If only he understood his own distrust; if only he had faith!

Hearing himself speak, his voice creakingly low, a whisper, a growl, remembering Robindraneth Tagore, an eastern polymath. "Faith is the bird that feels the light when the dawn is still dark."

Is acceptance of this gift the cure, or is acceptance the sweetest of infections? Tom wondered whether embracing the infection meant giving himself over to the Spirit, over to God, over to Christ. While some men resist in blatant pride, Tom resisted in metered, inappropriate intellect, but more importantly, Tom resisted because giving himself over felt like abandoning people who need him. It meant no longer being the rock for people he loved. It meant weakness in both intellect and philosophy. Though Tom could not fully articulate it, becoming part of the God-ness meant that he was no longer the deity of his patients. It meant he was no longer the deity of his children. It meant he was no longer the deity unto himself. This was the hardest part.

Chapter 6

PART I

I rode that fast black Vincent,
Hard and hunkered down,
That fast Black Shadow Vincent,
Wide open till the end.

—*BOBBY RAY CORBIN*

TOMMY THREW HIS LEG over his Ducati and pulled away from his mother's house. Grace hated him riding motorcycles but having grown up with and around them she accepted it as tradition. Her father had taught her son to ride when he was only eight years old on the trails through his property, weaving between trees and rocks on a 50cc Honda Monkey. Since day one, like his grandfather, Tommy knew he would ride a motorcycle.

Crossing Main, he rode down the hill over the river bridge and up toward the light on the other side, clearing the short ride from what was called traffic in a small town to the open countryside between Fredericksburg and Kerrville. In the heart of the Texas Hill Country, the roads wind and bend with sometimes steep slopes. Tommy knew the road well and rounding the bend from forty-five miles an hour to seventy miles an hour, held the clutch, ran the motor up and let go to bring the front wheel up high as he accelerated. The wheelie was part of his routine, day or night, morning or evening, bringing the wheel down in time for the first of many sweeping bends in the road. He was giving motorcyclists a bad name, in the way all good motorcyclists should.

With a deep creek on the west side and fields of sheep or cattle or maize or grapes or rusting cars on the right, Tommy leaned into the turns with the same glee his grandfather had felt in the summer of 1949, racing between Corpus and the naval base on his 1945 BSA, some sixty years later on a machine one hundred times better, with virtually no difference in joy.

In Kerrville, Texas, there were no Ducati dealerships, and in fact no motorcycle dealerships at all, so Tommy bought the 696 in San Antonio on order and had to ride it back for oil changes and maintenance according to his warranty schedule. He didn't mind because wide-open I-10 took him there, which meant he could go as fast as the bike would carry him. He did his best to follow speed limits, or at least did his best to think about doing his best, and while never in a hurry he rode like he was.

He'd gotten to work that morning at 6:00 a.m. to take care of the chickens, so leaving mid-afternoon left him a few hours before he was due for supper. His girlfriend Lori was cooking dinner for him at her parents' house, where they would eat and play cards and listen to George Jones, Patsy Cline, Willie Nelson and Johnny Cash records with her folks until it was time to leave. By 2009 it was far too late to be listening to vinyl, but Lori's dad Bob insisted that was the way country music was supposed to be heard, if, of course, you couldn't hear it in person.

Bob would regale them with tales of live Outlaw concerts, Willie Nelson picnics, and the time he ran into Johnny Paycheck at a Sac-n-Save outside of Pasadena, Texas, in 1975 when both men had stopped for gas. Bob had seen Paycheck play the night before at Gilley's. It was around noon and Paycheck was drunk, pumping gas into a converted school bus with "Johnny Paycheck" hand-painted on both sides. He wore a red bandana and a jean vest, no shirt, no shoes, with two pearl-handled revolvers on a belt. Bob was leaving the store with a bottle of Big Red stuffed with roasted peanuts, nearly driving away before he saw the bus and Paycheck.

"Johnny Paycheck!" he had shouted, extending his hand. Paycheck held a cigarette between his lips, unlit, taking Bob's hand with vigor. "I saw you last night at Gilley's," Bob continued.

Paycheck grinned and answered, "I reckon you remember more o' that than I do, partner."

According to Bob they talked for ten minutes, after which Paycheck climbed up into the bus and got in the driver's seat, heading out onto the highway drunk and driving his own bus.

On this day, speeding on State Highway 16, Tommy was hoping for catfish. Twenty years old with a job he loved, a shiny Italian motorcycle, church on Sundays, a pretty girlfriend who fried catfish and a beautiful place to live, Tommy's joy emanated from him. Kind but strong, no nonsense and eager to help, his aggression for life tempered by his relationship with God, the future belonged to him. With four hours left on a beautiful spring afternoon, he would go down to the dam and throw a hook in the water until he had to get ready. After dinner he would go home to work on a three-string electric diddly bow he was making. Cigar box body; hickory neck. He and the boys were working on some Albert King tunes and he wanted to sound authentic.

The trip was short, especially since he was speeding, so in no time he was riding past the police station heading for home. He owned a 1974 Winnebago with no motor, but had it towed out to fourteen acres he bought on the south side of the Guadalupe River, another four miles outside of town. With electricity but no running water, Tommy made do until he could afford something better. When and how made no difference to him, as long as he was pushing in that direction. For Tommy, life was sweet.

Meantime, Grace was taking muffins out of the oven, with Eric hovering close by to test the batch. While not part of the bed and breakfast package, she often made muffins for guests and anyone who wanted them. Some Saturday mornings she would collect a large carafe of coffee and a basket of muffins from their restaurant and set them out at the lawn entrance for all the foot traffic of weekend tourists and day-trippers. The lawn of the inn was manicured, with small tables and chairs hidden amongst the trees within a low rock wall. People she'd never met would pour a cup, take a muffin, and sit beneath oak or elm limbs for an hour or more, basking in the ambience of the sweet little inn.

PART II

A better day is comin' by and by,
A better day is comin' by and by.
No payback in my worry no payback in my hurry,
A better day is comin' by and by.

—SONNY ELKINS/BODIE SMITH

"Hello?" John answered, as everyone answers, with a question in their voice.

Hannah, calling from her hotel room in Brownsville, replied, "Hey, Johnny, any news on Dad?"

She thought she had given it enough time to be reasonable, to be casually asking. She was propped up in bed with the news on the television, her stocking feet crossed. She had crumbs from a granola bar on the front of her dress and in her lap.

"No," John answered. "We're here at the house waiting but I'm growing concerned. The garage was open, and he had meat in the sink, so he expects to come back, but we've been here for three hours and he's not home yet."

"That's not good, Johnny," Hannah sighed, "not good at all. What's next?"

He thought for a minute. "We'll plan on staying here. When we hang up, I'll call the sheriff, I guess. Better safe than sorry."

Even in his comment to Hannah, John could feel the growing delta between what he hoped and what he knew. Calling the police was becoming less and less alarmist, approaching that point of the pendulum's swing whereby not calling them was becoming the unreasonable thing. At least in his mind.

As she listened to John, Dianne picked up her own phone to call their neighbors, Angel and Rachel, to ask them to feed and look in on Hambone.

"Well," Hannah answered, "I'll call Grace and my clan and everyone at church to get everyone praying. You do the same, huh?" Then after a silence, she added, "Look, he could be broken down somewhere."

"Much more likely than anything else," John replied, relieved she'd suggested it.

Twenty minutes later a black and white Crown Vic pulled into the driveway, and John walked out to meet it. Stepping out of the car was a middle-aged DPS officer, pulling his gun belt and pants up while he stepped forward.

Lean and kind, he extended his hand to say, "I'm Officer Randal, Department of Public Safety." Then, as though his presence was a mystery to John, said, "I got a call about a missing senior?" He was new to the county, so John had never seen him before.

While the dispatcher had asked John for his father's age, hearing "missing senior" sounded so much more helpless, so much less virile, than his thoughts of his dad. Sure, his father was pushing eighty, but calling him a missing senior immediately struck John as hasty and misrepresentational. Before he protested, however, he knew both of these things were true. His father was missing. His father was a senior.

In his mind's eye John saw his dad, mid-forties, hard and lean with a camouflaged scar hidden on both cheeks by a full, robust beard. He was wearing scrubs with a stethoscope around his neck, clipping roses from the front bush before going inside. He saw his father, feet up in a lawn lounge-chair holding a spatula, waiting for the burgers to brown. His index finger was splinted and taped, after breaking it earlier in the day with a tire iron; a break he set himself. He saw his father, dancing with a five-year-old Grace, she standing on his feet while he twirled her in the garage. He saw his father, seventy-seven and one-half years old, thin in the shoulders, red-rimmed eyes under thick glasses, deep creases in his neck as he laughed with John about being unable to pee.

"Yes," John answered shaking the man's hand. "John Welton. I made the call. My dad is the missing senior. His name is Tom, Thomas Welton."

"How long's your dad been missing, John?" the officer asked.

John, eager to get through the questions and begin looking, answered quickly and thoroughly, "I've been calling him since this morning and have been here a few hours."

"And," the officer continued, "was the house in order and everything the way you would have expected it?"

"Exactly, but without him. All the doors were unlocked, the garage door was open, his coffee cup still out on the workbench."

Officer Randal's eyes widened a bit as he asked, "He doesn't lock up when he leaves?"

This frustrated the policeman, as he personally locked his house, locked his safe, locked his garage, locked his gate, locked his glove box, and locked his car. In fact, he often locked his phone and frequently changed his passwords. It made him feel better to think he was responsible, or that somehow, he could avoid being violated because he'd followed the rules and couldn't blame himself should he be robbed.

"Never has," was John's reply. "He always said he refused to be owned by the things he owns."

The officer pursed his lips a bit, then asked, "Does your father suffer from any illness, or is he forgetful?"

"No," John answered, "He's 100 percent healthy. I mean, he's seventy-seven, but still hikes and chops wood and mows his lawn. Works on cars. Hunts. He's missing on his motorcycle."

"His motorcycle?" came the surprised question, the officer's furrowed brow registering disdain, as though John was somehow responsible. Then, "Has he ever done this before?"

John hadn't anticipated this question and knew how problematic the answer could be. Had he ever done it before? Only a thousand times on a thousand days from the day John was born. This time was different but explaining the nuances of his father's disappearances and why eight or nine hours didn't fit the modus operandi, coupled with the family's growing concern over his living alone, simply wouldn't raise the red flags John wanted to raise.

John lied, "No, never. I mean, he goes off and rides sometimes, of course, but we always know about it and he's never gone long."

Guilty and tripping over his lie, he followed up by saying, "So I guess, yes, but no seventy-seven-year-old man comes up missing for nine hours without something wrong, right? I mean, the man doesn't leave his phone and steak if he's not coming back shortly."

Randal then asked, "Is he upset or depressed about anything? Anything happen recently that might make you think he could hurt himself or others?"

"No. No," John answered honestly, "I mean, he hasn't really been the same since Mom passed, but that was almost two years ago."

"Has he ever talked about hurting himself?" the officer asked.

"Never," was the answer. "Look, my dad is kind and smart, but a tough old bird. He was in Korea and a POW."

"So, would you say he was fairly predictable? Like you know his habits and patterns?" came the next question.

John thought for a minute, but not too long. His father set an alarm, drank coffee, hiked his seventy-three acres, ate brunch, worked in the yard or on cars, cooked dinner, read, or watched TV. He wrote a lot of notes and sometimes essays. On weekends he met friends for breakfast or at the shooting range or went to swap meets and then church on Sunday, at least until Roseanne had passed. Everything he did was within character and almost all of it predictable. Everything except when he would take off, where he would go, and when he might be back.

"Absolutely predictable, yes."

A man has his secrets, however, and while John and Hannah and Grace thought they knew everything about their dad, they truly only knew the things Tom wanted them to know.

In the spring of 1980, Tom had hidden a Smith & Wesson model .32 revolver in a 1971 Nova, between the seat back and the seat bottom, with just enough grip sticking out to be identified easily with a flashlight. It was not loaded. The car, parked outside of a roadhouse bar in Kema, belonged to a recent parolee and husband of Eleanor, Steven Moore. Tom had called the newly installed 911 emergency number from a pay phone, telling the operator he'd witnessed a man waving a gun around the parking lot of the roadhouse before going inside, giving a complete description of both the man and the car. Upon arrival, the police found the gun, a felony for the removal of the serial number and a parole violation for one Steven Moore.

Within months of Moore's initial release, El began coming to work late, sometimes missing the day entirely. There were stories of falling off of the porch and walking into a door, with heavy makeup over blackened eyes and swollen lips. Tom and Roseanne took Eleanor aside and told her what they could do. They would support her and help her and get her a doctor. They would pay for Steven's counseling and could help financially if she needed it. El, like so many, pretended they were wrong about Steven at first, eventually following with admission, but certain she could work it out and that he was a good man deep down. A good man deep down.

When Dennis showed up with bruising from what was clearly a man's grip marks around his upper arms, Tom took the gun to the garage, removed the serial number with a file, followed Moore until he went into the bar and hid it in the car. With ten years of probation revoked, Tom rescued Dennis and his mother.

"Why would he be so dumb, Rosie? Why did he have a gun?" El would ask as though losing him was, in fact, a loss.

Over the following few years Roseanne would comfort her and tell her the Lord works in mysterious ways and that sometimes people are just self-destructive. The alienation lead to divorce, the divorce to self-reliance, self-reliance to confidence and happiness and moving to Florida and Denny becoming an engineer.

Tom never told a soul. So, in character? Yes. Predictable? Also, yes.

"Well, John," said Officer Randal, "if he didn't have a particular place he might go, do you think he'd ride through the National Forest? It's pretty, so maybe that makes sense?"

John was embarrassed he hadn't thought of it. "Yeah, that makes sense."

Randal continued, "I can check hospitals and other departments from the car. If no one has heard anything, I'll issue a bulletin to keep an eye open for your dad. I'll drive down to 94 and through the Forest to Lufkin, and I'll ask the Sheriff's Department to head further south. I'll get the Crockett PD to head east through the Forest up there and I can meet them in Lufkin. That'll take care of most anyplace he might have gone. Then, if that doesn't work, we'll get a helicopter out here. Don't worry, John. We'll find him."

Officer Randal had no doubt that Tom would be found but took even odds Tom would be found alive. He'd had too much experience and had seen too many things to be completely hopeful, but simply let the work produce the result. He would drive north, Crockett police would drive east, and the Sheriff's department would drive south.

PART III

I'm just afraid of fire after I got burnt,
Didn't know no difference till then.
Lord, I keep touchin' that hot stove.
Think just one more time again.

—*SONNY ELKINS/BODIE SMITH*

The day, longer now than a month before; shorter than a month later, but fleeting as are all days, was warm. Fleeting, as are all days, this one warm where the sun shines kindly on infant grass and budding flowers, while they are still too fragile to suffer the coming Texas blaze. A temperate day in the 80s, perfect for sitting on porches and working in gardens and riding motorcycles and stretching your legs. Perfect for walks on the beach before the throngs descended, celebrating bulbs pushing their green through the dirt overhead; perfect for cooking outdoors, anxious for late-May peaches. Dianne poured a cup of coffee but dumped it into the sink, rinsing the cup after discovering Tom was out of milk; a transitory act as most acts are on a transitory afternoon as most afternoons are during a transitory spring as most springs are during a transitory year as most years are during a transitory life.

Taking her knitting, she stepped through the back of the house onto the patio, sitting next to John on an aging porch glider and putting her feet up. Silent as he gently rocked the glider, she sat next to him to work on a scarf she was making for her daughter Candice, who owned a gift shop in Ocean City, Maryland.

She spoke with her kids frequently but saw them only once a year, so these maternal machinations made her feel connected to them in ways only attention and intent can make a person feel connected. Quietly she sat, counting knits and pearls as part of a subconscious autonomic memory, her hands better than just practice would make them and certainly better than the attention she was giving it. There was magic in the knitting, as there is magic in all things hand-made, more so when hand-made things are for people you love.

John put his arm around her and kissed her head, peering into the woods he'd been in with his father many, many times. As it left the yard, the trail from the patio was quickly lost in the cool shade of the woods and underbrush and although he couldn't see it, he knew where it went. He knew it meandered through a winding and undulating hillside, not craggy or full of many rocks to speak of, as they were far away from the craggy and rocky parts of Texas, instead close to sea level where the deep loam served pine trees and native pecans forty and fifty feet high. Having sat in the yard many times, John knew the ground was comfortable and forgiving, allowing a certain cradle to a body's shape and hard spots.

John knew the trail well, different with every hike but the same nonetheless, forming a rough loop to the edge of the property and back with a deer blind in the middle, hidden by the trees and the vines and the dappling of the forest floor.

Made from cinderblock, the deer blind had been painted white when they'd built it some twenty-five years before over a three-day weekend, disregarding all manner of camouflage. More one-room cabin than deer blind, Tom had insisted on windows and a proper door so it could be used by the grandkids as a playhouse, with Hot Wheels cars, beach toys, and baby dolls still buried in the dirt outside of it, the flotsam and jetsam of childhood. John could see it in his mind's eye—that decked floor and tin roof, that orange door.

Without thinking he stood up and walked across the yard, entering the woods. Dianne watched as he walked, her adoration and sympathy compounded by her own worry of the state of Tom. Roseanne's cat had found her, jumping to her lap as John walked away.

"Lord," she implored knitting, "please bless Tom. He's an old man and we're worried about him. Please bring him home safe. Please make him whole, Lord."

The sun was dropping below the tree line as John brushed the light green leaves aside to enter the mottled shade. A cardinal raced down the trail ahead of him. Cool and a bit damp, his steps firm as his path straightened before him. Silent he stepped as he paced along a bed of pine needles, slowing only to pick up a stick for snakes and for moving new growth or spider webs from before his path. His stride was long and quick and while no longer and no quicker than it always was, his speed seemed to amplify as he whisked past the new growth and old growth and memories.

He saw deer tracks and more hog tracks than he could remember seeing before, as was true for the whole of the state. His kids knew these woods and this house, as did his nieces and his nephews and even a few friends. All were welcomed by his mother and by osmosis, his father. There were cookouts and fireworks shows. There were hunting week-ends and target practice. There were tetherball and horseshoes. There was the riding of small dirt bikes or go-carts and hide-and-seek and first outdoor camping trips. There were bonfires and foot races, rope swings and Easter egg hunts.

Walking to the cabin, John came upon the blind more quickly than he'd remembered. Specked with moss and a roof covered in fallen leaves, he pushed the door inward to find it as it had been left: watertight, rat droppings, a number of shell casings, a Honda QA50 minibike on a kickstand in a corner. There were a couple of faded shellback metal lawn chairs they used when they'd hunted, so he plunked down in one of them, using the minibike as a footstool with his gangly legs stretched out before him as a bridge.

The air was musty, so he stood to open the window, sitting again to do what, he didn't know. On a wall hung a modest chalkboard his mother had gotten from a restaurant supply, still with tic-tac-toe played half a dozen times in two colors. He could hear a rat under the floorboards.

On the windowsill behind him there were coloring books and cray-ons, a spiral notebook and a paperback copy of Spurgeon's devotional, *Morning and Evening*. Flipping through the notebook revealed games of hangman and treasure maps; with loose-leaf pages of paper tombstones and paper spy notes. On the inside back cover, that soft brown card-board pocked with dried water droplets and chafed by dirty fingers, John immediately recognized his mother's handwriting. As was her way, she would write a note or a thought or a poem when the muse struck her, often for no one. For no point beyond her expression; no goal beyond working out a thought; no reader beyond herself. Possibly inspired by Spurgeon, she'd left:

> My sin I sharpen to a razor, the shiny blade meant just for me
> And in my flesh my small incisions, compulsive satisfactions thee
> What was a test to feel my living
> A prick to tempt mortality
> Became a pattern, rage, malfeasance
> The scars became the shape of me
> Beneath the scars and skin and tissue, life it courses through my veins
> Somehow I know, to start all over
> I'd scar myself again, again.

John sat silent. Dumbfounded really. What had she been thinking? What was this about? He'd never known his mother to be anything less than hopeful and positive. Never less than faithful and courageous and celebratory. Never sardonic, only blissfully loving of everyone. Above all else, she was kind. He'd thought of her as sinless, which, begging the question, he knew was ridiculous, but in that question became suddenly aware of her frailty, of her humanity.

Reading the poem again he noticed the date, as was her way. As a doctor himself he'd committed to memory the date of his mother's first chemo treatment, last chemo treatment and the day of her diagnosis— the very day she had written the poem. She had come home and wandered off into the woods and wrote this. Likely the last time she'd been in the little cabin, and perhaps the last person to enter there until John sat down. She'd been afraid, knowing and afraid. John read the poem as understanding, not resignation. This was her comment on her humanity, understanding if she had it all to do over again, she would still fall to temptation as is our collective way. Her small incisions, like his small incisions, were self-inflicted wounds born in ego or pride. He knew too that he would fail as equally if given the chance to do it again. He hated that for her, for himself, and for humanity.

John sat, praying, not praying, staring through the open window at a darkening sky. He was thirsty but hadn't noticed until he'd gotten there, trading thirst for ruminating over his mother, frustration with his father, wishing he were on his balcony at home in Galveston with this day still in his future. This day, the day that always comes, was like an ensuing dog at distance, worthy of awareness but without much thought beyond that. But characteristic of the Day That Always Comes, this day had been nipping at his heels for years now and even began barking with the passing of his mother.

Every year, every month the barking became louder as the dog closes the distance to the point it must be addressed, finding that attention in uncomfortable conversations with siblings, agreements with locals to look in on, frequent phone calls to validate health and well-being. So, as he sat in the blind with The Day That Always Comes curled up and impatient at his feet, the morning seeming so long ago; the little concrete box quiet with rods and reels resting in the rafters alongside a pole saw, boat oars and long-dried, brittle stalks of sugar cane, while steaks thawed in the sink back at the house.

Waiting is the hard part, inaction so difficult to master. John had been working at it for years, braking on a never-ending drive to do the next thing and the thing after that and the thing after that. His father had been making up for lost time for the last fifty-five years, seemingly sprinting from goal to goal, accomplishment to accomplishment, chore to chore, task to task. This frantic pace made an impression on young John, compelling in him the same anxiety, the same dysfunction masquerading as ambition.

Always busy like his father, always restless, always driven to mask his fear of failure with his list of accomplishments, and always with a certainty his father expected it; forever unknowing his father suffered it. The brokenness, rewarded with status and big houses, was a treadmill difficult to abandon, at least until he saw it. When all you've ever done is run blind, how do you know what it is to walk? Growing in his peace through God's grace and the support of Dianne, this is how he landed in Galveston. This is how he was able to sit in a lawn chair in a deer blind with his feet up in east Texas. This is how he read his mother's poem and could feel her presence.

Having grown up at church on Sundays, he had an underlying joy since his youth through salvation and the promises of his faith, upon which was built his world view. Never even questioning, it was a permeation of purpose, even if that purpose was unknown to him. Then in college and in his burgeoning intellect, he was tempted with the notion that this was simply what he told himself, as meaninglessness was more difficult to embrace than being a part of something grand.

At eighteen he had stopped going to church and had moved away from the reinforced influence of his mother and stoic discipline of his father, exposed instead to bright university men and women who had no use for God. After all, existence followed by dust is mirthless and glum; so much more depressing than an eternal perspective, that John understood the draw to faith as a comfort. These ideas are what prompted his quitting the semester to catch shrimp and grouper and other fish, sailing out of Clearwater, Florida, after having been recruited by a high school buddy who said he was getting rich doing it. John's role was to bring in the nets and separate the keepers from the cast-offs.

While there, John prayed to a God he had grown uncertain of for a salvation he had grown uncertain of for an eternity he had grown uncertain of, as much out of habit than earnestness. He'd prayed for strength and wisdom, for insight and understanding, for focus and clarity, while reading voraciously both secular and theological philosophy from Martin Luther and the Apostles and Augustine to Confucius and Epicurus and Immanuel Kant and Soren Kierkegaard and Al-Ghazali. What he read at night he would think about during the day while separating fish, pushing the edible and the legal and the valuable into the hold while flipping the squirming masses back into the sea. All slimy, all equally desirous of living, but by rote John became fast and efficient, enabling his mind to be one place while his hands were another.

His back and shoulders became strong and brown, his hair light, and in this meditation, John began to experience the nuanced thoughts of a cynic. Cynicism is two-edged, however, and in his case, these were not the thoughts of a man cynical in regard to God and salvation. Instead, John's growing cynicism charged humanity and the nature of pseudo intellectuals with the immature fear of the faithless over being wrong or worse, the fear of appearing stupid or thought of as a lemming or denying the evidence versus denying the flesh. It became clear that the drive to disbelieve took more effort than the drive to believe, as he began to feel the need of God and existence of God within himself and to see the presence of God in all things.

In recognizing the sub specie aeternitatis—this universal and eternal and undeniable truth—it followed then that salvation became the natural extrapolation of ideas related to the folly of man.

As any examination of humanity becomes a study in transgression that requires rescue and absolution, John settled in on a lifetime commitment to stay on a path of understanding, lest he rest in the assembly of the dead. The intellectually dead; the emotionally dead; the spiritually dead. In these prayers and in this study John's faith grew that semester, whereupon his challenge stopped being whether his faith was warranted, becoming instead his resistance to judging the faithless as puerile dolts.

Returning to college the following semester, John never again wondered whether he was loved; never wondered whether there was an afterlife and where he would spend it; never wondered whether there was a plan for him; never wondered whether his life had meaning. While he would lie awake at times fretting over the temporal, the mundane, and the ultimately meaningless, his effort was only in growing and understanding, not in believing. In this commitment to faith he gained peace and understanding, fostering true underpinnings of joy independent of circumstance.

It had been years since he'd been in this blind, where he'd slept overnight instead of getting up at 3:00 a.m. and hiking through the woods with a rifle and thermos to be sure he beat the rising whitetails or rooting hogs. He and his father both would camp there, a circle of bricks a few yards away where their campfire would crackle. They would grill hot dogs on sticks, with open-canned chili on the bricks to heat up. In his younger years John would struggle with what to say; to be interesting in a way his father could accept, little knowing his dad accepted anything and everything about him.

As he grew older, however, they would sit up for hours, in the very chairs John sat in now, talking about most anything with the exception of Pearl Harbor or prison camps. It was those camping trips and hunting outings John relished most, having his father to himself without the distraction of chores and tasks and hyperactivity and even his siblings and mother. A child never outgrows a good father, and Tom being a good man had worked hard at being a good father, as likewise John had worked hard.

As he sat, remembering these trips and the time with his dad, John was grateful. Grateful for having been born to a man who loved him, considered him, wanted what was best for him, invested his time and his love and his experience in him. Amidst the memories, colliding in his mind and confounding the years and events, John found himself unable to remember what year they found a snake in the blind; what year he'd shot that nine-pointer; what year Tom had made a 300-yard shot with an open-site 1935 Mosin-Nagant, what year they'd seen their first hog tracks.

It didn't matter. It didn't matter whether his timelines and memories added up. It had all happened yesterday and had all happened 1,000 years ago. It had all happened last week and that morning. It was all happening that instant in John, the whirling mass of memory and affection and wisdom congealing into melancholy.

John could see his life in hindsight, and by virtue of experience, his life in foresight. Breathing deeply the forest's spring flora and last year's decay, the inhaling of both beginning and end struck John. Each breath held inception and cessation of a cycle, of a year, of a season, of a life. Each breath a cyclic triumph of its own; in as fresh and full of power, out as exhaust, spent and used. It had never occurred to him, these odors becoming a part of him, the familiar mulch filling his nose and lungs with comfort and hope.

"How is it," he maundered, "everything is a breath? Everything possesses that same metaphor of birth and death?"

He rocked the little motorcycle under his heels to listen for sloshing gasoline, with no intention to do anything regardless of the discovery, except to tell his father there was gas in it, if indeed there was. And after confirming the sloshing, he leaned forward to be sure the petcock was off, knowing his dad would have run the gas out of the carburetor before he let it sit.

Compulsively, John stood and mounted the little bike, turning the petcock to on and opening the throttle. Unfolding the kick starter with his right hand and opening the choke with his left, John brought his foot down. There was a sputter, and the sound of compression, but the little bike didn't start. Kicking again, John gave it some gas to another unsuccessful putt-putt-putt.

Frustrated and knowing better, he held the throttle wide open and kicked it over five times in succession, each with the same failure as the first tries. The rich, sweet smell of bad, varnished gasoline filled the tiny room as it worked its way through the carburetor throat and primary jet and intake valve, pushed through the exhaust valve and out through pinholes in the rusty pipe. The carburetor float was sticking, and it began to overflow, dripping from the bowl onto the frame and dusty floor until he turned the petcock back to the off position.

Lightning bugs began to twinkle on beyond the windows as the crickets warmed up for their coming night song. It was early yet, but the insects couldn't separate the shadows from sundown. Breathing heavily, John crossed his arms and collapsed on the crossbars, sobbing recklessly, knowingly.

A world away in Galveston, Hambone Happy Cheese had never known life without the sound of the ocean as a backdrop. He'd traveled with John and Dianne, but in lieu of understanding the absence of crashing waves in a new place, all he registered was excitement over hearing so much more and peeing someplace different. The sheer thrill of new smells and the potential new dogs he might meet was enough to forever keep him from understanding the ocean was gone. Still, however, that ambient tone, that sound of surge and crash and retreat was as much a part of him as were the seagulls, as was Mrs. Parker's annoying Pomeranian, as was the path he'd worn in the grass inside the fence line.

Hambone Happy Cheese knew no anxiety, had no need of introspection, dreamed the dreams of the unencumbered, chasing squirrels and splashing in the waves. Dianne was convinced he missed them, somehow pacing the fence line and crying, but when Angel and Rachel looked in on him he was sleeping as happy dogs do, his paw twitching with the excitement of the hunt, his tongue splayed out on the concrete pad beneath the picnic table.

PART IV

Lord, where't all that time go?!
Seems most o' mine done gone.
Now just a whole mess o' thens
With t'morrow hav'n today in it too.
Lord, I'm comin' to work late after noon,
But I'm workin' now. I'm workin' now.

—JUNIOR DONIE

Tom, still sitting, raised his eyebrow to find Ms. Flo standing above him, her eyes closed in reverie as she sang a song called *Gulf Coast Blues*. He could hear the music and hear Ms. Flo, but thought there was someone actually there with him, perhaps someone he was mistaking for Ms. Flo. He could hear the grainy record spin on the player, his trained ear knowing there was a warp, and while not skipping, there was a nearly inaudible change in speed as the needle rose and fell with the warp. Instinctively, he thought to sandwich the record between two books and leave it on the back porch of Springs Hardware for a couple of days.

Shouting, Flo raised, "Can't nobody sing the blues like her!"

"Who is that?" Tom asked, desperately hoping he was rescued, grasping at that glimmer as a man would grab a lifeline. Tom had things to do. Tom had feats to complete and goals to accomplish. Books to read and derring-do. He had a Volvo to restore and an 850T to ride. He could see Rosie's cat on the Volvo and the rust to be repaired around the rear windows and in the quarter panels. And he had this Triumph, after all. More than anything else, however, Tom had death to avoid. Tom wasn't through yet and the idea someone was there sparked again in him the notion there had not been enough time.

Alarmed he didn't know, and perhaps more alarmed she hadn't told him before, Flo shouted gleefully, "It's Bessie Smith, Tom! The Empress of the Blues, boy!" Then singing, "Some of you men sure do make me tired."

Tom, lucid, chuckled, knowing he was seeing an apparition of his own making and better yet, an apparition who misunderstood the question. "Can't nobody sing the blues like you, Ms. Flo!" Tom insisted.

Stopping, Flo smiled and earnestly said, "You're right about that, baby. We all sing our own blues, Tom. Can't nobody sing the blues like our own. Can't nobody."

He missed Ms. Flo badly, as he had since she'd passed. She'd died from uterine cancer when he was in a Korean prison, too good to be in the world any longer, he thought. Gone three years by the time he'd returned home, and well over fifty years ago now, the broken young man was further broken by her passing but was alone in it at the time. By the time he was aware she was gone, everyone who'd loved her had mourned and gotten through it. Her friends, neighbors and patrons had gathered for a grand funeral, crying and praying and carrying on, then got on about their lives as people do. Even good people. Maybe mostly good people.

His mother told him everything he wanted to know, which was everything. How she'd been diagnosed, her treatment, her weight loss and fatigue. She'd said it had been a beautiful service. "And Tommy, I think she was waiting for you like we all were. She knew you were coming home. She just knew it."

A few days after he'd gotten back, Mr. Leon Springs came over to the house with a box full of blues records and a record player. He left his new wife in the car, having remarried a woman from Rockport whose husband had been killed in Berlin during the war.

"Tom," he'd said, "Flo wanted you to have these," as he extended his arms with the box. His voice began to shake, and he began to break up, staring at Tom's monstrous scars. He could see Tom at nine years old, holding his mother's and his sister's hands at church. He could see him eating yesterday's pie in the front of the store by the register, an eager thirteen-year-old with a motorbike. "She loved you, Tom. Yes, indeed, loved you very much."

Tom took the box and set it on the kitchen table as Leon Springs went back out to the car for the record player. "Tom," he began again gaining composure, "she thought of you like a son and said so many times. If we'd been able to have kids, you would be the boy we'd wanted."

For the first time Tom understood Mr. Springs liked him after all, and he suddenly felt terrible for having punched him in the nuts all those years ago. He took the record player and put it on the ground beside him, standing to embrace Leon Springs as the man wept.

"She was so worried, Tom, so worried. We prayed every day." Then backing away and holding Tom by his shoulders at arm's length. "And I kept it up till last week when you got back."

Tom had spent the afternoon and the next three days sitting in his mother's garage, working on his BSA and listening to Willie Johnson sing *Jesus Gonna Make Up My Dying Bed* and *Let Your Light Shine on Me*. He'd spend the next five decades missing her.

"I missed you too, Tommy," Flo said when she stopped her singing, "Leon and I kept your picture on the nightstand when you were off fighting."

He followed her with his eyes, glad to have her, but also disappointed she wasn't truly there.

"You remember snapping peas with me on the back porch of the store, Tommy?" Flo asked. "We would snap those peas and flip on the box fan and the record player; singing with the records? I'm singing now, Lord knows. Sing with me again, Tommy Boy."

Tom's neck hurt as he started to crane, the sunburn on his ears and head and above the collar on his jacket flaming hot, even while the sun was hidden behind the tallest trees.

He answered her, "I do remember, Ms. Flo, yes ma'am, and think of it often. Some of my favorite memories. But I'm not much in the mood for singing right now."

Flo said, "You'd run up at the Piggly Wiggly for salt pork and those sweet Vidalia onions, and I'd cook up a pot of them purple hull peas you love. It was those onions what brought 'em to life! Tommy, everybody needs a pea-snapping memory, don't you think? Everybody."

Then, almost as a confession, "You know I never told anybody, but Howard Butt's place was closer and cheaper than Piggly Wiggly, but I sent you to the Piggly Wiggly anyhow. He opened that bakery in 1936 and I can't say I ever forgave him. And I didn't think it too smart to be shopping at my competition!"

Looking down at the premorse bones of his wrist, his ham of a hand nearly bursting, Tom found maggots squirming on the end of the dried spikes both on top of and within the marrow. He only cared inasmuch as he was curious.

"How long have I been here?" he wondered aloud, watching the white larvae squirm within his broken flesh; writhing on the shards of his protruding radius. Flies came in waves, lighting on his open limb and lips, circling the stench of his decaying foot in anticipation.

The flesh of his toes was gone now, the ants having relieved the appendages of the soft bits to expose the brown and white and bloody bone, dropping the aged nails to the ground around his heel. The connective tissue still held the digits together, seemingly growing from the stump of his foot, the dried edges of his derma retreating like the cooked rind of a baking pig to reveal the bone beneath. The ants, never satisfied, were hard at work on his oozing stump, where five separate rust-colored trails of the workers clamored over the ground in legion in order to disassemble his carrion with aplomb as Tom bore witness.

Anxious flies knew better than land on these bony seventy-seven-year-old stumps, flitting about the stark perches just long enough to flee in recognition of the ants, deciding instead to light on Tom's neck and ears and sunbaked scalp and open wound. His body odor rose up from his waist and from inside his jacket, having mixed with his sweat like a tincture, but there was something else. Tom had lost control of his bowel and bladder, and while little fluid was left in him, he could feel the warmth of his urine spread over the crotch of his old khakis, and the creamy distilled fecal matter fill the gaps between his buttock and testicles. The pungent mix of reeking man and rotten excrement made him swallow hard, but after a lifetime of these smells from patients he did not wretch. The sun, having dropped enough to light up the sides of tree trunks, was sliced thick and warm and orange as it streamed through the forest in cascading angles. It was beautiful.

Fearing local infection prompted his colon, Tom pulled his shirt up with his better hand to reveal what he'd dreaded: hot inflammation rising from below his waist into his abdomen. Strangely, he felt no pain. Not in the inflammation nor his foot nor his wrist nor his hip. His sunburn and lips bothered him mostly, but the grand wounds were numb. He didn't know what to make of it. He again swallowed hard and with great effort.

"Please Ms. Flo," Tom whispered, "please help. I'm in rough shape, Ms. Flo. I'm in rough shape."

Ms. Flo beamed with kindness and wisdom, everything Tom had known of her. "Tom, you can wallow in your own mud and misery or make the most of it. Make the most of it, young man. Make the most of it."

Then she held her head up and smiled lovingly, singing loudly, "You got a mouth full of 'gimme' and a handful of 'much oblige.'"

Then kindly, "But not you, Tommy. You never said gimme. You didn't even ask and should have."

Tom smiled back at her as she faded into the forest, becoming thinner and more translucent before evaporating completely. He could smell bread and pie and dollar bills. He could smell cheap perfume. He could smell old batteries and rust.

Awake now and looking beside him, he again opened the notebook for distraction. Distraction from the truth. This truth, coming to him now, was absolute, but no more absolute than it had been for seventy-seven years—just simply more immediate. That the truth was this: death is coming. He felt certain his desire and that alone was keeping him alive, but he could not pinpoint a desire for anything except the perpetuation of living.

He could not pinpoint a desire for accomplishment, a desire for adventure, a desire for a destination or a task left undone. No, his desire, as is the desire of mankind, was only to live for the sake of living. A primordial drive with no contribution from intellect or ambition or hope. He'd seen this hundreds of times in his practice, where patients would cling to living in ways that were neither admirable nor pathetic but were nonetheless hopeless given their age or malady.

He saw terminally ill patients with organ failure and centenarians with no hope of improvement in quality of life, but still fighting. It had become clear to Tom that this urge to survive had nothing to do with pride or fear and often not even love, but everything to do with existing. Existing is the guttural part, the component that is given us in different measure. The fight; the will; the refusal to go. This deathbed realization that the clock was ticking down, and while some went gladly, exhausted, others refused to go easily or quietly or peacefully. He'd had patients that almost refused to die, despite what their charts and his experience said. On the other hand, he'd had patients who had given up easily. These were patients he'd been surprised to find passed after a simple diagnosis or admittance into the hospital.

Tom hadn't felt as though he had a future for a long time now and could not honestly say he had consciously looked forward to anything beyond the completion of his Triumph. This Triumph was now a turncoat, his liberation becoming his prison. The rear rim was bent inward, broken spokes fingering out of the hub in hapless chaos. The forks were twisted in a way to point the front wheel skyward, anxious to breach the clouds while the weight and bulk of the motorcycle held him down.

"Where did it go?" he asked aloud, wondering not just where the time had gone but what he'd done with it, as though he'd lost or misplaced it. "I made a posy," he muttered, suddenly remembering a George Herbert poem he'd committed to memory as a boy, "while the day ran by."

Then he continued, "Here will I smell my remnant out, and tie my life within this band. But time did beckon to the flowers, and they, by noon most cunningly did steal away, and withered in my hand."

"Where did it go?" he asked again, as though he might actually find it if he looked hard enough.

He didn't ask in lamentation; he didn't ask in mourning or even regret. He asked in sincere curiosity, convinced, as he had been since being released from a Korean prison, that time is a concept we think we understand because we have a clock. As if we can understand time and space by viewing it. As if we can understand people by knowing them. As if we can understand motorcycles by riding one, or the blues by listening to it. Foregoing understanding, Tom came to believe time was the only currency and his sole focus had been on spending it wisely.

How had he done? Was he satisfied with what he'd accumulated intellectually and emotionally and psychologically? And to what good end? He had always considered the physician's credo—Primum Non Nocere (first, do no harm)—to be the credo for his life. How would he rate himself? Was he satisfied with what he'd accomplished, with what he'd come to understand? Was he satisfied in having spent his time wisely?

He would have said yes before he'd left that morning. He would have said he'd forced his awareness of time to the point that it became systemic, thereby feeling the spending of it with a joy and intensity and grief and anxiety and love in a way that was more fleeting because he could feel it passing. Surely, this meant something. Surely, his effort to squeeze the most from every minute would be satisfying enough to make dying easier. Because dying was on its way.

Certainly, there were occasions in his life, he'd supposed he'd been born out of time or at least out of place, certain a person with his interests and proclivities would have been better suited to another era. Like a lot of folks, he would daydream of bygone times, bygone events, bygone cultures and was certain he would have been better off there, or better off then.

Tom was more thoughtful, more insightful, wiser than most folks in post-war America, but truth told, he was more thoughtful, more insightful, wiser than most folks in pre-war America as well, which was a truth in all of his imagined bygone times, bygone events, bygone cultures. Misfits are not misfits during their lifetimes; they are misfits in all lifetimes.

Still, in his psyche he felt an ache, a tingling and gnawing feeling there was more. Perhaps this notion is what kept him upright in east Texas, broken beyond repair, blood pooling beneath his diaphragm, poring over a notebook he'd been keeping for forty years like there was something needing done. Like he'd been hearing a latent secret in a tone or a frequency he'd ignored or simply couldn't decipher. A whisper or less; the sound of nuance; the sound of knowing. His lips were cracked and metallic, his throat swollen, his forehead burned.

Below him lay a Polaroid of Richard "Dick" something. In the picture, he stood with Dick in a common room down a hall of a hospital Dick would never leave, with his arm around his patient smiling. Tom had taken pictures of an unusual skin malady Dick had, hoping to share it with a dermatologist colleague, and while the camera was out Dick had wanted a picture.

"Take a picture with me, Doc," he'd said, and obliging, Tom posed for it.

Tom couldn't remember his last name, but remembered him well, nonetheless. It was a group photo that included Dick's wife and middle-aged sons, along with Joanne Macon, an RN Tom had known for years and had slept with at a convention in Chicago. Joanne was the reason he'd kept the picture. She had come to his room after a dinner, drunk and insistent. It had only happened once and in fact was the only other woman Tom had ever been with in his life.

The next day, after getting his wits about him, Tom let her know it would never happen again. Joanne soon transferred to another hospital, and Tom kept the picture not as a trophy or reminder of his tryst, but as a reminder of his betrayal. He kept the picture as self-condemnation and to reinforce the idea in himself he did not deserve his wife. Lo and verily, he did not deserve anything.

"Those amoral hippy sons of bitches have no idea what's waiting for them." It was 1970, and Dick was talking about the college kids he saw on the news. "Their souls are cesspools, Doc, with no more moral character than an animal. Just a-humpin' and drinkin' and carryin' on. Sweet fancy Moses! These kids are empty but for whining and bitterness. Their daddies go to war for them and you think they give a rat's ass? No sir, because they don't have a code of honor. Damn Kennedys."

He went on, "You know what Lenin says about amoral youth? This generation is a damn shame, Doc, I tell ya what. Lenin said, 'The best revolutionaries are a youth devoid of morals' and you know why? I'll tell ya why, Doc. Amoral youth make great revolutionaries for two reasons, okay? First off, without any real sense of right and wrong, you—the king or the president or the grand potentate—can talk them into believing anything you want them to believe with emotion and impassioned speeches, and second off, or second or secondarily."

Pausing to think, Dick quickly began again, "Secondarily, I think. Anyhow, with no commitment to a moral foundation, amoral people can be driven to terrible acts in the name of the impassioned speech. Look no further than the Third Reich. A funny little man with a funny little mustache knew how to work a crowd, and because the crowd had a void in them the shape of God, that little Charlie Chaplain-lookin' bastard worked them into a froth."

Dick was earnest, certainly, and while his world view didn't allow for people unlike him, he was making a mottled point.

He continued, "It's easy to manipulate people who can't reason, and these draft-dodging school-skippers ain't got a brain in their head. They read what they're told and think what they're told and watch those soulless hack news reporters and someplace along the line flipped the switch on insight and deduction because they'd rather smoke wacky tabbacky and whore it up than learn any damn thing."

Dick was clearly passionate, and maybe felt his clock winding down. He was lamenting an America he couldn't recognize.

"You think for a minute God turns a blind eye to free love and dope? What the hell is happening in this country? You think for a minute He looks at their rejection of Him and lets them slide for their naiveté?"

"I can't tell you what God's thinking, Dick," Tom recalled saying, chuckling.

"Well I can, because it says so in the good book, Doc," Dick rambled. "These soulless heathens; these cafeteria Christians who pick the things they like and ignore the things they don't are going to hell all the same, the dumb-asses. Lord knows I'm not the best man, but I see these young women with their titties hangin' out and these boys you can't tell if they're men or women, and I don't know what to make of it. It's their mamas and daddies what it is. They ain't been raised right, that's what it is."

Dick's grown boys, standing behind him, both smiled and mouthed "sorry" as he rambled. One of them lived in Tom's neighborhood as he'd seen him many times walking a whippet.

Early on, perhaps even from the first ride on his Whizzer, riding had been an escape from the drudgery and responsibility of Tom's life, morphing instead into a daily meditation. On that road, in that helmet, he could reflect on whatever he'd been reading, whatever he'd been think-ing, whatever he'd witnessed and what it all might mean. He would think about his children and his wife, his gratefulness for them, their thoughts and ambitions. He would think about world events or art, gardening, his next project. Sometimes he would sing.

To and from home had become a daily opportunity to think about his patients and their treatment, and on occasion, a chance to think about their place in the world. Riding home that night on the Honda CL450, Tom thought a lot about Dick, and the reaction those young people or liberal-minded people would have to his judgment. They would say he was a bitter, hateful old man or worse because pigeonholing him was easier than understanding. They'd complain that he wanted to keep wom-en in their place and insisted everyone adhere to his brand of morality. Their rejection of Dick would mean a rejection of his Christianity and the moral code associated with his Christianity.

This, Tom thought, the rejection of a Judeo-Christian social con-tract, would be the downfall of the world. The Judeo-Christian ethic—regardless of denominational commitment or even a belief in God—was the backbone of American culture and would sadly be swept away with behaviors and beliefs incorrectly attributed to it, including Dick's judg-ment and hatred and prejudice. This hypocrisy is easy to cloak in the same robe as Christianity when looking at it from the outside in, and would be some of Satan's best work, if Tom believed in Satan. Instead, he attributed this willingness to taint a system with the behaviors of some of its adherents as stupidity at worst, and at best a lazy refusal to investigate.

These are the same thoughts Tom had himself as a young man, witnessing the congregation of Oceanside Baptist Church both in an out of their Sunday best. He himself had assigned behaviors to righteousness like indicators, before understanding righteousness lived independent of the execution or fulfillment of righteous behavior. That is to say, the value of a moral code cannot be judged entirely by the behavior of the people who are charged with executing the code's standard, but instead must be judged by the code itself.

Young Tom came to understand that if people are the way by which a credo's worth is evaluated, no credo will pass judgment. Ironically, no belief system can be evaluated by the people who espouse the beliefs within the system. The code simply has to stand on its own, with its disciples merely a poor reflection.

Ironically, and counterintuitively, thought Tom, the human inability to uphold an ethic transcends every belief system, from Methodist to Episcopalian to Aleister Crowley's version of Thelema to Catholicism to Hinduism to Islam to Baptist to Buddhist to LaVey's Church of Satan. No adherent performs their duties well, so to look at old angry Dick and judge his Christianity by his actions was simply immature.

Worse, perhaps, is the idea one can judge a philosophy or religion by the people who claim to espouse the religion instead of actually studying the religion oneself. These short-sighted judgments were certainly not the sign of intellect or source of truth Tom was looking for, so he paid no attention to observational judgment from either camp.

Tom believed observational judgment to be lazy. Truly, the amoral hippies would be as repulsed and judgmental about Dick's beliefs as he was about theirs. The difference, however, was in Dick having a theology he believed, even if unable to adhere to it, where the amoral youth clung to whatever plucked their heartstrings that day. It is fair to say, he thought, that the only thing they shared was hypocrisy.

Taking a farm road to get home, Tom leaned the light little twin cylinder around the corner and shifted up into third, the cool of the night numbing his lips and nose and knuckles. The temperature had dropped twenty-five degrees since he'd ridden in mid-morning, and as he wore an open-faced helmet and goggles, he reminded himself to put a shield on it before he rode it again. He could hear chain lash as he accelerated and shifted into fourth gear, indicating he was overdue in lubing the chain and sprockets as was necessary in those days.

This hypocrisy, Tom thought, is perhaps one of the reasons some people discard religion altogether. For them, religion bears only hypocrisy while condemning behaviors the amoral hippies support, like free love and marijuana. So Eastern religions became the draw for many young people, complete with meditation and sitars, without realizing their proponents are rife with hypocrisy, too. Buddhists want new cars, Hindus are sometimes malevolent, and Taoists take action into their own hands. But add a swarmandal to the Beatles' "Strawberry Fields Forever" and suddenly everyone thinks it's cool to be a Sikh because Dick was right: four funny little men with four funny little mustaches know how to work a crowd.

Atheists, and particularly vehement atheists, have a point when they refer to religion and cry "hypocrites!" The truth of the pandemic hypocrisy becomes the war cry, instead of what it should be: merely a symptom of an obvious illness.

The illness is not the religion but is human pride, self-interest and our lack of discipline. Hypocrisy cannot be the reason theology is abandoned, because theology and philosophy live independent of its adherents. The adherents are to blame, not necessarily the theology itself. Hypocrisy simply presents itself differently depending upon the collective agreement among a theology's adherents, and in the case of the easily swayed, unwise, disenfranchised and lazy nay-sayers, that agreement changes with the wind depending upon anything from mood to whoever is making the impassioned speech.

Tom believed that when a person's world view is tempered not in philosophy, theology, introspection, knowledge, and understanding but rather emotional reaction and knee-jerk cause-of-the-day, there is no winning them over.

As much as he had hoped to gain understanding from his patients' life experiences, he only found that rarely. Overall, Tom came to discover old people feel an obligation to be wise by virtue of experience, and even then, only when asked. Sadly, he found few old folks are, in fact, wise.

Time and again he witnessed an embarrassed look, minds searching for answers to questions they'd never answered and worse, had never even considered. He came to find over the course of his career and course of his desire, old people without a commitment to a theology were often no more wise than young people. They had simply re-played the emotional reactions of their youth, caught in an endless loop of rinse-and-repeat.

No smarter, no wiser, unaffected by age because they'd spent their lives satisfied in their ignorance, even celebrating it. He came to believe that a theological system was the fertile ground that produced wisdom, so a life without a spiritual commitment meant no wisdom would flourish. He thought it tragic they would go to their graves with experience, but no more enlightened than a child.

This idea helped compel in him a belief in God, or higher power, or benevolent creator. His desire for wisdom, coupled with observation, prompted the belief, as he couldn't embrace a desire for wisdom if there was no point. If there was no God. If there was no reckoning.

Chapter 7

PART I

Oh, Death don't keep a ledger,
Don't care what no one says,
Rich or poor, Death don't care,
Everybody pays.

—*Pastor Louis Claymore*

"Hey, Gracie," Hannah said when Grace answered.

She was calculating her inflection and concern against how much of it Grace could hear. Grace could hear much more than anyone knew but had been the little sister her entire life, so she played that part in return.

"Hey, sis," she answered, "any news about Dad?"

Hannah, as Grace was also her best friend, sighed, "Not yet. I was just calling to pray with you and see what's happening there. I prayed with Wayne, and he's calling the church."

Grace, while worried and anxious over what was to come, enjoyed a peace only her relationship with Christ could have given her. "He's been missing a long time, now, Han. I mean, John called me mid-morning and the sun is starting to go down."

Hannah, thinking, "Yeah, yes. Of course. I guess you're right. I don't even know how to think about it." She had poured a bourbon from the minibar and mixed it with Diet Coke. "I'm calling work and telling them I'm headed out there tomorrow morning. I can pick you up on the way if you want."

Grace, her conviction superseding her answer, jumped at the chance. "Absolutely I want you to. Can I meet you in San Antonio and leave my car someplace?"

"That would save a bunch of time," Hannah answered, "I'll just pick you up at that parking garage at River Center, if that works. Ten o'clock?"

"It's a date," Grace replied, "I'll see you in the morning."

While worried, she was also excited to see her sister and to be leaving town for a couple of days, then remembering, "Oh wait! Has anyone called Aunt Ruby yet?"

"No, at least I haven't, and I doubt John has. It seems premature now anyway; you know how she gets. She'd have Uncle Mac driving her to Dad's place five minutes after we told her. And Uncle Mac's not supposed to drive at night anyway."

"Makes sense," Grace answered, "Maybe we call her tomorrow depending upon what we know. I mean, if he isn't home tonight, we'll have to call her."

After hanging up, Hannah opened the sliding door of the hotel room onto the second-floor balcony. Walking through the clacking vertical blinds, she looked below to a swimming pool, a standard rectangular affair with aluminum chairs strapped with strips of heavy white vinyl. Still too early in the year for most people to be in the water, the concrete cool-deck was empty but for a woman, fully dressed, sitting on the far end reading and smoking a cigarette. She held a *People* magazine, getting caught up on Valerie Bertinelli's bikini body at forty-eight.

The ashtray on the table next to her was the sort you'd see in the 1970s, aluminum with curved butt rests and sand in the bottom for weight, giving indication as to when the hotel was built. The woman had red hair and wore a baseball cap, her orange lashes glinting in the sun when she squinted as she drew in the tobacco smoke. Mid-thirties, both too young and too old to be smoking, she wore a nurse's uniform and white leather clogs, one of which dangled from a bouncing foot. Beyond the deck was a narrow yard of sorts, mostly landscaped in rock and cactus with a few outcroppings of grass for guests with dogs. Beyond the yard a chain link fence and beyond that, the highway service road.

Hannah had poured the bourbon into the can itself, in part for convenience, in part to hide the cocktail. The former was true, the latter she didn't even know herself. Seeing the *People* magazine reminded her of a book she'd won at auction, adding to her collection of rare and first editions. *Her Privates We* by Frederic Manning was published in 1929 and signed by the author in 1934. Hannah had read it in high school as *The Middle Parts of Fortune*, the expurgated version meant to less offend the ears of parochial readers. Very few signed copies of the original full-length novel were known to exist. Hannah was very excited to now own one, having won it from a rare bookseller on eBay. She would tell Grace all about it on the road trip the following day; about how her collection was now large enough to arrange the books by century, then decade, then author within each section.

After all the kids left home, Wayne converted one of the upstairs bedrooms to a library and collection room with one full wall dedicated to Hannah's collection. He'd installed shutters over the window to block the light, and the bookcases for the first editions themselves had doors with glass treated to block harmful ultra-violet rays. The remaining shelves were filled with books they'd read but held no real value, along with trinkets they'd picked up over the course of their marriage. Tom had reveled in the room and in his daughter's passion many times, marveling at both her interests and her breadth of subjects. In fact, he was more impressed with what she'd read than with what she'd collected, promising many times to leave her his collection when the time came.

"I have an extensive collection of first editions myself," he would say, kidding her.

Hannah would tease him, "Only because you bought them when they were published. I think some of them are on papyrus!"

As a child he would read to her, wasting little time with nonsense picture books and stories he considered beneath most childrens' ability. "Our children," he would say to Roseanne even before there were children, "do not need to be coaxed into reading green eggs and ham. They need to be taught to think."

Roseanne, smart and funny and in complete agreement, was grateful for a man who thought what she thought, believed what she believed; she'd been magically drawn to Tom from the very day they'd met.

She'd told Tom, "We will not teach them to share. We will simply instruct them to share, and as they gain in understanding they will understand the morality of sharing. Obeying comes first and understanding later. Papi used to tell me, 'Do what I say and you'll understand when you grow up.'"

Tom would read Aesop's *Fables* and Mother Goose and Greek and Roman mythology, as his father had read to him. Roseanne would read Jonah and the whale and Daniel in the lion's den and David and Goliath.

Tom would talk about metaphor and the human psyche, while she would talk about faith and the lessons God gave us. Together, they represented an intellectual and theological foundation that would resonate within their children the rest of their lives, inspiring Hannah to cling to intellect and books in a way that fueled her passion.

She walked back into the room and pulled her hose off, then poured a second drink. The coke alone was ice cold, cooling the additional bourbon without ice. She couldn't bear the thought of leaving the room long enough to find an ice machine, so trading ice for convenience, she stepped back out onto the patio and closed the door behind her. There was a chair there, matching the patio chairs below, and careful to tuck her skirt around her bare legs, put her feet up on the glass-topped table.

"Lord," she prayed, "please take care of Dad. Please show us where he is and give him comfort. Please keep him safe and wherever he is and whatever's happened, be with him and help him feel your presence. In Your holy name I pray."

Mindlessly staring at the nurse below, Hannah watched her as she took off her shoes and, moving the chair closer to the pool edge, dipped her foot in the water as if to test the temperature.

"Still too cold!" she shouted, having noticed Hannah.

Hannah, embarrassed for being caught, shouted back, "You're braver than I am. I wouldn't even put my foot in it."

The truth of that bothered her. Her father was lost on a motorcycle at nearly eighty years old and she had grown so predictable she wouldn't put her foot in a cold pool.

The red-headed woman picked up her magazine and shoes, sliding the pack of cigarettes into the toe of one of them, then, looking back up at Hannah, said, "Have a good evening," and walked off.

At midnight, having not slept a wink, Hannah put her bra back on under her pajamas and, pulling the safety latch over so the front door wouldn't close all the way, walked down the only flight of stairs to the front of the building. With purpose, and afraid she would change her mind, she quickly walked between the buildings to the pool area and slipped in headfirst so as not to make a sound. Reaching the opposite side underwater, she breached the surface as her ripples slapped the tile around the sides, took a deep, frigid, whole breath and swam back.

PART II

I'm driftin' pretty baby,
My hitchin' come undone.
Hold on, pretty baby,
Fore I float away for good.

— *"Two-String Jonny" Baytown*

"You see what's happening with that Barney Clark, Doc?" Elmer asked, "I don't imagine the prognosis is that great, but who knows what the next twenty or thirty years will bring?"

Elmer, aging but still very interested in current events, was commenting on the first artificial heart recipient, Barney Clark.

"I've been following that pretty closely, Elmer, but I think it's too soon," Tom replied. "We're not refined enough yet to even transplant organic tissue without a litany of issues and rejection meds, so I can only imagine the complications of installing machines."

Then Tom continued, "Beyond the medicine and experiential research, what do you think about the ontology of such a thing?"

Elmer looked at Tom, head tilted, "Ethics, or portent?"

Tom answered, "Well, it would be tough to make a case against the ethics of keeping a man alive. No, I mean, where do you think it might lead?"

"Ah!" Elmer exclaimed, rejoicing over the turn the conversation had taken. He'd had enough of talking about his bowel movements and his sleeping habits and his blood pressure; enough of ball games and the weather. "My friend thinks too much!"

"So I've been told," Tom answered.

Elmer mused, "I suppose living with an answer follows whatever it is you think makes us human, Tom. In the classic example, if Odysseus had come home after twenty years and his fast black ship had every board replaced during that time, every nail and sail and oar, is it the same ship? Does the vessel exist simply because it travels under the same flag and name? Or does it exist independent of the flag and the name? Or does it exist only as the flag or the name? If you say it's the same ship, it doesn't matter whether Barney Clark has every organ and bone and all tissue replaced. Barney Clark could become a robot or bionic man and would still be Barney Clark because he is Barney Clark in his soul."

The sun was low on the horizon, hidden now by the oak trees and crepe myrtle in the courtyard; still light but cooling off. Elmer spit into the shrubbery and said flippantly, "Then again, I guess it doesn't matter what you think a human is, either. A lot of folks would love to be a robot."

"I can't put my finger on it," Tom said, "but I think you're right about a soul. I've decided it isn't ego that makes me believe it, or even hope. I'm convinced there is more to me and to you than this meat suit."

Elmer laughed hard. He had become Tom's patient some years earlier and enjoyed his company, now getting to see him every Friday. While Tom was his doctor, they had also become good friends. Sometimes they talked about bowel movements and weather; sometimes they did not.

It was 1982 and Elmer was in an old folks' home. In those years, they were called old folks' homes, somehow becoming senior care facilities over the years, but old folks know what they are. Tom volunteered on Fridays, followed by his late afternoon visits with Elmer. Some days, he would take Elmer out to dinner or sneak in an ice cold Lone Star or Löwenbräu beer in a small cooler, and sometimes cigars but on this day he'd brought Elmer a pack of Beech Nut chewing tobacco.

In Tom, Elmer had found a kindred spirit of sorts. Elmer was a retired general practitioner from Schulenburg, Texas, fought on the western front in Belgium during WWI, came home, went to medical school and got married. He had an indiscernible green blob of a tattoo on his right deltoid. Losing half of both feet to frostbite, he was sent home three months before the war ended.

"But a soul implies eternity," Tom continued, "and eternity implies God or an orchestrator. Do you believe in God, Elmer?"

Elmer, serious now, voice sounding as though it crawled over gravel and glass and phlegm and tobacco spit, answered, "Well I did. Then I didn't. Now I do again. I was mad at God for a long time, I guess, and thought I'd teach Him a lesson by not believing in Him." He chuckled at his hubris.

Tom laughed with him.

"Look Tom, to continue the ship metaphor, I believe with all my heart that we are on our own Odyssey. This "meat suit," as you said, this flesh and bone is a vague legend, just a story someone might tell once in a while after we're gone and eventually not at all. Our bodies are the vulgar, crude parts of our existence we sail through the universe in until they give out. Everything around us falls away, is replaced or changes until we are unrecognizable, as Odysseus wasn't recognized by anyone he'd known."

Elmer paused, then continued, "But God recognizes. Listen, for a long time, we doctors believed every cell in our bodies was replaced over seven to ten years, which worked well for this metaphor. What we now know is that it's true but for the neurons of the cerebral cortex. They are never replaced, and what is the cerebral cortex doing? Just memory, attention, perception, cognition, awareness, thought, language and consciousness, that's all. Just all the pieces that make us who we are."

Tom nodded as Elmer continued, "We, Tom and Elmer, are what's inside and what continues. And I believe with all my heart that eternity is real, and you live it either in concert with God, or out of fellowship with God entirely. That's it, those two choices, because that's all that makes sense. I'm not telling you this because I want it to be true or because I'm old and want God to hear me because I could see Him any minute."

Tom chuckled as Elmer smiled. "This is not my ego or fear of dying, Tom. This is a deep and abiding faith that can only be had through the acceptance of the gift. Get it? It is the simplest and the most difficult thing all at once. That's the hard part, because the faith comes after you sacrifice yourself, not before; it does not prove itself so you can then make the acceptance easy. And I believe with all my heart the only way to live eternally in concert with God is to simply accept the gift of passage, which is his Son Jesus Christ, as the only conduit by which to enter."

"Yeah," Tom said, almost to himself, "I have a hard time with that. Why did you give up on God?"

Tom bent down to the waiting cooler to pull two beers from the ice. He had a bottle opener in his pocket and, fishing it out, opened one and handed it to Elmer.

Elmer puckered and spit, then took a long, deep gulp from the amber bottle. "It's a hard thing, seeing your friends get killed, but harder still is losing a wife and child. Harder still, yessir. Soldiers sign up for dying, is the way I looked at it, so they can't be too damned surprised when it happens. I mean, hell, you signed up for it, didn't you? Signed up to die for something bigger than you. A way of life or an idea or for freedom, and in all of those, we signed up to protect the people trusting us not to fail."

They were sitting in the garden on the west side of the building, in the warm long shadows of a sycamore. Elmer stood to stretch his legs and put his hands in his pockets.

"Didn't we Tom? We stood up between the people we love and whatever was a danger to them. Our mothers and fathers and brothers and sisters and wives and children. When a soldier died next to me, he died with honor, because he stood up, knowing he could be killed. It was hard, and still hard on me today, but he'd stood up for it. He stood up with his hand raised, balls out and fierce."

He paused again, and a fleeting sadness crossed his face. "A wife and child are different. These are the people you did it for in the first place. If not the ones you have, then the ones you intend to have."

Tom listened, because that's what he did best. That's what he'd always done best.

Elmer said, "You know, I went to war without any shoes and came home without any feet. But that's not what did it because I raised my hand for that. I was twenty-seven when we lost my wife. She was pregnant with our third; a tubal and of course no one knew it in those days. Started hemorrhaging when I was at work and died in the kitchen with my kids standing there. No phone of course, and the kids thought they'd get in trouble if they left the yard. They were three and two and didn't know what to do but sit with her, which they did till I got home. I'd come in the house angry, having had a second flat tire in three days. You remember how bad tires were."

"Lord," was all Tom could say.

"In my anger and hubris, I insisted I was above believing. Intellectually, spiritually, emotionally. My subtle condescension and quiet judgment. I am ashamed now to say judgment of God Himself. My immature reaction was to stop believing in Him. So, I did, then I didn't, and now I do again."

Tom, pensive and slow to reply, asked, "Why was that immature?"

Elmer spit tobacco into the ivy and said, "God can take my anger just fine, but His absence was tough on me. Kept me from knowing things, from learning things, from having a more eternal perspective. My anger left me with no peace."

"What if you were right?" Tom said. "What if you were right about there not being a God?"

Elmer turned on his heel like a younger man would, eyebrow raised. "You fightin' with that, Tom?" the old man asked rhetorically. "When you believe, Tom, when you're a believer, the doubt is stripped from you as you see God in your life. When you don't believe, rather, before you believe, you question it because you can't see it in your life. Plainly, it's tough to believe something you don't see or feel or hear."

Elmer continued, "But first, and frankly, believing is just easier. Hate and anger are too heavy to carry around and there's no payoff in them anyway. And if God were the object of my anger, then of course I still believed because I had to have an object for my anger! Otherwise I was just crazy."

Tom, curious, as that was his way, asked, "How did you get over your wife's death, Elmer? How did you get those kids raised?"

He was marveling at Elmer being in the same position his mother had been in, at a time when few people trusted a man to raise his kids alone.

"I was alone for three years, doing the best I could. We moved in with my sister and her husband so she could help, and it turned out to be the best thing for the kids."

Elmer stared off into a much further distance than the courtyard allowed, seemingly seeing what had been his life. "My sister took the kids to church, and sooner or later got me to go back. There I met Sally, my second wife, and we finished raising those kids together, along with two more."

Tom thought for a moment and opened a second beer, handing it to Elmer. "So, what do you say about that? You made the most of a tragic situation?"

Elmer answered quickly, "God made the most of a tragic situation. And I never stopped being grateful for it."

He drew a long gulp from the cold bottle, then, "Tom, I'm an old man now. Feels strange even saying it. Strange to think no one in the world is afraid of me anymore. I was a soldier, a warrior like you. Young and strong and knew how to take care of people. I was fierce in my heart, like you are, Tom. And in all that I knew where my strength was. I knew I was only fierce and was only strong and was only driven because I had eternal perspective. In my hiatus from God I was weak, and self-centered in it."

Tom looked up at Elmer, still standing on the brick walk with one hand in a pocket, and one hand on the bottle, considering his words.

"These days, Tom," Elmer continued, "I wear adult diapers so when I sneeze, I don't piss myself, but I'm still fierce because I have a lion's heart. I'm as fierce as I ever was only because I'm a loved child of God."

Pausing, he continued in resignation, "Son, I haven't had a boner in seven years, but I'm as fierce as the day I left home because there is no frailty where I'm headed."

Then, almost in revelation, "Seven years, Tom! I can actually tell you the date: March 8, 1975. Sally was in the hospital and started talking about making love, and how much she loved me. That woman was seventy-five years old and talking about how much she loved me! Hot damn, that's some love right there, brother. I had this raging hard-on thinking about her and us, and if I'm being honest, it had been a while already. I mean, we both knew she was never going home, so I couldn't even put it to good use, but I have to say I was glad it happened there. I'm glad my last wood happened in a room with Sally instead of in my sleep or whatever."

"Anyway," said Elmer, returning to the present, "who are you to say you are smarter and more thoroughly considerate than Martin Luther, Rene' Descartes, Jean-Jacques Rousseau, Augustine, Thomas Aquinas? You're too old to be asking the question again. Too old to be open to the answer. You don't have any more time to wait to commit to the truth. Reject and burn or be open and burn. No matter, same result. God doesn't give you credit for being open to the possibility of His grace."

After taking another long drink from the bottle, Elmer sat back down next to Tom. He said, "Purity and impurity, that is all. Does it mean embracing the idea some loved ones won't be there with you? Yes. Will you be ridiculed sometimes? Yes, of course, by people who make comments and jokes in defense of their fear and insecurity. Or libertines in defense of their epicureanism. Will it benefit non-believers if you are open to the idea of salvation? Will it benefit them if you aren't?"

After a pause, Elmer asked, "What exactly are you waiting for, Tom? What are you waiting for?"

"I suppose I don't want to be silly, Elmer, or I want definitive clinical evidence. I want an epiphany or a burning bush, I guess. Or at least a good rationalization," Tom laughed.

Elmer looked at Tom earnestly. "Look, in my time and the atheists I knew? Most were tiresome bores, insisting they were too sophisticated for something as naïve as a belief in God."

Tom raised his eyebrows, "I hope I'm not a tiresome bore."

"Not tiresome at all, Tom," Elmer said, "because you're not an atheist. You're an agnostic. Agnosticism is worse than atheism."

They both laughed and Elmer continued, "Agnosticism is a way to keep from committing either way, gathering all atheists, believers and anyone on the fence into a nebulous belief in a higher power without hurting anyone's feelings. They get no further than their curiosity. This journey, the quest and inquisition, has no conclusion. After all, if I am more passionate about the question than I am the answer, I never have to choose, you see? Everything is theory; everything conjecture; everything is interesting because how can we know if we don't know? But if that's the criteria, how do we know anything at all, really?"

Elmer drank the rest of the bottle and tossed the empty into the cooler. "Hell's no place for you, Tom. Make sure you don't go there."

PART III

The wind come up this mornin', the leaves are comin' down.
The wind come up this mornin', the leaves are comin' down.
On the dirt around me, them leaves is all around.

— WASHINGTON BECKER

Tom opened a sweaty eye to his distended belly, bloated and hot. His lucidity, even alacrity, confused him. How could he be this broken and still be conscious, much less clear-headed? He could smell the petrichor of a coming rain, the tops of the trees above him nearly dancing with the potential. Spring made them giddy already, but the promise of rain was nearly enough to have them step out of the ground on their roots to leap with excitement. They likely would have but for concern over bird nests and the fear someone would see them.

Tom opened a sweaty eye to his distended belly, bloated and hot. His haze of fading consciousness was punctuated by minutes of distinct acuity further underscored by fantastic thoughts and questionable ideas. His foot, whole again; his arm intact and entire. Once again, he wore his watch and was certain he could slip his leg from beneath the motorcycle.

Tom opened a sweaty eye to his distended belly, bloated and hot, raking his gaze across his soiled pants to the current pages of his notebook. Splayed out from the binding was a yellow envelope marked "Fotomat" and thick with photos. Lifting the envelope revealed a quote in his own hand, "Death is not the worst that can happen to a man" and he remembered exactly when he had written it. It was 1963, only a few hours after having received the notebook from his sister and written with the Cross pencil she had given him. He couldn't think what should be done with his journal, hoping jotting down a few things might get him started.

He had no way of knowing it would be another decade before he wrote in the book again, and that on the heels of John using it as a sketch book, treating it more as keepsake than record.

Dropping the pictures from the envelope, Tom spread them out over his leg and the ground beside him. There were several pictures of Roseanne standing with Buddy Guy, his arm around her shoulder, and a final picture of John having a guitar signed by the blues artist. Beside John stood the same man in the picture of Tom and baby Tom-Tom he couldn't identify earlier. The pictures had been taken years apart, but the same man was in both of them. John's friend?

Tom couldn't remember. John looked to be about seventeen, having shown little interest in motorcycles but enormous interest in music. Tom could hear Buddy Guy's *Flesh and Bone* playing in his mind as he strained to focus on the image. Who was that? Was it Dennis?

"It doesn't matter who it is." Tom heard the voice coming through the woods, specifically from a large tree beyond the bike. "It only matters who it is not, and it is not anyone you know, so forget it."

Tom craned his aching neck in the spring dusk, not quite remembering whether he'd asked the question aloud. "Please," he said with as much conviction as he could muster, "please help me out of here."

A man in his late sixties in a dark woolen suit and high collar shirt stepped from the woods before him, standing at the end of the motorcycle. He wore a red silk ascot and an outrageously expensive gold Italian Diobolus watch with a whipstitch leather strap and red dial.

Surveying the wreckage before him, he said with an English accent, "Tom, I think this is past repairing. You've really made a mockery of it."

"Please help me out of here," Tom repeated.

The front rim of the bike, pointing skyward, made the perfect stool. The Englishman pulled a handkerchief from his inside breast pocket and, spreading it over the wheel's rubber, sat down on it to face Tom. Crossing his hands between his knees, he leaned in.

Handsome with a salt-and-pepper beard, wearing copper–framed glasses and surprisingly well-groomed for a man stomping through the woods, he replied half in jest, "After the fun you've made of me? You want my help?"

The man's shoes were remarkably polished—black split toe oxfords in shiny bonded leather with farrier tacks in the heels. They reminded Tom of his Sunday shoes when he was a kid.

Puzzled and weak, Tom's mind raced for recognition. "I'm only pullin' your chain Tom," the man said grinning, and somehow in that brilliant white smile Tom recognized him from a photograph in one of his motorcycle history books. The book jacket was the Union Jack.

"*A History of British Motorcycles,*" Tom mumbled.

The man, still smiling, answered "But you know it can hurt a man's pride being made fun of for his life's work, right?"

The man was Joe Lucas, the maker of the Triumph's faulty electrical system. Tom had suspected the man was a hallucination when he first heard the voice, and because Joe Lucas had been dead for many, many years he now had no doubt.

Dismayed over the hallucination, but not the electronics, Tom replied, "In the only picture I've ever seen of you, I think you were about forty."

Joe was currently wearing exactly what he'd worn in that photograph.

"Oh!" the man shouted, "but I was a handsome devil back then. Time gets the best of all of us, I guess. Now we're both old men, Tom. I'm older than you by a long shot, but both old, nonetheless. Now about this motorbike."

For some reason an English Joe Lucas could say "motorbike" reasonably, while coming from anyone else it was either naïve or insulting.

Lucas prodded Tom. "You didn't have that much trouble with your BSA, remember? You loved riding that bike."

Tom chuckled, "Riding, yes, but I was always trying to keep the electrics working. Have you ever tried riding without light? Half the time I rode the BSA I was terrified because I had no idea what was ahead of me. No matter now, I suppose." Then Tom added, "I was so proud of that bike."

"I remember!" Joe said, "British green and chrome, but that has been a long time now too. Long time indeed, and while I admit the headlight wouldn't burn holes in the asphalt, I take offense to your claim you had no idea what was ahead of you. A nod's as good as a wink, though, to a blind horse, eh? As far as the Triumph here, I don't think it's worth saving, mate."

Tom bandied, "Well, it's pretty rough for sure, but somebody could make it right again."

Lucas smiled wryly, looking over Tom like he'd looked over the bike. He pushed his glasses up firm on the bridge of his nose, exclaiming, "Crikey! You are looking like death warmed up, man!"

Joe reached down to pull the brake lever on the protruding bar. He stroked the cables and patted the tank curiously, absentmindedly.

Surveying the mangled pieces, the oil-soaked ground, the scrapes and bends, he said, "I have to disagree, Tom. Nothing here to salvage."

Something in his delivery seemed glad of it, relieved almost. Joe Lucas stood and retrieved his handkerchief, wiping his hands in habit. Wiping his hands of the bike and of Tom.

"Well, look at it this way," he said, turning, "You got all the life there was to get out of it. You used it up, so in that you should be happy."

"Well, I suppose I would want to have ridden it more. You know, restored," Tom answered. "I've only gotten a few miles after the complete restoration, after all."

Joe looked at him convincingly and said with a conviction he seemed to want Tom to share, "Restoration is out of the question, Tom. You have to let that idea go. Just let it loose and be glad for what you've had."

"Not true!" Tom heard a second voice coming around his right. Befuddled in recognition, Tom watched as his mother walked past him and scornfully shouted again, this time right at Joe Lucas, "Not true!"

She was thirty years old, the youngest he could remember her, and angry. Tom was so glad to see her he let slip the notion she was a figment of his imagination.

Turning to Tom, his mother said, "Don't listen to him, Tommy. It can be restored. I've seen it a thousand times. You just have to want it. You just have to believe it, Tommy."

"Mom?" Tom asked, "My hands are so cold, Mom. So cold. Hold my hands, won't you?"

His mother looked upon her boy, "I cannot warm them, Mijo," she said quietly. "Mine are not the hands you need."

Lucas, endearing and kind, almost mentoring, bordering on the uncanny, chimed in, "Look, Tom, everything ends. This bike, you, everything. I mean, nothing lasts forever, mate. Do you think these trees have been here forever? This forest? Hell, Texas itself is only one hundred and sixty years old. Even Lucas Industries went belly up a few years ago after more than a century!"

Tom sat quiet; half in delerium, half in understanding. Joe Lucas continued, "I thought the company was my monument, maybe in the way you think this bike and your legacy are your monuments."

Then raising his voice to the trees and quoting Shelley because he knew Tom would know it, Lucas cried out, "My name is Ozymandias! King of Kings; look on my works, ye mighty, and despair! Nothing beside remains. Round the decay of that colossal wreck, boundless and bare, the lone and level sands stretch far away!"

Lucas' shouting frightened the animals of the forest, causing birds to lunge from limbs in myriad panicked voices, and deer to flee their resting space. Esther only listened, knowing Tom had to hear it, but did not have to believe it. Still, knowing Tom had to hear it.

Hear it he must, because only in the hearing could he come to understanding. Frightening for Ester, surely, because her boy's understanding may fall short. Her boy's understanding may stop at the temporal. To a blind horse, a nod is indeed as good as a wink.

The shadows, now long and eager, bent into one another, overlapped, became black in spots. In Tom's private valley, trapped beneath the machine of his own creation, it was already night in the crooks and crannies and gullies of the Big Thicket. On the road and in the clearings the late day sun shone golden and yawning, soaking the treetops on their west sides, where the darkness rose higher on the trunks like a rising, drowning black water as the sun was beginning to set. Through his mother and at some distance, he could see a whitetail and her fawn, settling back down to lazily clip the indigenous spring grass and the leaves of saplings.

Joe Lucas continued, wearing kindness as a mask as he was increasingly obscured by the darkness. Kindly yes, but increasingly insistent, "Tom, the Triumph is lost. I would encourage you to embrace the loss, embrace the passing, embrace these growing shadows."

Then Lucas asked, "Have you ever read the *Ars moriendi—The Art of Dying*? Well, I have many times and if I'm being honest, Tom, you aren't doing this very well."

Esther stepped impatiently closer, in front of Lucas, waving him behind her. "Get behind me," she said to him motioning. "I don't want to stumble over you."

Then bending toward Tom she said, "Don't pay mind to that, Tommy. That's only true of the world, but not of the eternal."

With that, she bent down over the head of the crashed motorcycle to find the toggle switch on top of the headlight bucket. With a click of the enameled toggle she turned the headlight on to prove her point, the light beaming straight skyward within the crook of the forks and wheel.

In smug condescension, Joe Lucas asked Esther, chuckling, "If there is a light on in the forest and there is no one there to see it, is the light on at all?"

With that burning yellow trestle rising from the floor of the east Texas Big Thicket, both Joe Lucas and Esther Welton vanished in the wash of the glow. The headlight flickered and shone, flickered and hesitated off, flickered and was out. All that remained was the whitetail and fawn and closer in, Tom's decaying body. The top and secondary digits of his toes had fallen—the phalanges distales and mediae—but he cared none at all. Hours ago, he'd known the foot was lost. He could smell it now, the stench rising up and over the bike frame while the ants worked; while the flies frenzied about his wounds and face.

He missed his mother, grateful to hear her again, to see her again. His clarity had returned, and he puzzled over why his deprivation produced the hallucinations it did. Dehydration, certainly, but he wanted to drive the hallucination, not just have it visited upon him.

Gazing back down at the Polaroids of Roseanne and Buddy Guy, Tom began to hum John Lee Hooker's *Catch My Pony* and felt grateful for the music. Felt grateful for the lyrics. Felt grateful for having an outlet that expressed what he was thinking or thought, feeling or felt. As much as the Blues was a lifeline to Ms. Flo, it had been so much more to him, and for his entire life. This seemingly subtle, uncomplicated music encompassed the depths of human experience, of human emotion, and certainly Tom's. The Blues and this motorcycle—these motorcycles—were the only two manifestations of what it meant to be a human being for Tom.

The motorcycle, his humanity; the Blues, his prayer. Both certainly the closest he'd ever come to expressing the tangled mess within him. The thought of never hearing a record again was as painful as the thought of never riding a motorcycle again—maybe more so—and as this fresh idea came to him, Tom began to cry.

"I'm gonna catch my pony boys, gonna saddle up my black mare," he whispered, "I'm gonna leave ya joggin, joggin on away from here."

Cooling now, the day fading, Tom guessed five more minutes of reasonable light and after that, blackness. Anyone looking for him would be luckless now, as the darkness would hide his existence. In his mind's eye he remembered removing the reflectors and anything he felt the original designer never intended, which, sadly, included all of those safety annoyances, the absence of which would make him invisible.

He recalled distinctly pulling them from the fork tubes and rear shocks, cleaning the leftover adhesive off with gasoline and a rag, certain they were needless and sure he could avoid anything and anyone who couldn't see him on the road. Now the very people to whom he felt superior would be unable to help him.

PART IV

I got a pocketful o' dollars, the finest bourbon too,
Womens on my left and right, and Johnny Conqueroo.

— *STEAMSHIP BROWN*

By the late 1970s Tom's private practice was successful, as he had created a reputation for attending to patients as individuals. His treatment protocols looked at the patient holistically, incorporating not just traditional and state-of-the-art medicine, but also included herbal remedies for minor ailments, nutrition in a way that medicine mostly ignored at the time, and in being an empathetic friend to people. He'd always felt the body was only part of the treatment protocol, having witnessed many times the importance of attitude and of hope.

Still and always, Tom found himself getting close enough to patients to pry, forever curious about the way they saw the world and where they felt they fit within it. More than anything he was collecting perspective in the hope of one day formulating his own irrefutable, apodictic viewpoint. Because of his particular medical philosophy and the success in his approach, he was often referred patients by their primary doctors, who knew Tom could benefit the patient in a way they simply could not or more appropriately, would not.

These patients, whom Tom referred to as "the fighters," were as young as ten and as old as his oldest patient. Sent by specialists from oncology to endocrinology to dermatology and gynecology, Tom's role in their treatment was very often to treat the symptoms brought on by the treatment of their primary ailment. Such was the case of Jane Hythlodaeus, a beautiful, bald, Greek lung cancer patient Tom was treating for appetite loss and sleeplessness courtesy of radiation and chemotherapy.

"I don't know, man," Jane said in rehearsed sort of sophisticated kindness during one visit, "My life has been immeasurably easier because I don't believe in any of that." She was denying attachment to any theology.

Tom asked, admiring her candor, "Do you wonder about what happens when you pass, if anything?"

Jane, steeped in her needful conviction there is nothing, replied easily, "I don't wonder because it isn't a mystery to me. We just die, that's all. No eternal anything. No darkness, no new state of being, no anything at all. It's true I can't explain how we came to be, but that doesn't matter to me."

There was a defensiveness about her delivery, either from having felt the judgment of others or possibly from an avoidance of self-condemnation.

"But what if you're wrong?" Tom asked.

By this point in his life he was absolutely convinced there was a Creator, if not an eternity, because nothing else made any sense. He'd come to believe time as a concept was only meaningful to humanity, and only because we are aware of its passing. In this, he was satisfied with not understanding the beginning of time or the end of time because he'd made such an effort to understand and had never reached a conclusion he could live with. Having explored and exhausted every avenue he could imagine; he had just let it go as unfathomable. It is okay not to know everything, he reasoned.

"If I am wrong," Jane answered, "I'll find out then. Even if I'm wrong, I don't worry that there is some white-bearded man on a mountain ready to judge me for my sins. In fact, I don't think there are any such things as sins at all, just agreements between people and societies driven by what benefits us personally. All of life is just the selfish ambitions of mammals. Sorry if that sounds jaded or sour; I don't mean it to be. But look around."

"Well," Tom continued, "theology would tell you the point of Christianity is to deny those mammalian pieces of yourself in sacrifice to a greater sense of righteousness and to other people, at its most noble. Otherwise we're no better than any animal; unwilling to lessen our circumstances for the benefit of someone else's."

Jane smiled condescendingly, "We are no better than any other animal."

Tom could see his children in his mind's eye, fighting over toys and cookies and whose foot was there first. He could see the anger and venom in them as they needled one another growing up. He could see Hannah, sitting in the principal's office after punching a girl for making fun of her haircut, and again for cursing at a teacher. He could feel himself lift his drunk daughter from the front porch, putting her to bed at seven in the morning. In all of it he intuitively knew we don't outgrow behaviors; we just get better at managing the way they manifest.

Jane continued, "People are nasty to one another, doctor, including you. I'm not asking for confessions here, but for every moral law you regret breaking, there are a thousand more you've managed to erase. Not me. I embrace them. I mean, there have been times I was out of line, but for the most part I do not care because I am not responsible for everyone else."

Tom was listening, intensely curious over her conclusions. He knew she was right about humanity's turpitude, flashing back on his personal daily nastiness. He reviled the purposefully stupid, the unwise, a lack of discipline, people who spoke with authority while knowing little. He found joy in others' failures, then denigrated them for it. He loathed their insecurities and weaknesses and loathed their excuses. He loathed their excesses and their entitlement.

Where were they when he was in a concrete Korean cell? Where were they when he was twelve, hawking eggs and wild fig preserves? Where were they when he swam alone in stock tanks, wading through the snake-infested cane breaks to bring home some perch or sunfish? Where were they? They had no right to fail, no right to be stupid, no right to do anything less than he'd done. He reviled them, and no one but Tom knew it.

"Listen," Jane said, "I grew up in the 1940s and 1950s; a solid mid-westerner with mid-western Christian values. I went to college—the first woman from my family, mind you—with beatniks and hippies and other unsavory types. There I became an objectivist. Do you know what that is, Doc?"

She'd spoken on this topic many times over the decades; first, excitedly as a young women bent on the evangelism of the parsimonious, then, tiredly as a decades-old delivery of lines in a play by a weary traveling showman or a speech by a passionless politician.

Tom answered, "I'm guessing college was late 1950s, early 1960s?"

By her reference to objectivism he knew she was familiar with Ayn Rand, the queen of Don't-Tell-Me-What-To-Do. He was already judging her for what he knew was coming. She was a conveyor-belt product of a faulty philosophy machine, spitting out cookie-cutter examples of, ironically, enslaved free thinkers.

"Exactly," Jane answered knowingly. "Rand made a lot of sense to me, so in reading her and in pursuing my own happiness I was liberated. I didn't have to make the grandiose, meaningless sacrifices made by my mother, or by the religious, or by anyone who held some arbitrary nobility in being the dutiful, longsuffering housewife or dutiful, longsuffering citizen or dutiful, longsuffering anybody at the sacrifice of self. The droll pursuits and existence of my high school and college girlfriends was more than I could have born."

She laughed, thinking of those years and those friends. She said, "I decided my happiness would be my moral goal, which included doing whatever I wanted with my body and chasing economic dreams the way the most successful business owners, politicians and frankly, most men seemed to. I could do what I wanted without the idea there was an omnipresent overseer ready to condemn me for my actions."

Tom asked, as he had many times in different rooms of different people, "Did Rand make sense to you because you wanted her to make sense to you? Were you looking for preemptive absolution from an intellectual authority for all the things you wanted to do, but were held back by your moral upbringing?"

"At the time," Jane answered, "I suspect I did. I was a young, smart, rebellious, lusty woman and resented anyone telling me what I could and couldn't do for no reason but tradition. As I got a little older, I became more realistic, which still fit perfectly into an objectivist's point of view."

"Not to embarrass you," she said without embarrassment, "but I practiced my liberation at first by drinking and masturbating and smoking cigarettes. The cigarettes, I suppose, were my passion bearing fruit for death! I was militant about it at first, experimenting sexually to prove my point, having sex with strangers, including women, smoking reefer, taking drugs, and I don't apologize for any of it."

By this time Tom had cheated that one night on Roseanne, and Jane's laissez-faire recounting of her life stung him in the way betrayal stings the betrayer.

"I am both frog and scorpion," he thought. He had alienated people, ignored the bereft, lied when easiest, but on a scale he could live with. He'd held in contempt those who didn't measure up to his nebulous standard, holding them all to the standard he set for himself. In this he was stupid, unwise, lacked discipline. In this he had failed and was weak. In this he bore his hypocritical opprobrium. And no one but Tom knew it.

"I've had three very successful businesses and have enjoyed traveling the world," Jane bragged. "I was married twice and even though I loved my husbands, I cheated on both of them. I was divorced because they didn't see the world the way I see it, even though they sold themselves as evolved men. So, I made my way on my own. No kids because I couldn't be bothered with taking care of offspring. I had three abortions over the years. Weird, because as much as I was open to, um, temporary relationships," she said smiling, "it was embarrassing to be unclear about who the father was. Anyway, parenting isn't for everyone. It isn't some weird mandatory rite of passage required to make you complete or some nonsense."

"And," Tom asked, "do you feel your beliefs are rationalized by your financial successes? Which is to ask whether being successful confirmed your objectivism or do you feel more entitled to your objectivism as a function of your success?"

"Oh! Doctor!" she exclaimed, excited to be explored, "I think you and I would have made a great couple at one time," she began to answer. Then she winked at him flirtingly.

Terminal female patients often flirted with Tom, not because he was handsome but because it was their last chance. "In fact," she continued, "if it were five years ago, we may have made a great couple for a weekend!"

He was older than she was by a decade and even without hair she was pretty and clear-eyed. Instead of a scarf to cover her bald pate she wore a brown Garbo hat with an orange ribbon around the crown. She sat in the bed cross-legged, her bare feet poking from beneath her gown as she massaged them with her hands. The skin of her feet was thin, translucent, shining blue beneath.

Laughing for having made him uncomfortable, she answered, "No, success did not solidify my belief, but I am certain I would not be as rich or as powerful as I am without my beliefs. I didn't have to worry about someone else's feelings because I've always held that people are responsible for their own happiness and it wasn't my job as a business owner to make employees happy beyond retaining them to my benefit. So sure, I yelled at them and fired them if they yelled at me because it was mine; my business."

She paused, making a connection. "It also wasn't my job to make husbands or lovers happy beyond what payoff their happiness was for me or what payoff there was for them in my own happiness. Not being responsible for other peoples' feelings made objective decisions easy and as a result I could focus on the businesses, not the people."

Tom never stopped marveling over the intellectual's ability to rationalize any behavior with eloquence. Attaching objectivism as a philosophy to selfishness surely made life easier, but incredibly, alarmingly, destructively shallow. In much the same way eastern religions are only viable if the majority of adherents cannot perform the tenets of the religion, objectivism only works if the objectivist is surrounded by people who are not objectivists. Objectivism, in Tom's view, simply allowed the adherent to behave with little regard for anyone else, then blame the offended for their intellectually immature reaction to the offense.

"So it brings up the question," Tom thought aloud, "When you begin and maintain a life independent of your moral upbringing—in your case, your solid Midwestern religious upbringing—it seems to me you either fully embrace objectivism as a way to camouflage your inner guilt, run back to your solid Midwestern upbringing or divorce yourself entirely from your Christian ethic, which seems nearly impossible to me."

"Makes sense, Doctor," she said thinking, "but honestly I don't have any inner guilt. I'm dying and reflect on my life a lot, and there is very little there that I wouldn't do again, more often, or differently only because it would have been even more decadent. I haven't had enough wine; I haven't had enough sex; I haven't had enough conversation with smart people; I haven't smoked enough! I think desire for indulgence, even debauchery, is true of every person, but they don't have the nerve to admit it or the guts to pursue it. Or it makes for uncomfortable talk in polite society. What about you, Doctor? What do you believe?"

This was a rare thing for Tom to be asked, rarer still to be asked by a hedonist. "Hmm," Tom sounded, "I suppose I've had one foot in theology and one foot in the world since I was born. I'm still figuring it out."

"Well," Jane said, "It doesn't matter if you choose, really, because not choosing is a choice in itself."

"Of course," Jane continued, "I don't believe anyone who says they have no regrets, but everything is a trade, isn't it, Doctor? I, for example, regret smoking a pack and a half a day, but dammit, I enjoyed every one of those cigarettes. Every single one. If you cured me today, I would leave the hospital and go buy some. I would just smoke one pack instead of a pack and a half! I could have added a year or two back to my life, I suppose, by giving up cigarettes and gin, but hell, that would have been a year or two without cigarettes and gin!"

Jane laughed, glad to have an audience and to talk about herself. Glad to tell her stories and recount her adventures, without acknowledging her desperate belief that her stories somehow kept her alive, were somehow her lasting legacy.

Jane began to recount, "You know I've seen the Grateful Dead fourteen times? Sure have and was high as a kite every time."

Tom hated the Grateful Dead.

"And," she continued, staring into the ceiling to remember, "I've seen the Beatles, the Rolling Stones, the Doors, Yardbirds, Led Zeppelin, Credence, BTO, and a ton more. In my business we promoted bands locally when they came into a town, so we travelled a lot and bought a lot of newspaper and radio advertising."

Interested, and asking because it made her feel good, Tom said, "That's very exciting. Did you meet the bands as well?"

"Tons, almost everybody," she answered. "I dealt with their managers and production companies mostly, but would meet the band at after-parties when the shows were over. I never slept with any of the band members because I don't have sex where I eat, but I made out with Keith Richards at a party one time, and actually dated Paul Leka of the Lemon Pipers."

Tom had never even heard of the Lemon Pipers.

Then remembering a good story, she continued, "At one of the weird parties I went to I met Lyudmila Rudenko, do you know her? She's a famous Russian chess player. Funny, Steve Farmer of the Amboy Dukes couldn't pronounce her name, so he just called her 'Rudy' to her great annoyance. Anyway, I got to play chess with her for the entire evening. Maybe ten games total. I lost every one of the matches but was lasting much longer toward the end. I remember I was very tired as it had been a long day but enjoyed the hell out of it and was certain—still am—I could win if I'd kept trying. But no, I made a ton of money building that business, then sold it to EMI."

There was a darkness about her, that Jane. This look of knowing without acknowledging. He could feel an insatiability in her that one hundred lifetimes couldn't fill, because while smart and articulate and successful, she was superficial and had spent as much time avoiding her mortality as she had spent rushing it. She spoke rapidly, incessantly, almost because speaking meant she didn't have to think, filling conscientious gaps with vapid chatter. Tom had no sense whatsoever of her fatigue or winding down from her illness, her ever-present rationalization just a backup plan to her constant preoccupation.

"And what happens to your empire when you pass?" Tom queried.

Jane was casual, resolute even. "Rich people often talk about their legacy, and I suppose I'm no different. I want to be remembered for having built several businesses, employing lots of people, fighting hard when needed, as a good friend and lover, and as entertaining and fun."

Then, "I'm torn between leaving my money to animal charities or to Greenpeace. Greenpeace does great work but it's mostly political, where the animal charities benefit animals immediately. Plus, the animal shelter in Galveston committed to a new location and naming the building after me if I leave it to them."

"Seems clear to me," Tom said, as tongue in cheek as he'd ever gotten. "You get a building and help animals? I'd go with the Galveston shelter."

Many years later, Hambone Happy Cheese would be born into a dog shelter supported, in part, by Jane's legacy money. He would be adopted by Tom's son, John, and his second wife Dianne, whereupon they would take him home to live within earshot of the beach, feasting on bacon-flavored chunks of goo. He would be named by a grandchild, chase birds in the backyard and sleep under a picnic table while his loving owners searched for the man who had been the physician of the dead hedonist who had made his life possible.

All, while in blind, lethe ignorance Hambone licked the place where his balls once were and barked at anyone walking along the fence. Protective of his domain; fierce in his independence; assured in his kingdom; certain of his understanding.

PART V

When the sun goes down and there ain't no moon
And the darkness come in all around me,
Fear holdin' me like chains, I say a prayer,
'cause I know the sun is comin',
'cause I know the sun is comin'.

—MISS ALICE FORD

Officer Randal, driving under the speed limit, pulled his headlight switch as the sun was setting. Half an hour before sunset was the general rule, and teaching kids how to drive during summer school kept the rule fresh in his mind. His windows were down, and while he'd promised to check in with the other departments when he got to Lufkin, he pulled over at an empty rest stop to go to the bathroom and to call his wife. He wasn't supposed to make personal calls when he was on the clock, but he loved her and tried to catch her every night before she put the kids down.

"Hey baby," he said when she answered.

He was leaning against the deck lid of the cruiser, one hand in his pocket and the other holding his cell phone. He was facing west and had watched the sun set below the loblolly pine, bald cypress, redbud, white oak, and magnolia while he talked with his bride. Staring over the pebbled asphalt, the surface almost imperceptibly bowed and endless, he could make out the first mile before it twisted north. There was a chill in the air, but his thick undershirt helped stave off the cool of the coming darkness.

He and his wife were believers in Christ, and their love for one another transcended the ephemeral, transcended civility and obligation. He loved her, she him, and when they weren't together, they wanted to be.

"I'm looking for an old man that came up missing."

She asked with expectation, "Wander off? Senile?"

"Doesn't sound like it," Randal answered, "He left his house this morning on a motorcycle and his kids can't seem to reach him."

"Oh Lord," his wife responded, "What is an old man doing on a motorcycle?!"

Randal stopped her, "A man does what a man does, baby. He has his family raised and worried about him; he's alone in the world. If the old man wants to ride a motorcycle, he should ride a motorcycle. I ain't sayin' nothin' about that because my day is coming."

"Mmm, okay, but don't think for a hot minute you're taking off on a motorcycle when you're an old man. I need to keep my man safe!"

She laughed and he said, "You know what I do for a living, right?"

They laughed together for a minute in the warm chuckling of familiarity before Officer Randal asked her to pray for Tom. "Say a prayer for the old man?"

"I will, Love," she said, "What's his name?"

Randal couldn't remember, but said simply, "Oh, my pad's in the car, but God knows his name."

Then something caught his eye. About a mile toward the horizon he saw a shaft of light shoot skyward from the side of the road, flicker, then go out.

PART VI

Jesus, won't you make up my dying bed,
Jesus, won't you make up my dying bed.
It's gettin' too dark to see and I can hear trumpets far off away,
It's gettin' too dark to see and I can hear trumpets far off away.

—*Biloxi Willie James*

The cool night air was beginning to sharpen Tom and, combined with his slow internal bleeding, caused him to shiver. The cold woke him up, dispensing the sluggishness of coming death with an acuteness that felt too much like hope but nothing like confidence.

While the light was still strong enough to see, he turned the pages of the worn brown notebook for a last look; a last remembrance. Deep within the pages, photographs, notecards, and ideas in his own hand raced before him, each igniting a place and a time and people in his mind as anchors, as a tether to the world and to his life. Roseanne and Hannah and John and Grace, drawings and diagrams and notes. There were Christmas cards and gum wrappers with reminders on them—reminders for tasks and projects he would never remember, never get done.

"Seven degrees before top dead center," Tom mumbled, reading a scrawl in a corner.

He knew it was the timing setting on a 1965 Volvo Amazon he had rebuilt. He could feel his hand on the distributor, a timing light popping in strobe to reveal the numbers on the harmonic balancer like stop-motion film. Flipping another page revealed the last photograph Tom would see before dark. The last photograph Tom would see. He was standing beside a 1983 Honda CB1100 at the end of the Solstice Day Race, having ridden from Orange, Texas on the eastern border to El Paso on the western border, racing the sun. Taking off at sunup in Orange and riding 856 miles across the state under a blistering arc, the task was to reach El Paso before sunset.

Preparing to make up time, Tom had jetted the carbs, replaced the pipes and ignition, reduced the rear sprocket by four teeth to increase top speed. This golden orb, blazing overhead, followed him over the day, over the miles, over the highways of Beaumont and Houston and Katy, through San Antonio and northwest through the desert. When Tom cleared Boerne on the outskirts of San Antonio, he opened the bike up, the tuned 1100cc motor hitting its stride.

The sun on his back at one hundred and thirty miles per hour, Tom could see his shadow leading his front wheel on the asphalt below him. Nonchalant, effortless, his shadow mimicked him, feeling and knowing none of the stress on Tom's body and mind. He could see his shadow there, leaning forward over the blurred penumbra of the spokes within the dark oval of his wheel and tire, flat and quiet against the boiling asphalt.

Leaning, anxious, he could see that shadow stretching out before him like a runner leaning into a tape, desperate to reach the line before Tom. He could hear the sound of the motor, its effervescence rising up through the opening in the bottom of the very helmet he'd worn this day, whining in anger and purpose.

Racing the sun as the road wound west, the sun now in his eyes, Tom's shadow knew there was no winning, deciding to stretch out instead behind bike and rider one, two, three lengths as the sun dropped further into the horizon. Rolling first through Socorro, then El Paso, Tom made the Solstice race in under ten hours, where the First National Bank declared 103 degrees. The road had been built for him, he thought, as was that morning, as was the hour, as was the sun. El Paso—the step in Spanish—was indeed the sweet metaphor for victory as far as Tom was concerned. But a nod is as good as a wink to a blind horse, don't you know?

The photograph, a collection of the very few who made it in time and the many who didn't, was a celebration of having ended well. A celebration of men so desperate for a challenge and clarity of identity that they manufactured a challenge to gain the identity. In the image Tom had his arms around men he'd known from swap meets and motorcycle shows, dealerships and diners. In the image Tom was smoking a cigar, face beaming in an exhausted smile, and in that photograph was the same man he'd seen in the two photographs before.

"Who is that?!" he queried aloud, then felt satisfied it must have been someone from the cycle shows or swap meets. An acquaintance that had managed to be a part of his past.

Looking at the picture reminded Tom, after a full day of waiting, he had a cigar! He had matches! He'd had a cigar and matches all day!

The sheer joy of remembering a creature comfort at this late hour was overwhelming, causing Tom to whimper in anticipation. Searching the dark ground for his Pentax box, he raked his hands over several feet of leaves before finding it, snapped it open and plunged his good hand within. There was an inner sleeve on the underside of the lid, and even knowing the cigar was three years old, Tom didn't care. It was in a glass tube and corked, after all, and the matches should be with them.

"Why didn't I think of this?!" he admonished himself, "I could have done something sooner; made a difference earlier!"

Hastily sliding his fingers between the lid and sleeve, Tom poked his finger on something sharp; something not at all like a glass cigar tube, but he found the tube, nonetheless.

Pulling the cigar from the forgotten leather tomb, he put his hand back in to retrieve whatever had poked him. Suddenly astonished into near disbelief, Tom's hand told him what it was before he could withdraw the object. He could feel what it was and knew what it was, his brain reminding him through the tips of his fingers what it was.

Somehow, the Cross mechanical pencil turned up after all. Somehow, this slender silver spike had worked its way into the bottom of a sleeve in the back of a beat-up camera box, dislodged, Tom guessed, with the accident. Somehow, Ruby's lost graduation gift to him was found!

Dumbfounded, Tom pulled the cork from the cigar tube with his teeth and dumped the cigar into his mouth, biting the end off before lighting it. He normally would have used his pocketknife, but with one arm and little time, Tom wasted none of it. The matches, having ridden inside the tube with the cigar, were as fresh and dry as the day he'd put them in there; red-tipped with just a dot of phosphorous and potassium chlorate—enough to burst into flame when raked across a surface. Then striking a match on a dry limb end, Tom raised that flame to his lips and drew in, igniting the tobacco in a joyous flare. The fragrant smoke burned his eyes and pushed the flies out to a wonderful perimeter. He reveled in the joy of the temporary; the minor joys of a dying man.

The fire and the cigar quickened him, its burning an awareness of how quickly it all goes. In the fullness of truth and recognition of his moribund end, Tom wept in gratitude and conviction, understanding completely how little time there was to regret anything. How little time there was to forgive and to ask forgiveness. How little time there had always been.

PART VII

God almighty is comin' with a scythe,
God almighty is comin' with a scythe.
Tell the wheat and the chaff He's coming,
Lord, warn the wheat and chaff He's coming.
Gonna separate 'em out on the threshing floor,
You know He'll separate 'em out on the threshing floor.

—*EDNA ROSE*

With gasps and drawing of the sweet and bitter tobacco, inhaling the blinding understanding of his wickedness, of his desires, of his rage and his judgment, Tom could pretend no more; delay no more. He entertained no more his prideful abandon, guised as intellect and compassion. He could pretend no more his doubt for pride's sake.

In his exhaustion he was confronted with his lusts and insecurities; with the putrid festering pride within him—hidden from all, including himself but for glimpses when he was too tired to hide it or caught off guard by it—as he stared terrified into the dark of the woods. No time left to be convinced, no time left to maunder, no time left to suspend a commitment, he knew he must leap or perish, and he did.

In faith he made his Icarian plunge from the cretin labyrinth of his own making, crying out "God! Oh God I know!" Then in a whisper, "I've always known."

The forest, all ears raised in reaction to his cry, stood silent in anticipation. "Dear God, I know what I am. I know how I have run from you. I know how I hated you. I know, and I know you've seen through me; through all of it. I know."

Silence. Dead silence but for Tom's purging gasps.

"Father, I know. Father, I know you sent Christ in my place. I know I am not pure. I know. I know you sent Him to die for me because I cannot die enough or pay enough or beg enough or try enough to enter your kingdom without acceptance of that grace, of that gift. I accept that gift, your Son, Father. I accept your sacrifice. God, I'm sorry."

Then, from a Sunday school memory or needlepoint, Tom acknowledged, "For the wages of sin is death, but the free gift of God is eternal life in Christ."

On this day, Tom's last day, he prayed not as a beggar, but as an heir.

Then, drawing deeply on what was left of his cigar, in quietus Tom for an instant lit up the forest before him. In that glimpse—that orange instant—he saw his mother and father, Ms. Flo and Leon. He saw Rose-anne, smiling.

www.ingramcontent.com/pod-product-compliance
Lightning Source LLC
Chambersburg PA
CBHW051137020726
47501CB00005B/1552